STEPHEN DOWNING
IS DEAD

A NOVEL

DAN GOSS ANDERSON

PEER PUBLISHING

STEPHEN DOWNING IS DEAD
Dan Goss Anderson

Printed in the United States of America.
Peer Publishing
515 E. Grant Rd., Ste 141-351
Tucson AZ 85705-5797
www.Peer-Publishing.com

For more information about this book, visit www.DanGossAnderson.com

Edition ISBNs
Hardcover 978-0-9892009-2-9
Trade Paperback 978-0-9892009-0-5
E-book 978-0-9892009-1-2

First Edition 2013.

This edition was prepared for printing by The Editorial Department
7650 E. Broadway, #308, Tucson, Arizona 85710
www.editorialdepartment.com

Jacket design by Pete Garceau
Book design by Christopher Fisher

PUBLISHER'S NOTE: This is a work of fiction. Although certain minor characters are based on real persons (and one dog) who lived in the early 20th century, their portrayal herein is entirely fictional. Beyond that, no living person has been intentionally portrayed in any manner in this story, and no such portrayal should be inferred.

For Sherry Mullens
and for Adams Wofford

Author's note:

Because this story takes place in the first half of the 20th century, the narrator and other characters would have been unaware of terms such as Latino and Hispanic, now commonly used when referring to people whose culture or ancestry derives from Latin America. Instead, the narrator uses the terms that were common during his own lifetime.

STEPHEN
DOWNING
IS
DEAD

L ife changes in a moment. A woman's sharp cry outside my window. I scoot from my hotel bed and lift the curtain, blinking at the late-morning desert sunshine. One floor below, on the dirt street, the body is gone. Two men with shovels in hand, rolled up sleeves, pondering a dark brown stain. A black draft horse waits nearby, hitched to a flatbed wagon, ears drooping. Across the way a young woman stands, hand over her open mouth, that anguished cry still frozen in her face.

Beside her, a mustachioed man, burly, bracing her forearm with his own. Next to him, a large black and white dog, ears perked. The woman is twenty-five, I will learn, her black hair fashionably swept up and pinned, a few strands tumbling to her shoulders. An inch of white petticoat flashes from beneath her dark, ankle-length dress.

Later, I will come to know the exact smooth texture of her cheek, the ineffable scent of the smooth skin behind her ear, the swell of her lip. But in my memory of that first moment, there remains only this: She glances up, straight into my window and looks straight into my eyes. No warning. I feel myself blush and my breath catches. I step back to let the curtain fall, to break the sudden spell of those dark eyes. "Absurd," I say aloud, inexplicably embarrassed.

Absurd, yes, but even so my hand hesitates to lift the curtain again until I am sure she is no longer looking my way. I wait several slow breaths, my fingers playing with the coarse fabric of the curtain, then raise just a corner of it. They are walking away. My eyes play the line of her slender back and the slight sway of her rounded hips. Her head is bowed, and every few steps her hand goes up to her face, as if she is wiping away tears. She and the man and the dog finally disappear together around a distant corner.

She will tell me years later that she does not recall looking into a window that morning. No matter. What happened, happened.

S he is still a mystery to me. Wisps of gray-white hair rest now against her pale forehead. She lies awake, white in her hospital bed in this white hospital room. Her dark eyes are closed. With each breath, the pneumonia rattles through her lungs like crushed glass. A nurse pushes open the door and glances in for a second, then leaves. The hospital priest has come and gone, with his holy water and his candles and his blessed oil for the last rites. My hand covers her hand, hers now shriveled and small with nearly transparent white skin, and mine heavy and darkly discolored with age spots. Our hands have grown old together.

She has spoken only once since we arrived at the hospital. Two nights ago, late, she stirred in her sleep and grimaced. She murmured a word. A name, actually. "Stephen," she said. After a few more seconds, the knot of wrinkles in her forehead relaxed.

I am not Stephen. Across the bed from me sits Gabby in the other chair, taking her short turn for a visit in the room. Though she has put on some roundness in recent years, she still has the energy of a forty-year-old, with a Dolores del Rio kind of spark that turns the heads of men decades her junior. Only the whiteness of her carefully groomed hair, pulled back in a bun, gives away her seventy-five years. For her, white is not yet the color of death.

The half-smoked Pall Mall between her fingers infuses the air with a stifling cigarette odor that overpowers her omnipresent Chanel No. 5. She and Eva took up smoking in their early sixties, during the war when suddenly almost everyone was smoking. They wanted to look stylish. Not so long ago, as they strolled together through the downtown, Eva could have passed for Barbara Stanwyck, making an elegant little toss of her head after each drag. A cigarette between Eva's fingers looked like an extension of her hand. Gabby has never acquired the easy mannerisms of smoking. After a dozen years, she still grips the cigarette tightly in the very crook of her forefinger and middle finger, all five fingers splayed as if preparing to slap something. When she takes a drag she centers the cigarette in her puckered lips directly beneath her nose, instead of casually off to the side like Dolores del Rio.

Roy and Helen and the grandchildren are all out in the waiting room. Roy, though his mother lies dying here, maintains his usual middle-aged engineer impassiveness. Helen, who has been close to Eva since the day she married Roy twenty years ago, clutches a tissue and occasionally wipes the corner of her eye. Carl, long and skinny at sixteen, sits straight in imitation of his father, but his sorrowful eyes reflect the same grief his mother shows. The twins—Katie and Karen—in their always matching dresses, hold each other's hand.

In a seat nearby, Carmen grips her rosary in her arthritic fingers, a black lace scarf draped over her gray hair, her lips moving as she silently recites each Hail Mary. Beside her, Josue rests his straw cowboy hat on his paunch, the deep creases around his eyes pulled into the saddest expression I have ever seen on him. La señora is going away, and there is nothing he can do.

One or two at time, they have all been coming into the room to sit solemnly with Eva, patting her hand, speaking words of endearment or saying nothing at all. They depart after a few minutes, because that is the hospital rule, giving me an encouraging nod or pat on the shoulder on the way out. The twins kiss me on the cheek.

I am allowed to remain because I am the husband. Each night I have slept a few fitful hours in the chair beside the bed, alarmed by the increasing rattle and choke of Eva's pneumonia, and each morning I wash up and shave in the bathroom. Helen brings me a fresh change of clothes and minds Eva while I head off to the cafeteria for breakfast.

Gabby pushes herself up from the chair and stubs out her cigarette in the ashtray. She tucks her black patent leather purse under her arm. "*Mi amor*," she says quietly, "I must feed my cats. I will come back in a little while."

When I don't respond, she goes out and the door closes behind her. Eva stirs in the bed. Her right leg draws up slightly under the sheet, then straightens. Her eyes open slightly. She sees me, and, in a coarse whisper, says, "Are they gone? Owen … you have to know something. I tried to tell you … but …"

I straighten in the chair, glad to hear her voice, rough though it is. There is nothing important she can say that I don't already know. Perhaps she has hidden a little money away in a drawer. Perhaps she has an idea for the grandchildren. Or perhaps, after all these years, she finally wants to say something about what happened between Gabby and me.

"Tell me anything," I say, believing I am ready.

Her dark eyes fix on mine and she begins, and I feel the color drain slowly from my face as she whispers a story I could not have expected. Or rather, at some deep level I must have always known it, this secret, but now, forced out hoarsely in her dying whisper it splashes anew across time and our lives. In her dark eyes, as she speaks, I see her regret and her love. For a moment after she finishes, I am shaking as if from a passing ice-cold wind, but then it is over. The white room is quiet. Her eyes hold mine for what I know is the last time. There is no time for me to answer.

Through my trembling fingers, I feel her relax. Her eyes close, she smiles a little smile, and she whispers, "Amen." Then, just as the door opens and Roy comes in for his turn with his mother, she slips away and is gone.

I am alone, wandering the empty hospital corridor. The nurses said they would not be long, their faces politely somber and efficient. "If you want to wait outside," they said, "we'll be taking her to the morgue. You can walk with us."

Eva's words echo in my mind. A bit dizzy, I take a seat for a moment on a couch in a small waiting room. Her guilt lays over mine, crushing me. I feel like I am breathing sand. *Owen, you have to know something.* On a magazine table, today's *Daily Star* reports that President Eisenhower is still at Fitzsimon's Army Hospital in Colorado recovering from his heart attack. His wife, Mamie, is concerned. I imagine Mamie holding Ike's hand. I imagine the horror he has known in his life as a soldier, a life of causing other men to die, and wonder how he set it aside. Eva's burden weighs even heavier.

I leave the newspaper as I found it and start down the hall again. I hear Gabby's high heels coming up quick behind me on the checkerboard linoleum. She tugs at my sleeve, crying and babbling, her perfume a swirling, invisible cloud. Why didn't I call her? Everyone has left. Is Eva really ... she can't say the word.

I tell her I sent everyone else home, after they each had their moment to say goodbye. At this hour the hospital business office is closed, so there is nothing else to do until morning. Helen tried to insist on staying with me, then tried to coax me away with them. I couldn't leave. Not yet.

I remind Gabby she was gone a long time, feeding her cats.

"It wasn't that long. I wanted to relax for a few minutes. I fixed myself something to eat. Tell me, can I see her? Can we go back to the room?"

Sure, I say. Sure. Ask the nurses, I say.

She tugs again at my sleeve. "Walk with me. If you are there, they must let me see her."

I let her pull me by the hand. As we approach the closed door, I tell her we are supposed to wait outside.

She says, "I only want to say goodbye. Please come in with me." Clutching my sleeve with one hand, she pushes into the room with the other. Eva now lies on a gurney beside the bed, covered head to toe by a fresh white sheet. The two nurses are packing up the tubes and devices. The bed has been stripped and the sheets are piled in a corner. The older nurse nods to the younger one, who motions that we may approach the gurney. Gabby holds the edge of the sheet for a moment, then raises it slowly to reveal Eva's face. Her features have already begun to settle. The tension in her jaw is gone. Her eyelids lie flat, unblinking.

Gabby whispers, "She was so beautiful." She kisses Eva's forehead, then steps aside still holding the sheet, as if expecting me to join her in kissing Eva goodbye. I stand unmoving, unwilling to share my private moment. Gabby's mouth turns down into her familiar childish pout. "Thank you," she says to the nurses. "I'm glad I got to see her."

I nod to the nurses. "I'll be right back. Please wait."

In the hallway, Gabby grips my forearm as we walk. She pulls a new kerchief from her purse and dabs at her eyes. "I will miss her so. I know this is harder for you than for anybody. But I have lost my Eva too."

I only nod, afraid I might say the wrong thing. Until now I never understood Eva's guilt, or Gabby's importance in our lives.

She says, "Come. We must get you home. You need rest. So do I. I need rest."

I walk her out to her brand new car, a shiny blue and white Chevrolet Bel Air. 1955, only weeks old. When she is feeling stressed, she buys a new car. She says it makes her feel better to turn heads as she drives down the street in a new car. Eva's final illness made her feel very stressed.

Under the streetlight she hugs me tightly for a long moment as I pat her stiffly on the back. "We were close," she says. "No? So very close?"

I pull away and try to smile, without success. I tell her she has never had very good timing.

She smiles coyly and gets into her car. "I'm only trying to cheer you up. Good night, *mi amor*."

After she is gone, I stand for a moment in the darkness, the cool October air on my face, before I hurry back toward the door. In my distraction, I stumble over an edge of the sidewalk and stop to regain my balance. A hard fall at my age can be bad. A little moonlight would help, but the moon is not out. As a lawyer, under other circumstances, I would warn the hospital to put up better lighting here before somebody sues them. Not tonight, though. The hospital's problems are not mine. As I make it to the door, I remember. There was a full moon that other night, all those years ago. There was plenty of light.

A twelve-inch crucifix centers on the wall above the headboard
of our bed. I have always ascribed Eva's strong sense of guilt
to the church's teachings, and wondered at the way she seemed to
miss its more positive themes of forgiveness and redemption.

Owen, you must know something. Her whispered words come
back at odd moments, as if from nowhere. Or somewhere. The
heaviness of her guilt weighs on me. On the nightstand I've placed
the old sepia photo of her and Stephen, taken in front of their
house on Stone Avenue back in 1904, right after they moved in.
I came across it yesterday, as I sorted through some boxes in her
closet. I last saw it fifty years ago, the night after we returned from
our honeymoon. In the picture she wears a full-length skirt, dark,
and a white blouse with long puffy sleeves. It was the modern
look in those territorial days. She stands straight, shoulders back.
Something about the angle of the camera suggests that she is leaning away from him, ever so slightly, so that their shoulders do not
touch. Stephen, with his bushy mustache, holds himself stiffly,
a derby squared no-nonsense on his head. He is a bit taller than
she, a slender man. His chin is up slightly, a subtle challenge to
the camera. Eva described him as self-assured, but my years of
law practice have taught me that the truly self-assured don't issue
needless challenges.

There had been clues. I missed them.

The telephone rings jarringly. I stare for a moment, and pick
it up.

"Owen," Gabby's voice says. "*Cómo estás?*"

"Hello, Gabby." I wait. I don't feel like talking to her.

She waits, too. Finally she says, "I asked how you are. How are
you?"

I tell her I'm about as one would expect in my situation. I can
almost feel her pout.

She says, "Oh come on, Sweetie. Don't be that way. I have been part of your marriage for fifty years. Your Eva was my Eva, too. I am just checking to make sure you are all right. Do you have a ride to the funeral? You are not driving by yourself, are you?" She knows the answer, of course.

"I'm fine. Roy and Helen are coming for me. Actually, they should be here soon. I have to get dressed." In truth, they will not arrive for hours.

She is quiet for a moment. "All right. I'll see you there."

I put the phone back on its cradle. It is black and very sleek looking, with its round dial and numbers that are easy to see even for my old eyes.

I remember sitting on my hotel bed, that long-ago first morning after being startled awake by the woman in the street. Another surprise—a telephone on the wall. Right there in my hotel room. I had seen telephones in Boston, but I was no longer in Boston. This was the Territory of Arizona. A thousand miles from civilization. That large, prehistoric telephone looked elegant in those days—dark mahogany, the size and rectangular shape of a hat box, with a black funnel-shaped mouthpiece protruding straight out from the center of the box. On the side of the box hung a narrower, funnel-shaped black earpiece, connected to the mahogany box by a black cord the thickness of my small finger. In those days you had to nearly shout into the mouthpiece, and even with the earpiece pressed hard to your ear you could barely make out the tiny voice shouting back from the other end. Yet it seemed like a miracle of communication in 1905, and a sign above the hotel front desk boasted that just such a miracle device could be found in any of the 200 rooms of the Santa Rita Hotel.

Clearly, the modern age with its trains and telephones had beaten me to the Arizona territory. So had the modern age of lost baggage, as I discovered when I went to the front desk to inquire about my trunk.

"Mr. Bartlett?" the desk clerk repeated after me in some sort of southern drawl. He gazed with one accusatory eyebrow slightly elevated, like a righteous clergyman who has learned of an iniquity committed by me. He appeared only a few years older than I, but he wore imperiousness like some elderly Boston Brahmin. "You are Mr. Bartlett in room ...?" His eyebrows rose in synchrony with the rising tone of his question.

I leaned a forearm on the wooden counter. "I am Mr. Bartlett in room 54. I arrived last night. I believe you registered me."

"Ah. I remember. You arrived last night."

"I wonder if my trunk was delivered to the hotel."

He shook his head. "I have only just come in for my shift, but I know we have no trunks here, sir."

"Then I wonder if you could give me directions to the train station."

"Ah. And ... sir ... I take it, then, you did not arrive by train?"

"I did arrive by train, but that's not ..."

"Then, to which train station do you require directions, sir?"

"Is there more than one?"

"No sir. There is not."

I glanced around. Perhaps this was some kind of western practical joke. No doubt the locals would see me as a "dude," which, in the dime western novels I liked to read, was what a gentleman was called in these here parts. I said carefully, "I'm not sure why this is so difficult. If there is only one train station, I'd like directions to it."

He stiffened. "Nor am I certain why this is difficult, sir. If I understand you correctly, you are asking for directions to the very train station from which you came."

"That's correct." Arrogance has never sat well with me. I leaned forward, elbows on the counter. "And I'm beginning to think you are forgetting something very important."

"What could that be, sir?"

"You are the desk clerk, isn't that correct?"

"Clearly, sir."

"That is the point you seem to be forgetting. I am a guest of this hotel. The Santa Rita Hotel, by the placard on the wall behind you. You are an employee of the hotel. Am I correct so far? I arrived late at night, and I was tired, and after I got off the train I looked for the first hotel I could find. This morning I need to get to the train station and find my trunk."

"I thought you said you had been to the train station."

I felt my face reddening. "Yes. I was there. But it was late. I was tired. I was distracted. And no, I do not remember where it is."

The clerk shook his head. "Well, I don't know what you were distracted about, but Tucson is hardly a mile across, if that, and ..."

"Which," I said, slapping my hand on the counter, bam!, and causing his eyebrows to rise quite high, "is how I found this hotel in the middle of the night, and how I'll find the manager of this hotel very soon if you keep this up. First, however, I must get to the train station. The only train station. You, Mr. Desk Clerk, are going to give me directions. Or perhaps we should call the manager, now rather than later?"

His chin went up an inch. "As you wish, Mr. Baxter. If ..."

"Bartlett. Get it right. My name is Mr. Bartlett."

"Mr. Bartlett." He pointed toward the front doors. "You go out those doors, turn right and go to the end of the hotel, where you will find Broadway. Turn right and go two blocks east on Broadway, until you reach Fifth Avenue. Turn left. The train station will be straight ahead. You can't miss it." He shifted his gaze past my shoulder, and said, "May I help you, Mrs. Widdle?"

I moved over to intercept his gaze. "Wait. You may not dismiss me that way. You will get my name straight, and you will tell me

13

yours, so I can discuss this with the manager. I'm an attorney. My name is Mr. Bartlett. What is your name?"

He met my glare for barely a second, then lowered his gaze to the center of my chest. "My name is Billsley, sir. And do have a good morning."

"Thank you, *Mister* Billsley." As I turned around I nearly stumbled into the short, broad woman who was standing behind me.

She nodded, and said very solemnly, "*Mister* Bartlett."

I hurried across the lobby and out the door, my face burning, sure I must have seemed quite the pompous ass. In Boston, claiming to be an attorney might have served as a warning. Here, for all I knew, they hung dude lawyers from the nearest tree. If they could find a tree.

Outside, I squinted against the sunlight glare as I caught my first real glimpse of the dusty town that would become my home. So this was the wild west. It looked pretty tame. The Tucson versions of Broadway and Fifth Avenue were wide and sandy, lined with wooden and mud-brick one-story buildings housing hardware stores, clothiers, a farrier, a couple of barbershops. I kept an eye out for a law office where I might introduce myself later. My wool coat felt quite warm. In Boston, only the roughest of men would be in shirt-sleeves in mid-October, but here I alone was dressed for fall. I slipped the coat off and draped it over my shoulder.

At the old wooden train station, the heavy-bearded clerk was unable to locate my trunk. Maybe, he suggested, it had been delivered to the hotel? No? Well, then, a telegram would have to be sent. Maybe the trunk had gone on to a further destination, maybe it would end up in Los Angeles, California. Or maybe it had been taken off the train while I slept through some earlier stop before I arrived in Tucson. The clerk assured me he would do his best, and once my trunk was located, a message could be sent to my hotel. Fine, I told him. If I didn't receive a message in a day or two, I'd come back to check.

But without the trunk, I had only the clothes I was wearing. I would need a change or two. He gave me directions to the clothing store of Albert Steinfeld and Co., where I spent a half-hour being outfitted by a freckled Irishman named Mr. Finn, who fixed me up with two white cotton shirts and two pair of denim trousers and sent me next door for some sturdy high-topped leather boots to protect my ankles against rattlesnakes.

As I strode in my new boots back to my hotel, with packages under my arms, a steam-driven automobile machine hissed quietly past at what seemed a reckless speed, its mustachioed driver decked out in a flapping white driving coat and goggles. Looking around, I seemed to be the only person who was surprised to see such a sight.

There were other surprises, too, as I reconnoitered the town later in the day. The Mexican neighborhoods felt the most exotic, almost as if I had crossed the border into a foreign land. Almost every conversation I heard was in Spanish. I found myself wondering whether the authors of those dime westerns had ever visited the west—I didn't recall a mention of Mexicans at all. Many of the homes were long one-story row houses with front door after front door opening directly onto the street. There was a quiet Chinese neighborhood of a dozen small adobe buildings, near some agricultural fields, and at the other end of town I stumbled upon what was known at the time as Snob Hollow, where the Rockwells, Fishes, and Steinfelds presided over grand domiciles substantiating the prestige and social merit of those who lived in them.

Near sunset, when I returned to the hotel, the lobby bustled with young men, some in coats and ties, others in shirtsleeves, and nearly all of them in stylish boater hats. A half-dozen ladies in gowns clung to the arms of their beaus. The talk was boisterous and full of backslapping and laughter.

The stooped old desk clerk on duty, much more polite than Billsley, explained above the din that all these folks were here for a fundraising ball to send the town baseball team, known as the Grays, off to a baseball game in El Paso, Texas. The El Paso team was in town for a pair of games with the Grays, and it was thought that the Tucson team should make a return venture to El Paso. The desk clerk nodded toward a noisy knot of fifteen or twenty in the center of the crowd. "Those are some of the players. Both teams. One game today, and there'll be another tomorrow."

"Rather an informal ball, wouldn't you say?"

"Yes, sir. Folks here like to relax. I expect that baseball players enjoy their liquor, if you catch my meaning." He pointed toward a back corner of the lobby. "If you want some quiet, you can take the elevator to the roof and eat at our open-air dining room. Nice dinner, and no crowds."

The waiter seated me across from three men in dinner dress. I could see the whole town from this rooftop vantage, six stories high. I'd never considered myself as someone who could marvel at grand vistas, but I was surprised at how pretty the desert could be. The sun was just setting behind the jagged mountains, and overhead, threads of orange and pink light ran through the few sparse clouds. Around me the town spread out in rectangular grids, the railway cutting across one edge. From this height the drab row houses I'd passed in the Mexican neighborhoods showed courtyards behind their walls, with trees and gardens within. Farther out, beyond the town, lay the sparse desert vegetation. Off toward the sunset a line of tall cottonwoods and sycamores followed the path of the riverbed.

There were no mountains in Boston. I hadn't thought about

it while I was there, but trees and buildings always blocked the long view. Here, the landscape was so open. One could see forever. The sunset colors faded into gray, and stars appeared, and it all felt quiet and a bit magical. My waiter returned to my table three times before I was ready to order dinner. The men at a table across from me spoke of politics and gossiped, and from the sound of things they were movers and shakers. It seemed to them that Arizona was destined to be a state, but they disagreed about whether there should be joint statehood with New Mexico, or whether Arizona should be its own separate state. Two of them insisted that the joint statehood issue was balderdash, having been resolved years ago, but one persisted in the notion that a large combined state, Arizona plus New Mexico, could better compete with Texas. Either way, they all agreed, the recent murders in the area would not help dispel the image of a lawless and uncivilized people. Sheriff Pacheco had returned only two days earlier from up near Silver Bell, unsuccessfully chasing two Mexicans who had murdered two Americans in some kind of labor dispute. No sooner had the sheriff returned than there had been yet another killing last night, that young mining engineer, right outside this very hotel. A Mexican had been arrested for that, as well.

I must have given some sign of eavesdropping, because they lowered their voices. I busied myself with my food, trying to catch more, but all I made out was "Well, you're the mayor. Do something." I glanced quickly, but couldn't tell who had said it, or which one might be the mayor.

After they departed, I finished my dinner and sat for a few minutes taking in the star-filled sky. Most of the other tables were busy with diners. Over in one corner, a half-dozen chairs awaited an orchestra, facing toward the dining tables, the whole scene lit white now by electrical lights.

A man in a dark suit and polished boots approached my table.

"Excuse me," he said. "Are you Mr. Bartlett?" His skin was rather dark, his hair jet-black and straight. A handlebar mustache obscured his lips. Mexican, no doubt, by the look of him, but he said my name with no trace of an accent.

"Yes," I said. "Is there a problem?"

"Carlos Castillo." He extended his hand. "There is no problem. I went to the desk and asked to speak to the guest who is registered in your room number, which of course is yourself. The clerk said you were having dinner up here, so I decided to come up and look for you. I have a matter of business to discuss. Would you mind if I joined you? I could buy you a drink."

I sat with a cold tequila and lime drink in my hand, waiting for Mr. Castillo to get to his point. The tangy citrus flavor was new to me, and the night air was cool. I remember the moon was just up and full, its light transforming the dark architecture around us into stark silver rectangles and deep, angular shadows. Carlos, as Mr. Castillo insisted I call him, seemed oddly interested in me and in why I was in Tucson. Suspicious, I told him vaguely that I had arrived the night before, from Boston on business.

"Only last night?" Carlos said. "Did you arrive late?"

"To be honest, I don't recall the time. I was very tired. Why do you ask?"

"I'm sure it was a long trip. A long way to come on business. Were you in business in Boston?"

"No. Not exactly. I was a student most of the time."

"Ah. I thought you looked very young. You are only beginning your career, then. I believe the west is the best place for that. Better than the east, don't you agree? Much more opportunity for a young man."

I wondered if he had ever been to the east. "I don't know yet. I've only just arrived."

"What sort of business are you in, Owen? Mercantile? Shipping? Land? Mining?"

"I'm in law. And you, Mr. Castillo, what sort of business are you in?"

"Carlos. Call me Carlos. We are much more informal here than you are used to in Boston. I have a saddle and leather shop here in town, and I'm in ranching. I punch cows, as they say."

"Sounds very profitable, punching cows."

"It's a saying. It means I'm a cattle rancher. My family owns land to the east of Tucson. I'm also interested in mining. Then you are an attorney?"

"Yes."

"I see. Like any good attorney at law, you try not to reveal too much too soon." He rubbed his chin. "Speaking of law, you must have heard about the murder last night."

"Not much, really. Is this place as dangerous as it seems?"

He smiled. "No more dangerous than any other place. Eight or ten years ago, things were different. But we are becoming more civilized now. After all, the twentieth century is upon us—the future—and we cannot escape becoming civilized. We have not so many murders anymore. The one last night was the first in months."

"I overheard tonight that there was another one about a week ago."

"Yes, but not here in town."

"Who was killed last night?"

"A mining engineer who was putting together a business deal for a new mine south of town. He was a young man. He left behind a beautiful wife."

I sipped my drink, reminded once again of the woman outside my hotel window. "Do the authorities know who did it?"

"They arrested someone this morning. He is a friend of mine. I've known him all my life. He couldn't possibly have done it."

By the light of the electric lamps, my drink looked like water. The chips of ice had melted, and as it warmed to the night air, the flavor deepened. I felt the beginnings of a warmth in my head, as well, which probably loosened my tongue just a bit. I said, "Isn't that usually the case, in murders?"

His eyebrows went up a fraction. "Isn't what usually the case in murders?"

"Isn't it true that a murder is usually a crime of passion, committed by someone who would never have done such a thing but for the passion of the moment?"

"Perhaps. But this crime of passion, as you put it, was not committed by my friend. Did you know it happened right below where we are sitting? Outside the hotel?" He seemed to be watching me closely as he spoke. "As a matter of fact, it happened in the street right outside the window of your room."

"My window?" I set my glass on the table and leaned forward. "How do you know which window is mine? Who are you, Carlos? What do you want?"

He smiled again. "I told you. I'm Carlos Castillo. And you are Owen Bartlett, young lawyer from Boston."

I stood up, and kept my voice low. "I don't want to play this game, Mr. Castillo. This is an odd conversation and you have not stated the nature of your business with me."

Still smiling, he gestured toward my seat. "Please sit with me for another few moments, Owen. I need some information, and I simply wanted to get to know you a little better before asking."

When I didn't move, he glanced around at the other tables, then leaned toward me. "Please sit down. I don't mean to cause a scene. Please."

He waited until I resumed my seat, and went on. "As I

mentioned, the man who was arrested is a friend of mine. His name is Miguel Cordero. I do business with his family. Perhaps there were witnesses. Perhaps you heard something, looked out and saw someone standing there, outside your window. Perhaps someone was running away."

"I heard nothing in the night. When I heard voices outside my window, it was already morning. And a woman was there who must have had some connection. She was being escorted away when I looked out the window. Very lovely. From the way she acted, I suppose she might have been the widow."

He nodded. "It's tragic, isn't it, how the wife becomes a victim, too, when her husband is murdered. I wonder what her life will be like after this. It will be very different. I believe she loved her husband very much."

The Santa Rita Hotel and I are both showing our age, now. They closed that old rooftop restaurant years ago, though in the twenties and thirties the hotel itself became a hot spot for the likes of Tom Mix and Errol Flynn and other stars of movie westerns. I don't remember the last time I saw someone on a horse inside the city limits, except in the rodeo parade. But I do know that the widow came to love me, too, by and by. A rose opens slowly, and we had fifty years.

All these years I've kept busy with my law practice. During the war, I served on the draft board and she volunteered at the Red Cross, working on blood drives and chaperoning dances for the airmen stationed at the Davis-Monthan air field to the east of town. She liked those boys and they all knew her as Mrs. Bartlett. It was not unusual for me to arrive home from the office to find two or three uniformed young men in our living room listening to the radio, while she was in the kitchen cooking dinner. Even during those years of rationing she could turn the simplest rice and beans meal into a special moment with some subtle flavor she grew in her spice garden beside the back door. Those GIs appreciated every bite, and so did I.

At my entrance they would jump to their feet respectfully and call me sir. Eva, in the kitchen with an apron tied over her dress, would kiss me on the cheek and turn back to her stove while I laid my coat and tie over a chair and proceeded to fix a round of drinks. Over dinner the boys would speak of home—Birmingham, Chicago, Spokane, everywhere—and we would talk about the war news. They bragged about what they would do to the Germans or the Japanese, once pilot training was over.

Those evenings brought a sparkle to her eyes. When anyone asked, she would point to the pictures of Roy in his uniform, now somewhere in Africa serving as a supply officer. He wrote to his mother and me only occasionally, but nearly every day to Helen and the children, his letters arriving in batches of a dozen or more. Every couple of weeks, Helen would bring over the latest batch to share with Eva. Then, as the children played outside, they would put their ration books together and plan the week's shopping.

And nearly every day, Eva went to the stables to ride. Like so many parents in those days, she fretted about her son. Riding brought her solace and distraction. Perfecto, who had come to us as a five-year-old gelding just before the war, was her muscular antidote against worry as they cantered through the dry sands of the Santa Cruz riverbed.

Seeing her ride in just such a fashion had been the thing that brought us together. The morning after my conversation with Carlos Castillo in the rooftop restaurant, I peeked out the curtain of my hotel room. There, in the street where a man's life had ended in blood only a day and a half earlier, a heavy freight wagon was passing by, hauled by two straining mules piloted by a white-haired Mexican man with dark, leathery skin. Beneath the passing wheels there was no sign of the dark stain that had been there the day before.

I poured water into the washbasin and splashed my face. Back in Boston, the October weather would be chilly, the leaves outside changing to oranges and gold and reds. I might have a little fire going in the fireplace. Not here, not in this summery air. I pulled on one of my new cotton shirts, and a pair of the stiff denim trousers, and slipped my feet into the new high heel cowboy boots. I liked the feel of them. They gave me a bit more height, nudging me to six feet tall. In the mirror, I pushed my shoulders back. Yes, a good look, except for the black derby. I needed something more western looking, perhaps one of those wide-brimmed hats worn by the cowboys in dime novels.

At breakfast I read through the *Tucson Citizen*. Page one bore an article about the murder outside my room. Citizens were shocked at the finding of a body behind the Santa Rita Hotel. The nefarious assassination, carried out by means of a knife, had taken place without being noticed by any known witnesses in the dead of the night, and the body had lain in the street for an unknown number of hours before being reported at dawn to the sheriff. A Mexican man named Miguel Cordero, the son of a local rancher of good reputation, had been arrested and charged with the murder. Sheriff Pacheco assured the citizenry that the right man had been detained, and they could rest easy. The sheriff himself was only just returned from pursuing two other Mexicans who had murdered two Americans in a labor dispute in Silver Bell. The sheriff insisted there was no danger of an uprising against Americans by the Mexican community. Most local Mexicans, he was quoted as saying, were quiet, law-abiding folks. The article went on to recall that the sheriff himself came from a large Mexican family which had lived in the area for generations, and ended with an announcement that funeral services for Mr. Stephen Downing, the victim of the fatal assault near the Santa Rita Hotel, would be held at eleven that morning.

On my way to the train station to check for my trunk, I considered attending the funeral, curious to find out whether the widow had been the attractive woman I'd seen outside my window. There seemed little doubt, given the look on her face, and her slow, stunned retreat beside the big man and the dog.

Two automobile machines whizzed past me on the wide dirt street, one behind the other, careening at fifteen miles an hour around a one-horse dray that stood motionless in the street. At the train station, the bearded clerk still had seen no sign of my trunk. We agreed I should come back in the afternoon, after the 1:36 arrived from Casa Grande.

I walked on, across the tracks and out into the desert landscape. Before I left Boston, the talk among my friends had been of sand dunes and rattlesnakes. They ribbed me about becoming a camel rider. So far I'd seen neither dunes nor camels, just a scatter of cactus and the woody, spindly bushes I would come to know as creosote. The tough ground appeared not to have seen water in months, and yet the creosote plants were everywhere, spaced apart from each other by several feet and splaying their thin stems out into the warm air.

In the distance was a scatter of houses. A mile or two out was an outsized two-story frame building, and next to it, a boxy redbrick structure improbably fronted by tall, white Doric columns—the buildings of the territorial university, such as it was in those days.

A distant motion from the side caught my attention, and I turned to see a white horse cantering smoothly across my field of vision through the desert, ridden by a young woman. She rode astride the horse like a man, not sidesaddle the way a proper woman would ride in New England. Her dark riding skirt bounced against the horse's flank, and there was the most feminine grace in the confident way her body moved with the rhythm of the canter. I couldn't make out her face, but something about the flow of her dark hair and the way she held herself reminded me of the woman I had seen outside my window the morning before. How oddly charming that such a recent widow would be riding a horse through the desert on the very morning her slain husband was to be laid to rest. After she disappeared in the distance, I turned abruptly back toward town.

Back at the hotel, I dusted off my suit and put it on, along with my shiny new boots. I arrived half an hour early at the church and took a seat in the back, hoping to catch sight of the widow. I'd been to a Catholic church only once before, with a law school friend whose illiterate Irish parents obsessed that his study of law would lead him to godless heathenism. This territorial church resembled that one in Boston, with its musty air and banks of candles and figurines staring somberly from niches along the wall. I was struck by the human figure of a suffering Christ hanging right there before me on the cross, but it seemed to me that these Catholic churches wore a mantle of mystery not found in Protestant meeting houses I had visited.

The pews up front filled gradually, leaving the rows in back unoccupied except by me. The early arrivals were Mexican women, their heads covered by black lace scarves, and I wondered if I was at the right funeral—my impression had been that the murdered man was white. Then three fair-skinned men arrived together, followed singly by other clearly American men. I recognized Carlos among a group of Mexicans coming in. As the front of the church filled, nearly everyone—white or Mexican—genuflected in the aisle before stepping into a pew.

From somewhere, a small bell rang and a procession started

from the back of the church, led by a boy of perhaps ten holding a tall, thin cross nearly twice his height, followed by the priest in ceremonial robes, and then by the casket carried by six pallbearers, rough men in ill-fitting suits. As I learned later, they were hands from nearby ranches, available for hire. Stephen, as it turned out, did not have six friends to bear him to his grave. His funeral was attended instead mostly by the curious, and by Eva's well-wishers, and by elderly ladies in black who together made a career of never missing a funeral.

The small congregation rose to their feet as the procession passed slowly up the center aisle and stopped before the altar. The pallbearers parked the casket on a waiting table and moved off awkwardly to either side, looking to each other for direction. The priest and the boy took their places before the altar. As the mass progressed, I followed along as everyone else sat, then kneeled, then stood, then kneeled again. The priest chanted in Latin with his back to us, turning toward the congregation now and then to sing out in Latin and gesture ceremonially with his hands before turning back to the altar. His voice rang hollow in the long, high chamber. The casket rested heavily before us, Stephen's death the center of our gravity.

I remembered enough Latin from my school days to follow along in the missal I found in the pew. *Dominus vobiscum—The Lord be with you. Pax domini sit semper vobiscum—May the peace of the Lord be always with you.* Later on in life, I would memorize the Latin and translate it to myself as a diversion during mass, while Eva prayed earnestly beside me. But that day, the day of Stephen Downing's funeral, I didn't need diversion.

After the mass I waited outside the church alongside the ladies in black veils, as the pallbearers bore the casket out to a hearse drawn by two matched gray horses. Carlos nodded to me as he left with his group, crossing himself as he walked past the hearse.

The widow, coming behind with an impenetrable veil covering her face, boarded a carriage with two other women. The hearse started off, followed by the carriage and on foot by those remaining. We arrived at the cemetery a half-hour slow walk later, and I took up a spot within the group across the grave from the widow. She stood erect, her face hidden and her hands trembling, as the priest read prayers in Latin. I felt my own hands trembling in sympathy, unexpectedly, and I shoved them into my pockets, glancing around to see if anyone noticed. The priest paused now and then to sprinkle drops of water onto the casket from a small silver ornament. Afterward, the widow accepted condolences from the ladies around her and then quickly boarded the carriage. The driver giddapped the pair of horses into a trot, and she was gone.

It had been more painful to watch than I expected, bringing back the hurt of my mother's funeral, and the memory of frowning strangers who hurried to get her sealed casket and her contagion into the ground as quickly as possible, as I watched from the far side of the cemetery wall. I had kept my grief to myself, knowing they would have responded with impatience. It was time, they would have said, to be a man. After all, I was seventeen.

Reminded, I suddenly felt homesick. I regretted letting myself be talked into traveling across the country to this strange, almost desolate place. The other mourners straggled away. I stayed for a few minutes to watch, as the graveyard workers shoveled dirt into the grave, the first few shovelfuls thumping onto the casket until it was covered over. I wandered off toward a line of trees that suggested the possibility of water, only to find that the trees lined a dry riverbed that lay beside the town—the Santa Cruz riverbed, as I would come to know it. The high white-barked sycamores and cottonwoods, still green in October, reminded me of home, where rivers actually flowed with water, and where the greenness of trees would already be transformed into the colors of fall.

Mr. Norman had made it clear I had no real choice about leaving. Two summers before coming to Arizona, as I was crossing a broad lawn in Boston Gardens, I spotted him wearing a low topper, strolling with two younger men in boater hats. I paused to avoid crossing their paths. I recognized the two young men with him from the society page clippings Mother used to keep hidden under her bed—Albert was a year older than I, and Charles a year younger. Theirs was the life I might have had, had things been different. I imagined comfort and assured easy responsibility, a life free from worries. Board meetings, perhaps, and soirées. Cigars and port and substantial conversations in the parlor. I had yet to learn that wealth and privilege provide little protection from the real vicissitudes of human life. Albert, as things turned out, contracted mumps sometime in his twenties. He would never have children, and his wife would leave him for another man after the great crash in 1929, when, it was said, he lost everything. Cirrhosis of the liver finished him off later. Charles, though more cautious in his dealings, would lose both his sons to combat, one in France on D-Day, and the other in the Pacific during the fight for Okinawa, only a few months before Japan surrendered. In their grief, neither Charles nor his wife would be seen again in public after 1945. I'm sure none of us suspected such a future back in 1903, when I saw them in the Gardens. We were young and the green lawns of Boston Gardens bordered colorful plots of geraniums and foxglove, all carefully ordered.

What I did know was jealousy—jealousy in my youth as I pored over Mother's secret newspaper clippings when she was out, jealousy later as I walked past the Norman house on Chestnut Street in Beacon Hill, jealousy even in the Gardens when I saw the family together and knew I could not be part of it. But after Mother's death I had transformed that jealousy into ambition, and that ambition was what had gotten me into law.

I never met Albert and Charles, but I did meet Mr. Norman twice. I was ten the first time, and I met him at the public library, the old one later torn down in the 1890s to make room for the grand version still standing today. I used to love the booky smell of the old stacks. I would climb to the third floor, my footsteps echoing on the marble stairs. I would lean over the rail to spy on the heads of the patrons reading at the long tables below.

That morning, before we left for our library trip, Mother fussed more than usual with her hair, and donned a frilly yellow hat with a feathered plume sticking up in back. She shooed me away when I pestered her about it, her eyes fixed on her image in the mirror. "It's borrowed," was all she would say. Later, at the library, instead of wandering with me as usual through the upstairs stacks, she sent me up alone, promising to join me in a little while. "Go on," she whispered. "Find something good for me to read when I come up."

I climbed the stairs as she asked and walked up and down the stacks, my forefinger playing along the book bindings. After each row I glanced over the rail to keep an eye on Mother, who was seated at a first floor table with a book. On my third or fourth check, though, it occurred to me that she wasn't reading her book at all, but was mainly watching the door. She was waiting for someone. Curious, I took up a spot against the rail to watch. Who could she be waiting for like this? Why would she want me out of the way? Why was she wearing that borrowed yellow hat?

Her back straightened as a certain tall gentleman entered. His suit was dark, a black necktie braced his high white collar and he held a derby as he glanced around. He picked her out right away and went to her table. They spoke for a moment, he standing, she sitting, and then she rose to follow him outside. I'm sure I was bug-eyed with astonishment that she even knew a man who dressed like that, much less would walk outside with him just like that. I flew down the stairs to a ground floor window where

I could watch. Outside on the lawn, a man walked a large furry dog, and a man and woman strolled hand in hand, but there was no sign of Mother and the man. Another window, over on the far side of the reading room, revealed a horse and buggy trotting by on the street, and a woman sitting on a blanket beneath a tree. But no Mother. Exploding with nosiness, I finally dashed out the front door, tripped over something, and tumbled headlong on my face.

"Owen!" Mother's voice.

I whirled around and jumped to my feet, brushing at some gravel stuck to my hands. She fussed as she patted at the knees of my trousers, one hand steadying her yellow hat. What in the world, she wanted to know. What in the world, indeed!

The gentleman towered there, the calm center to this bit of ruckus, his eyes taking my measure, up and down. Then, smiling what I later concluded was an odd smile, he held out his hand. "Hello, Owen," he said. "My name is Christopher Norman."

In my ten-year-old lifespan, no man—and certainly no gentle-man with a derby—had ever offered to shake hands with me as if I were an adult. I looked to Mother for direction. She nodded without speaking, her eyes clouded by some rush of feelings I could not identify. I shook Mr. Christopher Norman's hand, once up, once down. I wasn't sure quite how to do it, but I remember his fingers lingered on mine an extra second before letting go. After an awkward pause, Mother told me they had some business to discuss and asked me to wait inside the library. "I won't be long," she said.

I wanted to protest, to watch this business discussion and figure out why she looked so—I didn't think of a word for it until later—alive. She did look so alive, her eyes moving from me to this Mr. Christopher Norman. I was fascinated. I protested and wanted to stay. Mr. Norman said nothing, and Mother grew stern for an instant. "Owen." Normally when she used that tone, her next words would be, "Don't make me ..." And normally I'd have continued to argue. But this wasn't normal. This was a new side to my mother I had never seen, and I liked this new side. I took a deep breath and decided to help her out.

"All right," I said as brightly as I could. "I'll wait inside." I looked up at Mr. Norman, unsure what to say, but he filled in the blank for me.

"It was nice to see you, Owen."

"Nice to see you, too," I said. Mother's warm hand on my shoulder. Mr. Norman's eyes on mine. I said, "I'll wait inside, then."

I felt their eyes on my back until the door closed behind me. Then I took another breath and abandoned my impulse to dash to another window and spy. This was clearly some kind of magic moment for Mother, and I didn't want to risk spoiling it. I climbed the stairs again to the third floor stacks and pulled out a random volume. The History of Pompeii and Its Destruction. A blue leather cover, I still recall. At a corner desk, I thumbed through the illustrations of bodies frozen into agonized death postures and began to discover how one's world can be turned upside down in one short morning. When Mother joined me, her eyes were moist. She put up a hand when my whispered questions started. "Not now," was all she would say.

Days later, after the constant barrage of my inquisitiveness, she finally sat me down at the kitchen table and confided the secret to me. She offered only the barest facts, and over the years I have filled them in from my imagination. At eighteen she had taken a job as a clerk in Mr. Norman's business. Her father had vehemently disapproved, but her mother encouraged her, secretly. In those years—that would have been about 1880, the year Mother was eighteen—women were beginning to speak of independence and her mother believed a young woman should learn something of the world before she settled down to marriage. Mr. Norman's father owned several warehouses, and it was young Mr. Norman's job to manage them. He was handsome and still in his twenties, but he was also married with an infant son. There were problems in the marriage.

A spark flashed somehow between them. I used to imagine that she became the love of his life, that he could not live without her, trapped in his unhappy marriage but secretly showering her with flowers and small but expensive gifts. More likely, though, she was merely a passing crush in a moment of his loneliness. However the affair progressed and however it fell apart—she never said and I never asked—one day it was over and she was left with me. Her embarrassed family turned their backs. She and Mr. Norman made a deal. Mother and I would be cared for, just as long as—and here Mother raised a significant forefinger to ensure my full attention at the kitchen table—just as long as we never revealed that he was my father. Not to a soul. Not ever.

I remember a searing heat in my lungs as I listened at the table, while this new vision of myself bore in upon me. No longer would I be, as Mother had always given me to believe, a boy whose father had died tragically on the docks where he worked. I was a boy whose father did not want him. I was a lie. A secret. A shame. I could feel her hand on my knee, though she was a blur through my tears. I fought for breath through what must have been a very long silence, and then, through the blur, I perceived the regret in her eyes. Regret that she had told me all this, perhaps, but certainly regret about what her life had become. I was part of what she regretted. If I hadn't happened ... She rose and moved heavily around the kitchen, preparing dinner. Had we spoken, I'm sure the thick, hot air would have muffled our words. But we did not speak.

I recall getting into a lot of fights over the next few months.

My friends fell away, as I challenged them angrily, singly and in groups, cocking my fists over small slights and disagreements. It was the bigger and stronger boys, though, who really drew my ire, boys who, like bigger boys everywhere, liked to have their way with smaller fry. I missed few chances to strike when they took a ball away, or pushed somebody down. I lost more fights than I won, but went home satisfied and bloodied many an evening, to Mother's distress. I slept well those nights, the ache of my bruises covering over the ache in my heart. By the end of that summer, there was almost no one left who would fight me. Even the really tough boys came to know that, win or lose, I kept swinging until I could no longer raise my arms.

Then, in a fight one afternoon, something happened to bring me back to myself. I had just knocked a boy to the ground, and he was slow at getting back up. The other boys around us were oddly quiet, not yelling as they often did while watching a fight. I stood my ground, fists at the ready, waiting. The boy's name was Peter, or maybe it was Michael. He was a couple of years older and had wanted to fight me to prove how tough he was, because I was getting a reputation. I remember we were behind Billy McGillicuddy's house, because I turned my head and in Billy's window caught a glimpse of another boy—a skinny but fearsome boy with fists raised, his nostrils flared, baring his teeth like an animal. I heard a growl and looked closer. That boy was me, my window reflection, glaring back at me, growling. I was growling. Suddenly seeing what I had become stopped me cold. The boy in the window and I dropped our fists. We stared at each other another moment. This was not what we wanted, not what we wanted to be like, no matter who had hurt us. And we turned and went our separate ways, my doppelganger and I, while the boys behind called. "Hey! Hey Owen! What are you doing? Hey!"

I was not magically healed, of course. Mother gradually soothed my lacerated ego. She loved me, my neighborhood compatriots respected me, and after a while, my friends became my friends again. I never lost my hair trigger when I felt threatened, or when someone weaker was threatened, but peace came back to me. Over many years since, I have even learned to respect what Mr. Norman did for Mother and me. After all was said and done, he was not a self-centered bully who took advantage and then pushed his son and lover away. He was just a man caught in the nets of his life, who tried to make things right for those who were trapped in the nets with him. In that way, I suppose, I became my father's son.

And so, that summer morning watching Mr. Norman and my half-brothers walking through the Commons, I followed at a discreet distance as they approached two girls seated on a bench in long, wide skirts, reading. The girls looked perhaps fourteen or fifteen, and they jumped to their feet to hug Mr. Norman. They might have been younger sisters, too young when Mother died to have become items in her clippings box. The family group was not thirty yards from me, but the distance was as unbreachable as the distance to the moon.

There was another day, later—the day of my law school graduation. The year before, the YMCA had changed the name of our program to the School of Law, and the bachelor of law degree I earned would come to be recognized everywhere in the country. My class was the first class of what, a decade or two later, would evolve into Northeastern University. Seated in my cap and gown among the dozen other young men, I listened to speaker after speaker. We were congratulated for graduating from this radical institution which provided working class men the opportunity of an education in the law. We were congratulated because from our ranks might come powerful men who would go on to have great influence in the world. We were congratulated because we would be attorneys and someday judges, perhaps even members of Congress, or governors. I wanted that destiny. I was ready to be a man of great moment.

But, like other young people, I secretly harbored other inclinations, and contrary, restless desires. Late at night, studying, I sometimes hankered to see more of the world. I devoured dime novels about the old west, novels peopled with prospectors and Indians and old Confederate veterans wandering the plains. And cowboys. The good guys were hard-bitten but warm-hearted, unpretentious and savvy, as ready to sling a gun as they were to sling a saddle. Being a cowboy certainly hadn't slowed up the president of the United States himself, Teddy Roosevelt—a real man's man. I hadn't been in a good fistfight in years, but I enjoyed the occasional rugby scrum and I could hit my share of long flies in baseball. Unlike a cowboy, though, I was not good with horses, even the tame drafters on the Boston streets. Lack of skill with horses would be a detriment to any cowboy, no doubt. And the prospect of sleeping in the rain on hard ground did not appeal to me.

Mother had raised me to be a realist. After graduation I went to work at the prestigious law firm of Herrington and Hines, where I was assigned to be the associate for a Mr. Jacquelyn Davenport. Mr. Davenport was ten years older and newly made a partner in the firm, a Harvard man. He seemed scarcely ever to notice me when I surfaced after whole weeks hunched over fat volumes in the firm's basement library, researching the common law of topics like misrepresentation and specific performance in a contract for the sale of real property. He would leave nearly illegible notes on my work stool, wishing to be informed as to opinions of the courts of Maine or Pennsylvania or Illinois regarding methods of terminating a tenancy in common in which one owner had committed a tort against another. I crafted legal memoranda on the requested issues, left them in the safekeeping of Charles Blaise, Mr. Davenport's secretary, and moved on to my next assignment.

One sunny early-June day, while I was poring over a thick file of invoices intended to help Mr. Davenport prepare for the deposition of a shipping company accountant, I decided to sneak out to the water closet. In a hurry, I cut through the elegant second floor waiting room, where only the elite and most well-heeled clients were ever invited. There—I froze in my tracks—sat Mr. Norman, reading the morning *Globe* in one of the leather-upholstered seats. I carefully turned away.

Two days later, on a Sunday morning, there came a knock at my apartment door, and I opened it to find Mr. Norman standing in the hallway, a felt top hat under his arm, his black bowtie squared. I stared until he said, "May I come in, Owen?" When I still hesitated, he brushed past me and stood in the middle of the sitting room, looking around at the furnishings. I collected myself enough to move a pile of books from the overstuffed chair so he could be seated. I offered him a cup of coffee or tea before I realized I was fresh out of both.

"No thanks," he said, settling into the chair. "Owen, let me get to my point. I think we would both agree that I have done my duty by you, and by your mother, rest her soul. I didn't hear of her passing until weeks later, from my property manager. I trust her funeral was dignified?"

After a pause in which I couldn't yet answer, he went on. "As I was saying, I believe I did my duty by both of you. Would you agree?"

After another pause I was able to get out, "Yes, sir. You have." So much to say, so much to ask. So many years. Mother. The past, tumbling in all at once, memories, questions, absences, impressions, more questions. Beneath it all, my anger. I fought it back by focusing on his face. His face was the future of my face—my own brown eyes couched in a slight puffiness, my cheeks laden with new weight, my wide mouth brought down at the corners by three additional decades of life. I wondered if my brown hair would gray first at the temples, like his. Up close, I saw that I resembled him more than did either Charles or Albert.

He said, "And up until now, you have respected your part of the bargain, as well. I think you know what I'm referring to."

"Yes," I said. "Of course."

"The point, Owen, is that you have now come to the end of a good education, the foundation of which I provided through my support, and the rest of which you sought out yourself. You have begun your career at a fine law firm. I did see you, by the way, day before yesterday when you tried to escape my notice. I hadn't known you were working at Herrington and Hines, and I made some inquiries. You'll be happy to know you are well thought of. Mr. Davenport, your superior, has convinced the senior partners that you are quite diligent and may have a good future with the firm. As I understand it, they thought they were taking a chance when they hired you because you were trained in that odd YMCA program. Not the usual path to a position at Herrington and Hines. You've impressed them enough that they will be looking at others from your program in the future. Under other circumstances, it would also be useful for you to know that Robert Hines has been a friend of mine since our school days. Under other circumstances, I might enjoy the irony of your employment there. But circumstances are what they are. Let's think practically. About your future, I mean."

I knew what he meant and I waited. He wanted me out of the way. I fought back the old impulse to raise my fists to this bully. I reminded myself that I had made myself into the gentleman he now faced, a gentleman who understood restraint and knew how to deal.

He said, "Owen, you have equipped yourself with the tools and background to make your way in some substantial fashion in the world. Wide vistas are open to you, and with the ambition and ability you have already demonstrated, you will go far. I have no doubt about that. Boston, however, would not be the best place for you, wouldn't you agree?"

I drew a deep breath. "Sir, my status as an attorney is something I achieved myself, without direct help from anyone, including you. I believe I have earned the right to choose where I wish to practice law."

He ran a finger along the brim of the top hat on his knee. "You are right. You have earned the right to practice any career, in any place. On the other hand, the life you have now is in part the result of my support. Things could have been very different for you and for your mother. I know you understand that. And we both understand that we are in a position to hurt each other. I have no desire, absolutely no desire, to engage with you in that way. Instead, I am asking, as a favor, that you start a new life somewhere else. I am in a position to help you, with money, with connections, with enough resources to give you a good start. What would you say to that?"

This was not a bluff. He could ruin my chances at Herrington and Hines. He could arrange for trouble to follow me if I moved to a different firm in the Boston area. Of course, I could embarrass him by crashing into his life as the bastard son. But the embarrassment for him would be mild and momentary, and his elevated life would go on. Mistresses and bastard children were not so uncommon among successful men. My reputation would suffer more than his—after all, I was the bastard. Whispers would follow me as I applied to other firms. Doors would close. And he was making a reasonable offer.

He was good. He had me. I understood now how the deal had come about between him and Mother. She had approached him about her condition and her circumstances. He weighed his choices. He made her an offer, a more generous offer than he really needed to make. I searched his eyes and was surprised to find sadness there. The same deep regret I had seen in Mother's eyes. Perhaps, once upon a time, she really had been the love of his life. Perhaps he would have liked a chance to be a real father to me.

I said, "How much money and support are we talking about, sir? I recall being shoved into the world rather abruptly after my mother died."

"That happened before I was aware, and I apologize. I had given instructions for the eventualities, but never imagined it would be like that, or so soon. She was young. So were you." He leaned forward for a moment. "I'm very sorry. This time, now, to set you up, I would expect to offer, oh, two or three thousand. Let's say I make it three. I could also provide some introductions. I was thinking of the Arizona territory. Plenty of opportunity for a trained lawyer, with all the talk about statehood."

Arizona. I thought of my dime novel daydreams. And three thousand. I tried to keep my eyebrows from going up. Three thousand dollars was a lot of money in 1905. His carrot was certainly bigger than his stick. "That's generous."

He nodded. "I mean for it to be, Owen. I mean for you to have a real chance. I hadn't expected you to put yourself through law school, though I did intend to help you a bit once you started a family. But since you have demonstrated real ambition, it would give me some satisfaction to see you rise in your fortunes. Only ..." He paused and smiled. "... not here. You understand."

I nodded. He knew how to offer a bribe. I could have learned much from him.

He reached into his coat pocket, extracted a thin envelope, and handed it to me. "This is a letter of introduction to an acquaintance of mine, Mr. Epes Randolph. He is with the Southern Pacific railroad, and has business interests in California and the Arizona Territory. I understand he recently moved to a little town called Tucson, near the Mexican border. It's a place to start. In my letter to Epes, I have introduced you as the son of a dear friend. Which is true, of course."

We shook hands at the door. He said, "I will send you account information and how we shall manage the funds. Goodbye, Owen. You looked good at your graduation."

"Sir?"

"You looked good as you walked across the stage in your cap and gown, and took your diploma. I was proud. I am proud. You've done well under difficult circumstances."

I swallowed hard. "Thank you, sir. I hadn't known you were there."

I watched from the doorway as he walked away down the hall. Then I closed the door as softly as I could manage.

A week later, I boarded a steamer for Liverpool, on a ticket I purchased with a little of Mr. Norman's money. I wanted to experience something of Europe, in the way other educated men did, before heading off into my new future. I made my way to Scotland, to the cool highlands near Invernesse, where I spent July and most of August. Days, I wandered the green loch shores and imagined my future life out west, in the land of the cowboys. Nights, I drank ale with a quiet farmer and his wife who rented me a cheap room above their three-table pub. Una, the wife, would grill me about my plans for marriage and what she perceived as my lack of interest in finding a wife. Past her third glass, she would touch my arm and lean her heavy round bosom close as she extolled the warmth and loving kindness a woman could bestow unto my life. Taran, her man, nodded agreeably and gripped his mug, his eyes increasingly glazed as the night went along. At evening's end, off they would go up the stairs, stumbling and steadying one another, to demonstrate from inside their bedroom walls, with regular thumps and irregular sharp groans, their own rough version of marital bliss.

When they saw me off at the Edinburgh and Northern station, Una counseled me one last time. "Get yourself a good wife, Owen. A good wife." Taran grunted in assent, his green eyes matching hers. They stood shoulder to shoulder on the railroad platform, watching impassively as the train slid away.

U na would have been pleased to know I met my good wife only two months later, a day or two after I attended the funeral of her slain husband. I was eating breakfast at the Santa Rita Hotel, and reading the newspaper, getting the lay of my new hometown. An editorial pontificated about the need for better relations between Americans and Mexicans. As to the murder that had happened outside my window, a front-page story said that the grand jury would meet tomorrow and would no doubt issue an indictment charging a Mr. Miguel Cordero with the crime of murder of the first degree. Mr. Cordero and the murder victim had been business partners on a mining venture on land belonging to the Cordero family. Witnesses said the two men had seemed on friendly terms, and were surprised that Mr. Cordero would commit such a terrible act. The victim, Mr. Stephen Downing, was a mining engineer, and was exactly the sort of educated, professional man needed to help turn the territory into a modern State of Arizona.

As I read, a young runner for the hotel brought a white envelope to my table, addressed to me, care of the Santa Rita Hotel. I tipped him and slit open the envelope with my butter knife. In a firm hand, the note inside read, "Dear Mr. Bartlett, I would be pleased if you would come for a small luncheon today at noon. I have a matter of urgent business with you. You needn't RSVP. Simply come at noon." The note gave the address, and concluded, "Sincerely, Mrs. Stephen Downing."

The widow. My mind's eye went to the woman outside my window. Those intense eyes. I leaned back in my chair, my palms suddenly moist. I reminded myself that this would be about business. No doubt she would have questions regarding the estate, or the disposition of property. Her late husband had failed to provide a will, or perhaps he had prepared a will but she (or someone else) wanted to dispute it. She must have heard I was a new lawyer in town—probably from Carlos Castillo, or perhaps from the clothier where I had purchased my new outfits. Who knew how news travelled in a town like this. I had expected my new law practice to take some time getting off the ground, but circumstances seemed to be veering in my favor.

South Meyer Avenue turned out to be in a Mexican neighborhood of narrow streets and flat-roofed adobe rowhouses whose doors opened directly onto the street. The faces were mostly brown, nearly all the conversations in Spanish. I wondered if I had somehow got the wrong address. When I found the house number, I glanced around. No one was watching. No one seemed to think me out of place. I knocked, then knocked again. After a minute a tiny Mexican woman opened the door, so tiny the top of her head barely came up to my chest. Her gray hair was tied back in a long braid that draped across her shoulder, falling almost to her waist. She greeted me in Spanish.

I glanced again at the number beside the door. "I'm sorry. Can you tell me …"

"Señor Bartlett?"

"Yes, I'm Bartlett. Is this … I'm sorry, but do you speak English?"

She opened the door wider and gestured with a sweep of her hand for me to enter. "*Pásele.*"

I followed through a covered foyer that opened abruptly out onto a large walled-in garden. Two men and a woman sat at a small table under a spreading shade tree. She, in a black dress, was strikingly pretty. Her dark eyes regarded me with that same flame-inducing intensity as the first time, but this time I could not escape behind a window curtain. Though her face looked drawn, she smiled. "Mr. Bartlett," she said as the two men rose in greeting. "I'm so glad you could come. I am Mrs. Downing. I'd like you to meet Mr. Cecilio Amado Borboa, and Father Arnold."

I shook hands with each. Father Arnold I recognized as the priest from the funeral. His roman collar checked a burgeoning double chin, and his flaccid handshake spoke, perhaps, of otherworldly concerns. Mr. Borboa, shorter and slighter of build, gripped my hand dominantly, his eyes measuring mine. At his gesture I took an empty seat at the table. Mrs. Downing spoke in Spanish to the Mexican woman, who nodded and disappeared back into the house.

Mr. Borboa said, "Mr. Bartlett, we are glad you decided to come."

Father Arnold rubbed his hands together. "Yes, we're glad indeed. It's such a gorgeous afternoon, don't you think, now that autumn has finally arrived."

"It's pleasant," I said. "I wouldn't have thought October could be so mild." I kept my eyes on Father Arnold, though I really wanted to stare at Mrs. Downing.

He said, "That's exactly what I thought when I first arrived last year. But after the hot summer, I think I can get very used to having a mild October. For one thing, October is a good month for gardening. This ..." His hands spread to indicate the enclosed yard. "... this is beautiful."

Two or three small sheds stood at the far end of the courtyard. At the near end were flowerbeds and a large plot of vegetables mulched by straw. Staked tomatoes reminded me of Mother's summer vegetable gardens, except that here there was no lawn around it, only bare ground. A large vine covered with brilliant red flowers tumbled over the corner of the high, whitewashed wall.

I said, "This is all so hidden away behind the walls."

She said, "It's the Mexican way. I've always liked it. It gives a person an easy sense of privacy with the family." She nodded toward the house. "Chela is bringing refreshments. We are also waiting for another guest … Ah, here he is, as we speak. Mr. Bartlett, I believe you met Mr. Castillo at the hotel?"

Carlos Castillo strode confidently across the yard, his black boots polished, his black coat and tie pressed and neat. He shook hands warmly with Mrs. Downing and then turned to me to extend his hand. "Mr. Bartlett. It is good to see you again." His handshake was genuine and firm. He greeted the priest and Mr. Borboa, and after a few pleasantries about the weather, he wasted no time getting to the point of the meeting. "Mrs. Downing, have you …?"

When she shook her head, he said, "Would you mind if I do?" His eyes engaged mine. "You see, Mr. Bartlett, we wanted to discuss something, and please forgive me if I seem rude by rushing into this. Time is important. As you would probably guess, we wish to discuss what happened the other night. When Mrs. Downing's husband passed away." He glanced at her, then at me. He paused, waiting. They all waited.

I said, "You said there has been an arrest in the case."

He leaned forward. "Yes. But as I also mentioned, they have arrested the wrong person. And there will be trouble because of it."

I said, "The editorial in the newspaper didn't seem to question whether the wrong man had been arrested."

Carlos and Mr. Borboa stiffened, and glanced at each other.

"I'm sorry," I went on. "I don't mean to demean your friend. But what would I have to do with all that?"

Carlos cleared his throat. "You mentioned to me that you are a lawyer."

I shifted in my seat, feeling suddenly more awkward. "Mrs. Downing, if there is a problem with your husband's estate, I'm sure I could find a way to help you. I would need a few days to set up my office. My credentials haven't even arrived. I'm still waiting for my trunk."

She smiled. "Mr. Bartlett, there is no estate. Just a little money we saved, and our house. Under the territorial law, it's mine now. But our friend is in trouble. Deep trouble. The only thing that can help him is a good lawyer. His name is Miguel Cordero. The Cordero family is well known in Tucson, and well regarded. Miguel Cordero is in jail for the murder of my husband. Are you interested?"

Father Arnold was staring off at a little patch of flowers near the house. Carlos and Mr. Borboa watched me as Mrs. Downing went on. "Miguel was my husband's business partner. The Cordero ranch borders the gold mining district at Greaterville, in the mountains south of town. With Stephen's help, the Corderos staked a claim and established a mining company. They started constructing a system of pipes from high up in the mountains, to bring in water for processing the gold. That's as far as they got before Stephen was killed."

I said, "Then I suppose I would need a few extra days to learn something about mining law, if that is where this is headed."

Mr. Borboa spoke up. "Mr. Bartlett, we want to hire you to defend Miguel Cordero."

My mouth must have dropped open. "I don't mean to be disrespectful, and please pardon me for saying this. But Mrs. Downing,

45

why in the world would you want to hire a lawyer to defend the man who killed your husband?"

Her cheeks flushed. "Miguel did not kill my husband. He's a good man, and he wouldn't do such a thing. He wouldn't kill Stephen."

"I see. Well. This is a bit of a shock, you know. I ... Let's be realistic." I weighed my words. My law practice needed to start somewhere, but a murder case—and this murder case in particular—would surely be over my head. "You haven't asked how much experience I've had."

She smiled. "All right. How much experience do you have?"

"Well, to start with, I have no experience in criminal law."

"But you have experience in law."

"Yes. Mostly in matters of business, which is why I assumed you needed help with the estate. In fact, when I was planning to leave Boston, I was given the name of a businessman here who might help me get started with that sort of practice."

"What is his name?"

"Something Randolph. An odd first name. A friend of someone I know."

Mr. Borboa said, "Epes Randolph?"

"Yes, that was the name."

Carlos and Mr. Borboa glanced at each other and the air felt abruptly cooler.

"To be honest," I added, "I haven't been at all sure I would look up Mr. Randolph. I was just offering an example of the sort of business matters the law firm in Boston was involved in."

Mrs. Downing said, "I see. Well, you won't have any trouble getting invited to the Gentlemen's Club."

I said, "Considering the man who referred me to him, I would expect Mr. Randolph to be a man of the highest stature in the community. But I've never met him and I have other priorities than joining a gentlemen's club."

Carlos abruptly stood up and extended his hand toward me for a handshake. "I have to get back to my shop. I very much appreciate your frankness, Mr. Bartlett. Maybe you are right. Maybe you would not be the right lawyer to represent Miguel."

Mr. Borboa stood up to leave. "Thank you for coming," he said, "I wish you good luck, whatever you choose to be doing. I am sure with your connections you will have many opportunities."

I rose to my feet as well. Clearly, I'd said the wrong thing.

Mrs. Downing looked distressed. "Chela is bringing out some food. Please stay, all of you. There is more to discuss."

There was sympathy in Mr. Borboa's eyes, but firmness in his voice. "Señora Downing, thank you for inviting us to discuss this. I think we have heard what we needed to hear. Please excuse me." He bowed slightly in my direction, and turned away.

Mrs. Downing gestured for me to remain and walked with them toward the house, speaking quietly, her hands gesturing urgently. Carlos shook his head.

Father Arnold, who had remained seated, watched them leave. "I'm sure I have no idea what that was about. But I haven't been here long myself, and I don't know everyone."

"Perhaps it was my mention of Epes Randolph."

"Maybe. Or maybe it was something else. Mrs. Downing can fill us in when she returns." He gestured toward the showy red vine in the corner of the yard. "Are you familiar with the flora here, Mr. Bartlett? That large vine over there is one of my favorites. Bougainvillea. Curiously, the red flowers that you see aren't flowers at all. They are colored leaves, called bracts. You have to get quite close to see the flowers themselves, which are yellow and very small. Tiny, in fact."

I would come to know over the years that Father Arnold's mind dwelt mainly on flowers and food, even as he performed his spiritual functions. A few months later, when he was teaching me the catechism so that I could convert to Catholicism and marry

Eva, he spoke of milk as a metaphor for the soul, in comparing the effects of a venial sin and a mortal sin. The soul, like fresh milk, was pure and white. A venial sin made a dark spot in the milk, but a mortal sin turned the milk black. "Ah, but milk," he said. "Pure milk." His eyes lit up at the thought. "There's the thing. I'd love a cup of pure milk right now. Wouldn't you?" And off he went to his kitchen, to return with two cups of fresh, white, free-from-sin milk. He raised his cup in a toast. "Our sign of God's love!" He drained the cup in a single swig and smiled brightly, his upper lip white with a milk mustache.

The gray flecks in his dark hair suggested he was in his forties, but his unlined forehead and uncomplicated eyes suggested an age more youthful. Eva believed him to be wise. He would be her priest and confessor for the next two decades, and I know now he must have known her secret all along. But I recall nothing in his uncomplicated face that morning to give him away. Those bright red bracts on the bougainvillea sure looked like flowers to me.

When Mrs. Downing returned a few moments later with Chela, they each carried a tray of food and drinks, which they set before us. To my surprise, Chela took the seat where Mr. Castillo had been sitting. I had presumed her to be a servant, but here she was, joining us. Mrs. Downing, handing us each a cup of tea, said, "Mr. Bartlett, this is my good friend, Señora Graciela Salgado. Her nickname is Chela. She doesn't speak English. This is her home."

"Ah. That explains it. So this isn't where you live, Mrs. Downing?"

"My friends have been taking turns watching over me. They've been so wonderful. They don't want me to be alone. Chela invited me to stay with her while things were taken care of. The funeral, and so forth."

"I'm sure this has all been very difficult. What a nice place for a respite."

Father Arnold stirred his tea. "The other gentlemen left rather suddenly, don't you think? I was hoping we could all enjoy lunch together."

"Not to worry, Father," Mrs. Downing said. "Another time, perhaps. They had been planning something that didn't seem to work out." Her eyes flickered to mine briefly.

As the two women watched, Father Arnold showed me how to prepare my first taco, wrapping a warm corn tortilla around small pieces of the sliced beef, adding a mix of chopped vegetables he called a salsa. As he watched me take my first bite, his mouth opened in sympathy with mine. He waited. "Good, yes?"

I nodded, my mouth hot with the flavors. "Mmm. A bit spicy, I must say. Where did you learn Spanish, Mrs. Downing?"

"I don't speak it very well, but I'm trying to learn. When my husband and I met, I had a dream to live in a foreign country. He said we could do that later, after he made some money in mining here in America."

Father Arnold said, "From what I understand, there's plenty of money to be made in mining."

"I've heard that," I said. "Mrs. Downing, have you been here in the Arizona territory long?"

"Two years, more or less. My husband and I came here from Wyoming. He was from the east, and he studied mining at the Missouri School of Mines. We met when he came to Wyoming to visit his cousin. Stephen and I moved to Arizona because he heard there was a possibility of some gold mining near Tucson. If the gold mining didn't work out, he planned to work for one of the copper mining companies."

Later, as our life together began, she would tell me the rest of the story. How her father was a Wyoming rancher who died in a cattle stampede when she was an infant. How her mother, self-educated and well-lettered for a woman of that time and place, tried to land a position as a country teacher and, turned away because she had a baby daughter, moved to Laramie to establish a boarding house. How the baby daughter grew to womanhood among drummers and pitch men and quiet alcoholics, scrubbing and helping in the kitchen and reading books for hours in her mother's room. And how her mother was killed one night, reading in lamp light beside her window, by a stray bullet from a drunken ruckus on the street, and the sixteen-year-old Eva, fending off the lawyers and refusing to lose everything, gritted her teeth through her tears and took command of the boarding house, which she ran until Stephen Downing came along, bringing the respectability of marriage and the promise to take her off to foreign lands someday.

Of course, she said nothing about all that on the day we met. She had other intentions. I said, "You seem to have picked up the Spanish quickly, then, at least to my untrained ear."

She said, "In front of our house there is a big prickly pear cactus. The Mexicans call it a *nopal*. Not long after we moved in, a couple of Mexican ladies came to my door asking permission to take a few of the *nopalitos*, the new little cactus pads that were growing on it. *Nopalitos* are a delicacy. Well, the ladies came another time, and another, even though they had removed most of the *nopalitos* on their first visit. Before long they were inviting me to their homes and introducing me to their friends. Now I am like part of their families. They really are the best friends one could ever find, and they help me with my Spanish. In some ways, I got part of my wish to live in a foreign country. Until only a generation ago, this part of the territory was actually a part of Mexico. America swallowed it up. Last week, after the news about Stephen, my friends scooped me up like a little bird, and brought me here to stay with Chela for a few days. They knew I could not be home alone. They helped me through all the funeral arrangements. Everything." She touched Chela's knee. "Chela has been so wonderful. I don't know what I would have done without them."

Waving his fork over his plate, Father Arnold nodded and said, "I have often said friends make all the difference in difficult times."

I said, "I'm very sorry about your husband. This must all be very painful."

She sat erect in her seat, her back straight and hands holding the small painted plate on her lap, her eyes lowered for a few moments. My eyes followed the lace pattern of her high-necked white blouse down over the rounded swell of her breasts. When I glanced back up, her eyes were on mine.

She lifted her chin slightly. "Right now I'm very concerned about Miguel Cordero. No matter what anybody says, he did not kill Stephen. He is not that type of man, and for him to be convicted would add tragedy to tragedy. When I found out that you are a lawyer, I decided to invite you here for lunch today. There are other lawyers I could speak to, but you are new and not yet full of the local gossip and prejudices. You say you don't have a lot of experience, but it seems to me there are other things that matter. Perhaps you have ideas that are different than some of the people who have been here awhile. I think once you meet Miguel you will see what I mean, that he couldn't kill another person."

I said, "Let me be honest, Mrs. Downing. I do intend to start a law practice here, and I do intend to be successful. But I believe your other guests were wise to decide I am not the best man for the job of defending this Mr. Cordero. At a minimum, one ought to have a bit more experience than I do, before taking on a murder case—in fairness to your Miguel."

She shook her head. "Mr. Borboa and Mr. Castillo are not concerned about your lack of experience. They simply got the impression that you will turn out to be just another white American. The man you came to meet, Epes Randolph, is a rich railroad man who is happy to use Mexicans as laborers on his tracks, but has no interest in mixing with the local Mexican businessmen. I can see in your eyes that you are independent, whatever your connection to Mr. Epes Randolph. You look like you would be a good lawyer. You will be successful, I have no doubt. And I believe you should start by looking at this case."

"I appreciate your vote of confidence, but being a good lawyer isn't something one wears for everyone to see, like a good suit. I'm sure your Mr. Cordero would like to have someone who has experience as a criminal defense attorney. I have a little experience, but not that kind."

"Miguel's father has already hired one of the local attorneys. Myself, I don't really care for him, the other lawyer. He's very unpleasant."

"In my short time in the profession I've met a number of lawyers who are unpleasant men. That doesn't mean they aren't good lawyers."

"He is well thought of, but I don't think he will take the case seriously."

"There you go. If he is well thought of, perhaps Miguel would be better served to have him as his lawyer."

She paused, her eyes dwelling on mine, thoughtful and distant but melting something warm in my belly nonetheless. She said, "Maybe it would be better for Mr. Cordero himself to hear that from you. I wonder. Would you do it if he asked you?"

"Would I do what?"

"Would you represent Miguel Cordero if he asked you himself?"

"Why would he ask me? He's never even heard of me."

"You aren't answering my question. Some things only become clear with the passing of time. Wouldn't you agree, Father Arnold? This may be one of those things. I don't know why, but I believe you are more capable than you think. I'd like to ask one favor of you. Just one. This awful time would be a tiny bit easier for me to bear if I knew Miguel had someone good to defend him. Would you go to the jail and speak with him yourself? That's the favor. Just speak with him. After that, whatever you decide will be fine."

I hesitated. Her hands lay folded in her lap. One hand went up to tuck loose hair strands behind her ear, drawing my eyes back to hers. We seemed alone in the universe, and I knew she was right. I had nothing to lose by visiting the poor man in jail.

The image of Mr. Norman came to my mind. Perfectly mantled in his perfect dark suit, his air of authority filling my apartment. People in his world had surely never seen the inside of a lockup. "All right. I'll talk to your Mr. Cordero. But I will tell him to stick with the lawyer his father has hired. He shouldn't be hanged because of his lawyer's lack of experience."

That night I dreamed such hot dreams. I had been with only one woman in my life—the youngish wife of the fat building superintendent. And only once. She knocked at my door to inquire about the neighbor across the hall, about when she might find him at home to discuss some matter of rent. She and I talked at the door, and then, because the neighbor might arrive any moment, we sat on my sofa, the door ajar so she could watch for the neighbor. I was captivated by her voice, by the music of a woman's voice in my little apartment. Her black hair spilled over her shoulders and her eyes danced as they played with mine. She threw back her head to laugh and when she asked questions she touched my forearm with her fingertips—each touch more electric than the last. She and her husband were new to the building. She wanted to know about the books that lined my walls and filled the space under my desk, about the thick law textbook I still

53

held with a finger marking my place. She asked about my life as a student, about the ladies in my life. I told her there were no ladies in my life, or at least not in my life that way. She thought I must be lonely here with nothing but all these books.

One thing led to another. There was a kiss. Her hand guided my hand inside her blouse and I remember my surprise at the pudding-softness of her breast and the way her nipple stiffened at my touch. Her hand slipped between the buttons of my shirt and everywhere she touched my skin caught fire. The door closed, our clothing came off in a tumble, and once she learned I had never before been with a woman her passion grew boundless. I lost myself in her fire, in the texture of her hot, moist skin and the pitch of her soft cries as my cock discovered the amazing heat inside her. She moved against me, her thrusts informing my thrusts, her body teaching my body, and as I caught on she gripped my thighs so tightly that the red marks would be visible hours later. Then—to my surprise—she began to sob, her face against my naked shoulder. Concerned, I tried to pull away to look at her, but she held me hard against her as we rocked and the passion subsided. I kissed her wet eyes and asked if she were all right. She whispered, "Silly man. Sometimes tears are happy tears."

Afterwards she dressed quickly, smiling all the while. She pressed her lips one more time against my forehead, and gazed into my eyes. "My, oh my. You do have a talent. Whoever marries you will be one lucky woman." A week later I heard a rumor that she had run off, leaving her fat husband, who huffed and moped around the building for another month before he too disappeared.

Now, in my sleep, those skin-on-skin memories confused with dream images of Mrs. Downing's body and at last the fire in me drove me awake and out into the cool night air. Long walks have always been my antidote to disquiet and sleeplessness. The hotel lobby was quiet as I passed through. The desk clerk on duty was nowhere to be seen. Outside, a bicycle lay propped against the hotel wall, and across the street I could just make out the rectangular shapes of buildings. I walked the quiet streets, passing the occasional lighted window. A hint of pink light began to spread across the curved black line of the horizon, and dark gray clouds mounded above the silhouetted mountains. The dawn reminded me of a certain morning at the beach with some friends from law school, back in Massachusetts. I had walked the edge of the water as daylight came on, listening to the cries of the sea birds and the rhythmic hiss of the waves. Far beyond that watery eastern horizon was Europe, and over to the right, somewhere, was Africa. The earth felt magical and whole, and I felt a wholesome oneness with it.

Here in the desert, I felt something of the same. The pinks and yellows of dawn spread through the sky and there was an expectancy in the dry air. A breeze picked up against my face.

"Owen?" a voice says.

I awaken slowly.

"Owen." Gabby's voice, not Eva's. The jasmine scent of Chanel No. 5.

I am in my easy chair, in black slacks and white dress shirt. My stocking feet up on the ottoman. I am old again, and my Eva is gone.

I sit upright, wiping my hand across my chin. Gabby is perched on the edge of the ottoman, next to my feet. She shakes my toe gently with her fingertips. She is all in black, with a black scarf across her shoulders. She is smiling.

"*Mi amor*. Shame, shame. Asleep in your easy chair on the morning of your wife's funeral. You said they were coming to pick you up soon, but I didn't believe you. The funeral isn't so early." She rises and takes a seat on the sofa across from me, her black handbag on her knees. "I do feel bad for you. I want to do something to make you feel better. What can I do?"

There was a time when I knew those eyes so well, and they knew me. Now I am tired and she has too much energy.

When I don't respond, her lips pucker into that childish pout. Then she brightens as if she has only just thought of something. "Listen, my love, there were some earrings. I gave them to Eva many years ago. Every time she has worn them, I have felt jealous because they are so beautiful, but she was my friend and I could not take them back. Would you mind if I take a look in her jewelry box? I'm sure Helen would not want them, and their look is too old for your granddaughters. Would you mind? I'll just be a moment."

I pass my hand across my chin again, my mind still fuzzy. "Couldn't hurt, I suppose. I'll get it."

"You're a prince."

Eva was always simple in her choice of jewelry. She liked a single strand of pearls, a plain silver bracelet. Even later in life, when we could afford a bit of ostentation, she had no interest in replacing her gold wedding band with a fancier diamond setting. Her jewelry box is pretty and unpretentious, with its tan wood *fleur d'lis* designs inlaid into the smooth blue-green enamel finish, an heirloom passed down to her from her pioneer grandmother. I remember Eva saying she wanted Helen to have it someday.

I bring it out and set it on the ottoman between us, and open the lid. It once played a music box tune when the lid was lifted, but the music mechanism no longer works. Inside, Eva's earrings and rings are organized in compartments in the red-felt top tray. Under the tray, her necklaces are in the bottom section.

Gabby purses her lips when she doesn't see what she is looking for. She glances back toward the bedroom. "Maybe … maybe she left them in a dresser drawer?"

I don't want to turn her loose to snoop through Eva's things. I suggest that after Helen has a chance to go through with the girls and pick out what they want, she can have what's left.

She pouts her pout again. "Oh, I know Eva would have wanted me to have these earrings." She watches my face, and then drops the pout. Anger flashes across her eyes, and then is gone. "Anyway," she says, rising and smoothing her skirt, "I must be going. I'm sure the flowers are arranged wrong at the church. I'll straighten them up before everyone gets there. And last night at the rosary, the mortician had her makeup wrong. Maybe I can help them to fix it. Are you sure you don't need a ride?"

"You know I don't."

At the door, she kisses me on the cheek. "You are a good man, Owen Bartlett. Your wife was very lucky. You were very lucky, too. But we'll have lots of time to talk about these things, won't we?" Without waiting for a response, she winks and hurries away down the sidewalk to her car.

She is one confident woman, I'll give her that. She has never let herself give up on anything. During the long years of the Great Depression, when privation was a part of life for so many, her non-stop hard work and clever door-to-door marketing made her "Gaby's" stores a success among her southside clientele. She knew her customers, knew what would attract them, even using the Mexican spelling of her nickname as the name of the business. She made sure they knew her, too. She offered inexpensive dresses and clothing for Mexican women and their daughters. Any woman or girl who showed talent with a needle could barter a week or two of sewing time for a dress or blouse, and many times the family of the seamstress would wind up buying their daughter's handiwork as a mark of family pride.

Even the war didn't stop her. The economy picked up and there were more jobs, which meant her customers finally had more money to spend, but the war effort demanded fabrics for military needs, which meant that new and fashionable dresses remained as hard to get as ever. Ever creative, Gabby took her cue from patriotic automobile dealers. She held gala sales events at which women could trade in their used clothing for a discount on new and good quality used outfits. Her seamstresses culled the trade-ins for promising material that could be refurbished and remade into saleable "new" dresses. Then she made well-publicized donations of the remaining used clothing to the war effort. She decorated her stores with war bonds posters and American flags. Her ostentatious American-ness raised people's spirits and her standing in the community. It raised her bottom line, as well.

During those war years, Eva and Gabby remained as close as ever, though Gabby was often busy. When she was able, she would come over to cook with Eva. If the weather wasn't too hot, they went for long strolls. They took up cigarette smoking, and used their walks to get the hang of it. At dinner or at get-togethers with Josue's family, Eva usually arranged for Gabby and me to be near each other or sitting together. Nobody noticed, because that was the way we'd all been doing things for as long as anybody remembered—Owen and Gabby sat together. Even if just the three of us were in our living room, Eva took the antique wooden rocker, leaving the sofa for Gabby and me. That's the way it had always been.

But away from family and close friends, Gabby and I mostly avoided each other. An old spark still remained between us that made us uncomfortable. So, in the fall of 1946, I was surprised when Gabby called me at my hotel while I was in Phoenix on business.

"*Mi amor*," she began, when I answered the phone. "I have missed you."

We met for dinner at a small restaurant away from the center of town. She hugged me in the parking lot, and held my arm tightly as we walked in. We spoke of business. During the war, she had closed her two Phoenix stores because of gas rationing, but still had all the stores in Tucson and Nogales. Now she wanted to open up a new Phoenix store. She talked about the problems of getting old and trying to run a business spread over three cities. I sympathized. Before the war I had had a thriving office in Phoenix, as well as my main office in Tucson, but with the war on, and with gas rationing and all the attendant limits on travel, my Phoenix associates eventually caught on to the fact that they didn't need me. I decided it didn't matter. I was getting tired and slower. They got a good price when they bought the Phoenix practice.

Neither of us mentioned Eva until nearly the end of dinner. There was a long moment of quiet. Gabby looked up at me and said, "Do you ever feel guilty, Owen?"

I poked at the vegetables still on my plate. "Sometimes. But not often. You know, it's strange. She always meant for something to happen between us. I can't say why, and I know we'll never talk about it."

"I wonder why she feels like she owes me something. It's really the other way around."

"I know. As I said, it's strange. It was almost as if she was saying that you are as much a part of us as we are, if that makes any sense. I probably shouldn't say this, but back when you and I were seeing each other she wanted me more. In bed. You know?"

Gabby laughed. She reached across the table and put her hand on mine. Her fingers still bore the strength of her sewing years, but though her touch was soft, the skin looked more sinewy now, no longer the smooth, callow skin of youth. She said, "I used to wonder if you were too much man for her. But there is more to it than that. Something in her needs us to be together."

It was true. There was a magnetism in the air between the three of us that was as old as our time together. I never caught a glimpse of its meaning until the moment before Eva died. Amazing, that I could have missed it all those years.

Later in that evening, no one paid any attention to the old couple in their sixties strolling through the lobby, holding hands in the garden, looking up at the bright desert stars. We slept through the night in my hotel room wrapped tightly together. In the morning we made love, slowly and deliciously, but as breathlessly as always. Gabby's hunger was undiminished.

Now, holding Eva's jewelry box by my side at the front door, I watch as she drives away. Back in my easy chair I open it, picking through the half-dozen pairs of earrings. I pull away the earring tray to look again at the necklaces underneath. Like the earrings, they are feminine and simple. A delicate gold chain. A sterling chain and locket engraved with the name Molly, her first horse.

Under the necklaces, in one corner, there is a felt tab. I pull it gently up, expecting to find the now-defunct mechanism for making the mechanical music. Instead, there is another compartment, long and thin, that contains a white handkerchief, wrapped carefully into a cylinder so that a monogrammed letter S rests precisely at the tip. I take it out, and unwrap what turns out to be a silver, dagger-shaped letter opener. A tiny chip is missing from the pointed tip. A chill seizes my spine as I realize what I am holding.

The county jail stood behind the Victorian county courthouse, a redbrick building with a second story law library and gabled attics and a cupola that could have come straight from Boston. The jail itself was a flat-topped brick structure with barred windows set high in the wall so that air could get in but a man could not get out. Dusty sunlight streamed in from the high windows to illumine the two large cells, each holding a half-dozen bored men seated or lying on the dirt floor. The stink of urine and feces hung in the air from the uncovered slop buckets in a corner of each cell.

A big redheaded jailer in khaki pants and a white shirt relaxed behind a desk. I had seen many Irishmen just like him in Boston. I introduced myself and told him I'd like to speak to Miguel Cordero.

"Are you family?"

"No. I'm a lawyer."

"I believe he's already got a lawyer."

"Be that as it may, I'd like a word with him. I received a message through his family that he wanted to speak with me."

"If you ask me, he gets too many visitors. His whole family's been here, his father and his uncle, brothers, his damn cousins, you name it. You'd think they wouldn't want anything to do with him, considering what he did."

"The message I received was that he wants to speak to me in my capacity as a lawyer. He has that right, I believe."

The Irishman's tongue played against the inside of his cheek as his eyes measured me. I could tell he wasn't sure Miguel really had a right to be visited by a new lawyer under these circumstances, but something flickered in his eyes and he decided not to challenge me. "Cordero! You got a visitor."

A tall man of about my age approached the bars. His face was dirty and his dark hair disheveled. A few days' beard growth stubbled his chin. His intelligent eyes sized me up.

The Irish jailer took a position beside me. I said, "I'd prefer to speak to Mr. Cordero in private."

He grinned. "This is as private as it gets, counselor." I leveled my gaze at him until he sidled back over to the nearby table, still well within hearing range, and resumed his seat. "Take as long as you need."

I extended my hand toward the bars. "Mr. Cordero, my name is Owen Bartlett. I was asked to come talk to you about your case."

Miguel looked at the hand and then over at the jailer. He said very quietly, "Nice to meet you. You are the lawyer?"

"I am. You knew I was coming?"

"They said there was a new lawyer coming to take my case."

"Then you were given incorrect information. I came here as a favor, but not to take your case. There are more experienced lawyers who could do you much more good than I can. You do already have an attorney."

He glanced back toward his cellmates. He whispered so quietly I had to lean forward to hear him. "I heard you are very smart."

"Who did you hear that from?"

"Somebody I trust. Look, I am a rancher. My grandfather came to Arizona sixty years ago, when this was all still Mexico. We have three generations here. I work hard. I read and write two languages, but I don't know nothing about law. I know about people and cattle. The lawyer my father hired is a rancher, and that man has been my father's lawyer for a long time. He is friends with the judge. But I think he doesn't care so much about me and my case. He doesn't look at me when I talk. I have heard you would care about my case. Sir."

"Mr. Cordero, perhaps you are not being entirely fair to this other man. The way he looks at you when you speak is no indicator of whether he's a good lawyer."

He shook his head. "Maybe I can't tell a good lawyer from a bad lawyer, but I have heard you are a good man. I think it is better to have a good man than a good lawyer."

"That doesn't make any sense, Mr. Cordero. If I understand correctly, your life is on the line. You need an experienced lawyer.

Period. I can be a good lawyer, but I have no experience in criminal law. I could not, in good conscience, take on such a responsibility. I don't think it would be good judgment, either for you or for me. What if they hang you because I didn't do a good enough job?"

"What if they hang me because my lawyer didn't really try to defend me?"

"I can't imagine that such a thing could happen."

He stared at the floor for a moment. "Would you talk to the other lawyer before you decide?"

"Why would I do that? What would I say? That he ought to care more about you?"

"No. Ask him what he thinks of Mexicans."

"What he thinks of Mexicans?"

"Yes."

"Why in the world would I ask him that?"

"To find out how hard he's going to fight for me."

"I don't understand. Why would your family hire someone who won't do a good job for you, whether he likes Mexicans or not?"

"That's because you are American, Mr. Bartlett. You think it doesn't matter that a lawyer sees Mexicans like they are below him. But if I lose this case, to him I'll be just another Mexican who gets hanged. There aren't any Mexican lawyers here in town who would fight for me the same as they would for a white man. There used to be a Mexican lawyer here, a good one my father says, but he passed away. So my father wants me to rely on a white lawyer who is busy with his own cattle ranch. There are other lawyers here, but my father trusts only this one. I don't trust any of them."

"Mr. Cordero, has it occurred to you to wonder what I think of Mexicans? Perhaps I would give the same answer as the other lawyer. I'm American, as you noticed."

"Yes. But I heard you might be different."

"You heard that from whom?"

"Somebody I trust, like I said. And since you want to know, it was somebody white."

"Was it Mrs. Downing?"

His eyes narrowed, as if he were about to expose a secret. "Yes."

I considered for a moment. I wanted to impress Mrs. Downing. And part of me wanted to take the case because it would get me noticed right away, which would be good for starting my law practice. On the other hand, I knew I was not ready to do a murder trial, and if I did a terrible job, nobody else in town would hire me. "I'll tell you what. If it will make you feel better, give me your attorney's name and I'll speak to him. Perhaps he would let me help him with the case. If not, I think my involvement will end there. There is too much at stake. You could die in prison, or you could be hanged."

His face brightened. "So you will talk to him?"

"Yes."

"His name is Hyram Winthrop. His office is only a block from here. Will you come back after you talk to him?"

"I will speak to him for you. I'll do that much."

My first meeting with Hyram Winthrop did not go well. Or perhaps it did. It changed the course of my life. His handshake was brusque, and his flicking motion for me to have a seat could as easily have been a motion to flick tobacco spit from his fingertip. He could have been drawn from a dime western novel, his face lean and weathered, his handlebar mustache drooping an inch below the line of his jaw. Dark eyes glared from the deep sockets above his prominent cheekbones. "I've got work to do, sir," he said, his voice surprisingly smooth coming from such a rough aspect. "What do you need?"

"I came to speak with you about Miguel Cordero."

"What about him?"

"He told me you are representing him in the murder case."

The dark eyes narrowed. Seconds passed. "And?"

"He asked me to come and talk to you about it."

He leaned back in his chair. "Why would he do that?"

"I don't know. Someone suggested to him that he should have me represent him. He sent a message to me, and I visited him at the jail."

"You a lawyer?"

"Yes. Sort of. I'm ..."

"Seems to me a man either is a lawyer or isn't a lawyer, and if he's got average intelligence he can probably tell for himself which it is at any given moment of any given day. It's not a hard question. You a lawyer or not?"

I felt the hairs on my forearms rise, that old facing-the-neighborhood-bully feeling. "I have been admitted to the Massachusetts bar, if that answers your question. I received a message from Mr. Cordero that ..."

"You're not in Massachusetts."

"No, I'm not. That's why ..."

"You practiced law in Massachusetts?"

"I worked for a firm in Boston, after I graduated from law school."

"Law school!" His face lit up, but the acerbic grin did nothing to make him seem friendlier. "Law school! What the hell can you learn about practicing law in a law school?"

I rubbed my finger over the smooth wood on the armrest of the chair. "I take it you did not go to law school?"

"Hell no. I read the law, like every other lawyer worth a tinker's damn. I apprenticed and I studied. I've been practicing in the Arizona territory for twenty-eight years, and when I wasn't

65

practicing law I was working my ranch. So I believe I understand which end of a pleading to start reading from, and I also understand a hard day's honest work. You didn't learn any of that in a damn law school. I don't think they even had law schools when I started."

"Harvard Law first held classes thirty-five years ago, in 1870. So they did have them when you started." I tried to inject enough sarcasm into my voice to echo his. "For your information, a number of law schools have been started on the Harvard model since then. And there have been law curricula in some colleges since the days of the Revolutionary War. John Marshall himself studied law at the first such program, in Virginia, before he enlisted in the Continental Army under George Washington."

Winthrop's jaw hung open for a moment. "Marshall?"

"Chief Justice, U.S. Supreme Court. Marbury versus Madison, among other important decisions? You've heard of judicial review?"

He reached down for something beside his chair. His hand came up with a silver spittoon, into which he spit a nickel-sized wad of brown drool as I watched. He swirled the contents of the spittoon thoughtfully, as if he were holding a brandy snifter. "Counselor, I wouldn't trade the two inches of goop that's in here for what you learned at Harvard Law School."

"I didn't say I went to Harvard. I attended law classes at the Boston YMCA, where I received a bachelor of law degree."

"You went to law school at the YMCA?" His eyes squinted into what could have been a smirk. "This is good. So, what do you want to know about the Cordero kid?"

"I'm not sure. He asked me to represent him. I told him he was better off with an experienced attorney ..."

"Good thinking."

"... And he pressed the issue. I'm not sure he's happy with your representation."

Hyram shrugged, setting the spittoon back onto the floor. "Fine. You want him, he's yours."

"That isn't why I'm here. He simply …"

"Look, don't waste my time with these little games. I've got more things to do than a yellow dog's got ticks. Tempus, as the Romans used to say, is fugiting."

"Mr. Cordero said to ask you what you think about Mexicans."

Without taking his eyes from mine, Winthrop leaned to the side and let drop another wet wad. There was no splash, and I tried not to imagine what the floor looked like on his side of the desk. "Is that Cordero's problem? He doesn't like the way I see Mexicans?"

"I have no idea. He simply suggested I ask the question."

He pursed his lips for a long moment. "I'll tell you what, law school boy. I've been old man Cordero's neighbor since Miguel was in swaddling clothes. I've helped the Corderos buy and sell land and horses and cattle and the good Lord knows what else. I wrote old man Cordero's damn will. And rewrote it five years later. I represented him in a lawsuit against Colonel Manning himself, and Manning settled up rather than deal with my disagreeable self. If that kid Stephen Downing hadn't got himself stabbed to death, I probably would have drawn up the papers on the mining deal between him and the Cordero family and all their damn Alianza investors. I was the first person Miguel Cordero thought of when he was being examined by the judge, after he was arrested for killing Downing. His father trusted me enough to ask me to continue the representation on the case. So don't you ask me what I think about Mexicans. I've been dealing with them practically all my life. I've never been their friend, but they know they can trust me."

"That doesn't tell me what you think of them."

"I think the same thing you think of them. If they work hard and speak English and take a bath every week like a white man, they're fine."

"And that's what you believe I think about them?"

Hyram stood up violently, slamming his chair against the wall behind him. "Don't give me your hypocritical bullshit, fella! You're whiter'n I am, and a lot less experienced. So get the hell out of my office. If Miguel wants you to represent him, he's yours. Tell him I said he can go to Mexican hell. And I'll laugh my ass off watching you blow smoke through that law school diploma while they convict your client. The grand jury is meeting right now, as we speak, to get him indicted. He'll be tried, convicted, and probably hanged by the end of next week."

I rose slowly to my feet, straightening myself to my full height. Hyram was taller yet, his chin high and his eyes fierce. He would no doubt be very good in a bare-knuckle fight with a mountain lion. As would I. "Very well," I said.

I closed the office door behind me, and stood motionless in the hallway for a full minute, my face hot as if I'd stood too close to a bonfire. Very well, indeed. If a crude rancher like Hyram Winthrop could practice law in this desolate territory, then Owen Bartlett of the School of Law of the Boston YMCA, Class of 1904, could do no worse. I strode briskly out into the bright desert sunshine, conscious that I had no idea what to do next, but determined that I would figure it out. And God help Miguel Cordero.

H yram died of a stroke twenty-four years later, in the winter of 1929. By then, I thought of myself as almost his friend, though I'm not sure he would have acknowledged such a relationship. As I came to know him, I realized he didn't just have a dislike for Mexicans. He had a dislike for everybody. Equally. He was exactly the pugnacious, bitter man I could have become if I had remained that angry boy I saw reflected in Billy McGillicuddy's back window. There was something of Hyram still in me, and I could not bring myself to dislike him.

He was one of the best trial lawyers I would ever know. He had an unerring sense of how a jury would perceive the facts of a case, and of how the appellate courts would rule on almost any issue. Outside the courtroom, though, he missed few opportunities to be harsh. At the end of his life, having offended nearly every human being he ever came into contact with—American or Mexican or otherwise—he died alone and nearly broke, too crippled from strokes to maintain his ranch with no help, and too unflinchingly rude to his clients to make much money practicing law. Ironically, the only client who stuck with him until the end was Don Antonio, Miguel Cordero's father. From what Gabby told me, the two were alike in many ways. Disagreeable ranchers, all business, no soft touches at all. She reminded me a number of times how lucky Eva was to have found such a respectful, gentle husband as me.

They buried Hyram at Evergreen Cemetery, on the highway north to Oracle. His brother, a pudgy merchant whose first name I can't recall, a man as laconic as Hyram himself but somewhat more pleasant, came down from Globe with his pudgy wife in tow. Eva refused to attend, and so it was just the three of us, shivering beside the grave in the January breeze. The workmen lowered the casket with two ropes, then waited respectfully under nearby trees. Hyram had wanted no clergyman, so the brother stood awkwardly at the head of the grave, staring into the hole for a long minute. He picked up a fistful of dirt from the dirt pile and let it fall through his fingers into the hole. "Well, there he is," he pronounced. "Rest in peace. Didn't know him too well. Raised in different families, and his was the worst, I heard. I remember he was always reading books when he wasn't running away. Lost track of him and found out just a few years ago he was a lawyer. No idea how that happened." He paused, then said to me, "You want to say anything?"

I considered for a moment. "He was a good lawyer. I think he was proud of that."

The brother waited, and when I said nothing more, he said to his wife, "You ready?"

As they drove away and the workmen came back to fill in the hole, I wandered across the fifty yards of brown winter grass to the grave of Stephen Downing. The original cemetery had been dug up and the bodies moved to make room for Tucson's northward expansion. I paid to have Stephen's remains transferred to Evergreen, including the original headstone, which read "Stephen Downing, Husband of Eva, 1878-1905." After a dozen years, the grave looked well settled again under a tall pine.

I shivered in the cold, wondering what Stephen's life would have been, had things turned out differently that fateful night. With me, Eva talked little about her life with Stephen. I knew through Gabby that things had been difficult. Stephen was ambitious and jealous, hard on Eva when she wanted to go out of the house alone. Oddly, Eva apparently told Gabby, he didn't seem to be jealous of Mexican men, and didn't mind her socializing with the Mexican families who were befriending her. Gabby believed Stephen just couldn't imagine Eva being attracted to Mexican men. Clearly, I see now, there were things about Stephen's jealousy that Eva did not want to share with Gabby.

We talked about all this as we lay in bed together in the Phoenix hotel we referred to, in code, as my office. By then we had been seeing each other for many months. It wasn't anything we had planned to happen. My law practice was thriving, mostly because of the Eighteenth Amendment to the Constitution—Prohibition.

My hands were full with clients charged with liquor crimes. Prohibition did not solve many social ills, but it sure kept a lot of prosecutors and defense attorneys employed. I opened a second office in Phoenix, and traveled all over the state. At one point I employed nine associate attorneys.

By then, as well, Gabby's clothing business had expanded to seven stores, three each in Tucson and Phoenix, and one in Nogales, five minutes from the Mexico line.

After years of raising eyebrows because she refused to lead the secluded life of a traditional Mexican widow, she had finally won social acceptance in the Mexican community by becoming wealthy. Money always talks. Like me, she traveled often to Phoenix on business, and one evening I spotted her eating alone in the hotel restaurant.

Her face lit up as I approached. "Owen, how nice. What are you doing here?"

I told her I was having dinner with the attorney who managed my Phoenix office. She offered me a seat at her table. "How are you? It's so nice to see you here." She asked how my new Phoenix practice was doing, and I inquired about her stores. Like me, she made the trip a couple of times a week, and usually stayed in this very hotel. I said this was my first time here, that I usually stayed over at the Exelsior because it was closer to the office, but the Exelsior was full this particular night.

Just then my Phoenix manager arrived for dinner. Gabby scribbled her room number on a napkin. "Give me a ring, after you finish with your dinner. I'd love to talk and catch up." Her hand was warm when she squeezed mine. "It really is nice to see you, Owen."

She left shortly afterwards, as my manager and I talked office business and looked over the menu. The practice was getting very busy. We probably needed to hire another secretary. As we ate I tried to keep my mind on business, but it kept veering to Gabby's room, up the stairs and down the hall, where she awaited my call.

Later, in my room, I sat on the bed staring at the napkin with Gabby's room number. Eva would be asleep by now. If I were home, I would be reading beside her. We had ended each day that way for years, I on my side of the bed, and Eva on hers. It happens to a lot of married couples, I suppose. Daily life creeps in. The mundane stifles the exciting.

Now and then, of course, Eva and I still found our moments. Like the Saturday morning when I slipped my hands under her blouse as she washed the breakfast dishes, and she reached back to fondle my crotch. Had Roy come home early from whatever he was doing with his friends, he'd have found me with my trousers around my ankles, thrusting up against his mother's bare bottom, her skirt and apron tossed onto the small of her back, and the two of us giggling as her hands splashed in the dishwater. Or the time she surprised me during an autumn picnic by the Rillito Wash. We had invited the two young attorneys from my Tucson office and their wives. They all tramped off across the big wash and into the foothills for a little after-lunch hike. The moment they were out of earshot, Eva grabbed my hand and tugged me off to a thicket of desert broom, dense after the heavy late-summer rains. In seconds she was out of her blouse and corset, smiling and tugging my belt. We lay on her wide blue skirt on the soft sand, and her hand guided me inside her as soon as she was on her back. Her body reached for mine, matching my rhythm, her face concentrating, our eyes measuring each other. She kissed my shoulder while we arrived together in a soft, spreading, warm climax. We lay quietly afterwards, side by side, staring up at the clear blueness of the sky, holding hands until we jumped up at the distant sound of approaching voices. We were fully dressed and standing over the picnic supplies by the time our friends scrambled up the bank of the wash, excited about a small herd of deer they had startled minutes before. I brushed a couple of airy white desert broom flowers from Eva's hair. If anyone noticed our smiles, they said nothing.

But those moments of closeness and passion had grown farther and farther between. We got along fine, rarely even arguing, but she mostly fussed and worried about Roy, his grades, his sports, his girlfriends, as he wended through his high school years. Roy was her project. My project was my law practice. I lay awake at night parsing the next day's arguments with opposing lawyers in civil cases, or fretting over personnel issues—should I let this or that secretary go, or offer an associate's job to a certain young man fresh from passing his bar exam. Our preoccupations were separate preoccupations.

Something else hung between us. I couldn't identify it, back then, but now I know what it was—Stephen Downing, and how he died, and all that happened afterward. Eva's guilt weighed on her, though I didn't understand what it was that was bothering her, and I think one day she came up with a way to assuage that guilt. She offered Gabby a gift: me, her husband. Not consciously, I'm sure, and not overtly. She didn't direct me to become Gabby's lover. She began to put Gabby between us at gatherings, when a bunch of us were seated in the living room or at Carmen's and Josue's long dinner table. Sometimes she put herself at the far end of the table, down with Carmen and the children, and somehow made sure I was sitting next to Gabby at the other end. She insisted I meet with Gabby to help her with issues about her business—issues Gabby was quite capable of resolving herself. When Gabby came over for Sunday dinner, Eva would leave us alone while she ran off to pick up some eggs or a box of flour she'd forgotten. In the evenings before bed, she spoke of how important Gabby was to her, and how she wanted Gabby and me to be friends.

And here we were in a hotel far from home, together by accident rather than by Eva's design. Gabby had been over for dinner only a week or two before, but this felt different. Far from home, just the two of us, and, no doubt, we felt the effect of Eva's inexplicable efforts to put us together. I left Gabby's napkin on the dresser and took a shower, and when I came out I picked it up again. Room 212. I pulled on a shirt and some pants. Gabby smiled as she opened her door in a white lace negligee, a hint of her perfume wafting around me in the hallway. "I knew you would come," she said.

After that, we often arranged to meet when we were both in Phoenix. I never discussed these rendezvous with anyone. Nor did Gabby, as far as I know. I would phone her at her office, still located in the back corner of her first store. If one of her employees answered, I said I was her attorney. In our clumsy code, her favorite hotel in Phoenix was "my office," and our rendezvous were "appointments." We would set an "appointment" to meet at "my office." We were in our late forties, by then, and our nights were filled with the wonder of youthful passion, our bodies straining together for sometimes hours and hours. Sometimes, walking down a sidewalk to court, or speaking to my secretary, or thumbing through a file, I felt light and airy. At family get-togethers with Josue and Carmen and the kids, we tried to avoid sitting together so that the sparks wouldn't be too obvious, but found ways to bump shoulders or touch hands in passing. I caught myself smiling at inappropriate moments. I knew this wasn't love. It was excitement, it was lust, it was release from middle-age boredom. It was not love, but it felt good.

In those days we never discussed what Eva would think if she found out, though it would turn out we both thought she suspected and we both suspected she would not disapprove. For me, though, it couldn't last. As months passed, I would lie awake at night fretting, feeling lousy. The time came when I felt bad being with Gabby, and felt bad when I was at home with Eva. Gabby noticed my increasing distance and pretended it did not hurt. Our "appointments" grew brief, and longer in between. I told her the law office in Phoenix didn't need me as much as before.

Finally, that morning at the cemetery, looking down at Stephen Downing's headstone, I made up my mind. I walked past the workmen at Hyram's grave and headed to my car. The time had come to end things with Gabby, and make peace with myself and my life at home.

A s I finish dressing for Eva's funeral, the doorbell rings. I peek through the curtain. There stands Josue. He is alone. I open the door wide for him. "My friend," I say. La Señora, as he always called Eva, would have told him how handsome he looks. I just say, "How are you?"

"I'm fine, amigo." He enters and stands in the living room, hands first in his pockets, then at his sides, then back in his pockets. In his dark suit he looks both younger and taller than his sixty-seven years and his five-foot seven or eight. The solemnity of the moment hangs between us like an awkward cloud. Neither knows what to say. We are better talking about golf. I taught him to swing thirty years ago, or at least I taught him as much as I had to teach. Then, because a Mexican could never be admitted to the private club at El Rio, we played at the "muny"—the municipal dirt course at Randolph Park, named for Mr. Norman's friend, Epes Randolph. By my own choosing, golfing with Josue at Randolph Park was the closest I ever came to knowing its namesake.

Josue shrugs at our awkwardness. "How are you?"

"I'll be all right." I take a seat on the sofa.

He settles heavily into the overstuffed chair. After a moment, he looks at the empty antique rocker across from us, where La Señora always sat. "The rosary last night was very nice. We all wished you were there."

My turn to shrug. "I couldn't go. Just, you know, at the last minute it was too much for me."

He nods. We are both quiet, each staring into his own thoughts. I'm wondering if he has ever had an inkling of the real truth about what happened to Stephen, the real truth that brought us all together. But no. He was too young and callow at the time to suspect anything. He ran the errands Eva asked him to run, took me where she told him to take me. He practiced his English. He knew nothing.

Finally, he says, "It's hard to know what to say."

"*Sí. Ni modo.*"

He smiles at the inside joke. Nearly five decades ago, Eva sat with him afternoon after afternoon, slowly enunciating English words, trying to help him form them through his Mexican palate. They both eventually agreed that the Spanish of his childhood had permanently shaped the vowels and consonants of his lifetime. Despite his desire and efforts, he would always have an accent. "*Ni modo,*" he would say. A sort of Mexican verbal shrug of the shoulders. *Ni modo*—as in, There's nothing to be done about it. He taught her the phrase, and she used it often.

Ni modo, I think as we sit here together, the empty rocker between us. I ask him if Carmen will be coming, and he says she is with Veronica, helping get the grandchildren ready. Carmen was only fifteen or sixteen herself when Josue, then in his early twenties, began courting her. She was immediately jealous of the way he seemed to worship Eva, though Eva was long since married to me. According to Gabby, who made a point of knowing everything about everybody, Josue spoke of Eva almost constantly during his courtship of Carmen. Later, with her sisters and girl cousins gathered around, Carmen would wrinkle her nose and imitate him. "La Señora" this, she would say, tossing her hair. "La Señora" that. Gabby finally stepped in and resolved the problem, convincing Carmen that Eva was way too old for Josue. Eva and Carmen later became great friends. Carmen was "Aunt Carmen" to our son Roy. Eva was "*Tía* Eva" to the eight children of Josue and Carmen. But to Josue, Eva would always be La Señora.

Grief lines his face. Minutes pass, and finally he rises to go. "Do you need anything, amigo? Anything I can take care of for you?" The words come in a rush, now that he is leaving. "I'll be looking in on Perfecto, you know. He will get his treats and oats. Who is picking you up for the funeral? Maybe you should not be here by yourself?"

I tell him I'm fine. "Roy and Helen will be here before long. Really. They'll be here soon. And after, everybody is going over to Roy and Helen's house. Plenty of food, I hear."

"Lots of food," he says. He smiles and hitches up the waistband of his trousers. Over the years, his girth has grown with his prosperity. "Carmen was up most of the night. Tacos, burros, enchiladas." His native tongue trills long on the bur-r-r-os in the way neither Eva nor I could ever achieve, with our gringo tongues. "Carne asada. You name it. And lots of good American food, too, I hear."

I put a hand on his shoulder as we walk to the door. "We all had some times together, didn't we?"

"We did, we did, *pues*. But don't speak of them like they are over. We will have a lot of times still. You still have to beat me on the golf course."

"Are you kidding? The only reason you think you're winning is that funny Mexican math you use to figure up the score. You aren't supposed to subtract one stroke from your score for every swing I take. That isn't the way it's done."

He grins at our old joke. "Ok. You can make any excuse you want, amigo. Only for today. Carmen is already worrying that you won't get enough to eat. She'll be inviting you over for dinner five or six times a week."

We give each other a quick *abrazo*, two quick pats on the back, and I wait on the doorstep in my stocking feet as he gets in his car. A good man, Josue. I recall the difficulty I had, in those early days, trying to learn to pronounce his name. I kept calling him Jose. "No señor," he would say. "No Hose-say. I am Josue. Como Hose-sway. Hose-sway." Not until Eva finally explained to me that his name was the Spanish version of the English Joshua did I finally get it right. Hose-sway, not Hose-say.

"Josue," I repeat to myself, waving to his car as it pulls away. "Josue."

Hyram was right—law school had done nothing to prepare me to practice law. With my classmates, I read "cases," long written opinions by high courts about why they had decided a certain case the way they had. The cases were named after the people involved, like Marbury vs. Madison, and Pennoyer vs. Neff. We argued learnedly (we thought) about the legal principles involved, like whether courts should be the only ones to decide what a law means, or whether the courts of one state should have power over someone in another state, or whether providing separate facilities for people of different races really satisfied the right to be treated equally. We learned to toss around words like "writ" and "assumpsit," and phrases like "fee simple absolute," "stare decisis" and "covenants running with the land."

But we learned nothing about how to handle facts. Facts were unquestionable in our discussions—Plaintiff sold a horse to Defendant, who paid Plaintiff a deposit of five dollars and promised to pay ten more dollars when the horse was delivered. The horse died before it could be delivered, and Plaintiff delivered a horse he claimed was just as good. Defendant refused to pay. Plaintiff sued. That was it, as far as the facts went—they were simply given to us, and we argued about the legal issues. Should Defendant be required to pay? Should Plaintiff return the deposit and keep the second horse? What theory of law applied? We learned very little about doing a trial, which of course is mostly about facts. What caused Stephen Downing to die? Where was Miguel at the time? What evidence—what facts—could prove Miguel caused the death?

And then there was the simple matter of procedure. I had no idea how to do a trial, let alone a jury trial. I was in way over my head. I knew it, and a man's life depended on how quickly I could learn to swim in these waters.

For the briefest of moments, I considered humbling myself to Hyram and asking him for a job so he could teach me the nuts and bolts of being a criminal defense lawyer. But I knew he would humiliate me from morning to night, and the moment passed. To be honest, I mainly wanted to impress Mrs. Downing. Her image haunted me as I sat in my room that night making lists and strewing them all around my bed. I listed things I needed to start my law practice. Statute books. A desk and paper. A sign for the office door. I listed questions. Did I need to apply for admission to the territorial bar? Was there even a territorial bar? I fell asleep trying to start a list of steps in the defense of Miguel Cordero.

When dawn arrived, I awoke still dressed, lying on the notes scattered on the bed. I walked quietly out through the empty hotel lobby. I wandered aimlessly through the town, block after block. It was too early to stop by the railway station to check for my trunk. The big, bearded clerk's name was Robert, I knew by now, and I would continue stopping by, nearly every day, until Robert convinced me that the trunk was lost. We were both surprised, two months later, when it turned up in a Los Angeles warehouse. By that point, the trial of Miguel Cordero was long since over.

As the sun rose I walked along the tracks and the edge of town, then in a long circle along the riverbed and back toward the hotel. I passed the house where I'd met Mrs. Downing. A few women were out, sweeping the streets in front of their homes with straw brooms. After a few more blocks, I came upon the corner of Stone Avenue and 14th Street. There it was, just as she had described it—a small corner house with a ten-foot-high prickly pear cactus at one corner. Plastered walls, with a flat roof. White, recently painted. Two large shrubs framed the door, but the yard otherwise was bare dirt, like the yards all over town. In 1905, grassy lawns were still a thing of the future in Tucson. I stood before the door. Stephen Downing had walked in and out of that door a thousand times. Then one day, or one night, he walked out, over the spot where I was standing, and never returned.

"Señor?" A young Mexican man stopped at the edge of the yard. I'd seen him approaching on the street. He was perhaps eighteen—a boy, really—and he carried a large envelope in one hand. He looked familiar, but I couldn't place him.

At that moment, the door opened and Mrs. Downing stepped out carrying a pail and a broom. Her hair fell across her eyes, and she stopped when she noticed us standing there. She set the pail down, and her hand went up to tuck her hair behind her ear. Her face looked drawn, and her eyes red. "*Buenos días,*" she said to the boy.

The boy nodded. "*Buenos días,* Señora." He said something else, and held out the envelope.

She took it and spoke to him again in Spanish. Then, still looking at the envelope and not at me, she said, "Mr. Bartlett. What a surprise. What brings you here so early?"

I felt myself blushing, as if I'd been caught spying at her door.

"I was, you see ... I was walking. I do walk quite a lot, when I'm thinking."

The boy said something, and she nodded. "Josue recognizes you from the funeral. And as for me, housework is something that can be done anytime, especially when I can't sleep." She adjusted her hair again. "Mr. Bartlett, this is Josue. Josue drove the hearse in my husband's funeral. His uncle owns the mortuary." She spoke to Josue and he stepped forward with one hand extended.

We shook hands in a firm, once-up, once-down motion I would come to associate with the Mexican working class. I said, "Tell him I'm glad to meet him. I'm sorry I don't speak Spanish."

She spoke to him and he answered, shaking his head. She smiled and said something else, and he nodded enthusiastically. She said, "Josue says he would like very much to learn English. I told him you are a lawyer, and perhaps you might be able to use him as your assistant. He says that would be fine."

"How would I use an assistant who doesn't even speak English?"

"He would have to learn English, then, wouldn't he?" She smiled. "Did you decide to take Miguel's case?"

"I spoke with him at the jail. He's interested."

"And you'll take his case?"

"He has another attorney at the moment. As you know."

"Mr. Bartlett, you are avoiding my question."

I looked away. "To be honest, I'm on my way to visit him right now. I mean, later, after breakfast." I hesitated to say the words, because once I said them and made the commitment, Miguel's life lay in my hands. But her smile broadened. I added, "I'm on my way to tell him I'm willing to represent him."

"Excellent!" She clapped her hands, and communicated the news to Josue, gesturing toward me. He grinned and answered. She translated. "He wants to know when you would like him to come to work."

"Mrs. Downing, tell him I'm not hiring at the moment. Not even a secretary."

She repeated this to Josue, who shrugged and nodded. We shook hands again, once-up, once-down, and he said something polite, setting off down the street and looking not at all like a young man who had just been turned down for a job. Over the years I would come to know how optimistic he could be in all things, but my impression at that moment was simply that he didn't understand what I'd meant.

I asked, "Did you tell him what I said?"

"Of course."

"I hope he won't be camped at my door tomorrow morning."

"No, but he wants me to teach him English. Maybe I'll start with him soon. He's very bright. And chipper. He's always in a good mood."

"You look chipper yourself, for so early in the morning."

"I doubt it, but thank you. I really couldn't sleep, so I came home from Chela's to do a bit of house cleaning. I think I'm still not ready to be here for long, though. Which brings us to the reason you are here."

"Which is?"

She leaned on her broom. "I don't know. You haven't said. I assume you didn't come to talk to me about hiring Josue."

"No." I felt my face redden again. "I didn't. As a matter of fact, I really was simply, you know, passing by. It was coincidental. I was out for a morning walk, a constitutional walk. It's quite the thing back east, walking for one's health. And you had described your house, where it was." I watched her eyes. "And here I was, passing your door, as it were, when this young fellow Jose said something to me, and then you came out and, well, there you have it."

"Josue," she said. "His name is not Jose. It's pronounced Hose-sway."

"Ah. As I said. And now, I suppose I should leave you to your project, and be off to finish my walk. So that I can visit Mr. Cordero."

"Yes. I'm glad. He is a good man."

"Yes. I suppose so. And now, well …"

"Yes. Enjoy your constitutional walk."

"Yes. And thank you." I walked away stiffly, sure I could feel her eyes on my back.

A different jailer was on duty, this one a Mexican, tall and energetic. He nodded. "You are the new lawyer." He waved his arm toward the cell, where there were now only three inmates. Two sat quietly in a corner. Miguel Cordero stood apart, his hair unkempt, eyes red, a week's worth of scruffy beard on his face.

I walked over and leaned against the bars. "Good morning, Mr. Cordero. You don't look very well."

Miguel leaned on the bars. He shook his head. "I don't feel good. Isn't there some kind of bail to get me out? Have you talked to my family?"

"Not yet. I wanted to think over whether I should represent you. Are you sure you don't want to use Mr. Winthrop?"

"My father came to see me yesterday. He told me I'm loco for doing this, but I told him I trust you. But even though he wants to use Mr. Winthrop, he will pay you. I told him you are the lawyer I want."

"We can worry about the money later. We need to talk about your case." I lowered my voice to a whisper. "Tell me what happened that night."

"The night Stephen was killed?" He paused, eyes on the floor. "I wish I could tell you."

"Were you there?"

"Was I where? At the hotel? Yes. I was in my room."

"Why were you staying at the hotel?"

"Our ranch is a day's ride from Tucson. A long day. My *tío* lives …"

"What's a teeyo?"

"It means uncle. My *tío* lives here in town, and I could stay with him, but he and my father don't get along, so it's better if I stay at the hotel."

"All right. You stayed at the hotel. Was anybody else with you that night?"

"I was by myself in my room."

"The murder victim, Mr. Downing, did he come to see you that night?"

"Stephen? Yes. He was in a hurry, but he came to the hotel and told me we needed to call a meeting of the investors. He said there was good news. We talked a little bit about some equipment, and then he left. He didn't say what the good news was."

"Did you have problems between you? Did you get along?"

"We were business partners. I didn't know him before he came to talk to my father about starting a gold mine on the ranch. My family, we are ranchers. All we have is cattle and land. Stephen was a mining engineer. He used a lot of big words about geology and mining. He had a theory about where the gold is in the mountains, where it comes from when it washes down into the canyons. He said he thought the source was on our land, high up. My father talked it over with the other members of La Alianza, about investing. Stephen really believed we would be rich. I don't know what will happen now."

"What's La Alianza?"

"*La Alianza de Hispano-Americanos*. La Alianza, for short. It's a kind of mutual aid society. The members are businessmen and ranchers around Tucson. Mexicans. Friends of my father. We got them to invest in the mine."

"So you were friends, you and Stephen?"

"We were good business partners. We didn't agree about everything, but we got along."

"What didn't you agree about?"

"Money. Stephen wanted to move fast to get the mine going. He kept saying we could be rich in two or three years if we moved fast. Maybe five years. You know, buy a lot of equipment and hire a big crew, and like that. I thought it was better to go slow and be careful. Some of the men in La Alianza have experience as miners in Cananea and Morenci. They said we could lose a lot of money trying to find the gold there in the Santa Rita mountains. It's rough country."

"And there wasn't any trouble between you and Stephen? Personal trouble?"

He shook his head. "There wasn't any trouble. He was strange in some ways. He was kind of jealous about his wife, and who could blame him? She is beautiful. He never said anything to me about it, but you could tell by the way he looked, I guess. I stayed out of it. I have my own beautiful wife."

"Did the sheriff say why you are a suspect?"

"He said it was about my knife. That morning, I was washing my face in the basin, and I heard a key in the door, and the door opened, and in walked a man from the front desk, and behind him the sheriff with two deputies. They told me to sit down on the bed, and said Stephen had been murdered during the night. They started going through my clothes, and when they found my knife, the sheriff told me I was under arrest."

"How did they know about your knife?"

He shrugged. "Around here, all the ranchers carry a knife or a gun. I like a knife. You can't cut off a piece of meat or clean your fingernails with a gun."

"Why would they think your particular knife was the murder weapon? Why would they arrest you just because you had a knife?"

"I don't know. All I know is they looked at it, and one of the deputies said it looked about right. They put me in handcuffs, and took me out of the hotel in front of everybody and made me walk down the street to the jail. In handcuffs. It was embarrassing. I'm glad my father didn't see it."

"I still don't understand why they would immediately think of you as the suspect."

"Neither do I."

"This doesn't make sense."

"I know. That's why I need a lawyer who will fight for me. Are you going to fight for me?"

———

Judge George Davis sat across from me, elbows on the desk, his bony fingers folded into a steeple. A partially smoked cigar lay cold in the ashtray, but there was no odor of tobacco in the room. His lips pursed into something like a mild expression of concern. "It's nice of you to stop by, Mr. Bartlett. I like to get to know the new lawyers in town. You are from Boston."

"Yes, sir. News does travel, doesn't it?"

"This is a small town, Mr. Bartlett. You graduated from Harvard Law School?"

"No, sir."

He leaned back, and then leaned forward again, returning his elbows to the desk. His hands resumed their steeple, and his tone grew a bit more insistent. "What I heard was that you went to Harvard Law School."

"No, sir. I attended the law program at the Boston YMCA."

His fingertips tapped together two or three times. "I see. I heard that, too. The truth, I understand, is most likely that you went to Harvard."

"No, sir. The Boston YMCA. Some of our teachers came in the evenings from Harvard, and I attended a few lectures there, but that's as close as I got."

The judge's fingers tapped together once and then he let the point go. "I can't say as I've met many lawyers out here who've been to law school, even a law school at a YMCA. Do you think law schools are necessary?"

"I can't really say, sir. I suppose time will tell."

He nodded, his eyes narrowing at my dodge. "I can't really say, either, since you are the first specimen I've run across here in the territory. Seems to me that law school might give a man a little better grounding in the law than the old fashioned way of reading and apprenticing. But so far I'm in the minority in Arizona. Wouldn't you agree?"

"With what, sir?"

"With the notion that law school gives a better grounding in preparation for a legal career. Although it doesn't help much in the actual practice of law."

"I couldn't say, sir. I would hope my training helps."

"Then we'll see together. So be it. The world turns, as they say. Now, as for your practicing law here in the Arizona territory, even though you've been to law school, we need to see that the proprieties are met. The statutory requirements."

"Yes, sir. I was hoping you would tell me what those proprieties are."

He tapped his steepled fingers together again. "That would be giving you legal advice, which isn't my job. An attorney should be able to research the law for himself. However, since you were kind enough to stop by, I will tell you. Under the statutes as they have existed in the four years since the United States Congress enacted them in 1901, one must reside for six months in the Territory of Arizona, and must declare an intent to remain. You do intend to remain, don't you? Good. You must then be examined in open court concerning your knowledge of the law by three attorneys whom I would appoint. Such an examination would be easy, no doubt, for someone with a law degree from the YMCA. I've also heard you wish to be involved in the Cordero murder case. That's probably not possible, since you have not yet been admitted to the territorial bar."

"Would it make a difference that I've already been admitted to practice law in Massachusetts?"

"Ah." His fingertips separated and remained erect and spread as if he expected me to toss a baseball into them. "I had understood that you were less experienced. Now that you mention it, however, I did hear something about the Massachusetts bar. It would indeed make a difference that you were already admitted there. You would merely present a copy of your credentials to the clerk of the court, along with a written declaration of your intent to reside in the territory, and a motion for the court to admit you to the bar. You do have your certificate of admission?"

"No, sir." I shifted in my chair. "You see, my trunk was misplaced during my travel west. I'm still waiting for it to be recovered by the railroad. My certificates and credentials are in it. It should arrive any day. I hope."

He leaned back, the corners of his mouth curling upward in something like a smile. "Then if your credentials have not arrived, you won't be able to represent the Cordero boy. I believe the arraignment is set for tomorrow. If he pleads not guilty and goes to trial, the trial will be held day after tomorrow."

I caught my breath. "Isn't that rather quick, Judge?"

"No, Mr. Bartlett, it's the law." His eyes peered into mine. "The grand jury returned a true bill yesterday. The arraignment will be tomorrow. The defendant is in custody and his case therefore takes precedence on the court calendar. The law requires that after arraignment I give him at least one day to prepare for trial, if he requests it. I'm a fair man, and I shall insist that he request it. Which means he will be tried on Friday, day after tomorrow."

He picked up the half-smoked cigar from the ashtray and ran his forefinger along its length. "Take it from me, Mr. Bartlett, you would be in over your head with that case. Best you should leave it in Hyram Winthrop's capable hands. I will send word to him this afternoon that he is still on the case. From what I know of the unfortunate circumstances surrounding the crime, Miguel Cordero will be convicted no matter who represents him. You wouldn't want to have a client convicted of murder in your first week out here in the territory. That would be a bad beginning." He smiled and leaned back smugly in his chair. "And there you have it. It's settled."

I can't say I slept well that night, but at least the pressure was gone about representing Miguel Cordero. I took a leisurely dinner in the rooftop cafe of the hotel. I sat at a small corner table listening to the six-piece Mexican orchestra, and thinking of Mrs. Downing over several of those delicious tequila drinks Carlos had introduced me to. She was lost to me, no doubt, because I could not fight the fight for Miguel Cordero, and I had no other way to impress her. I told myself I would simply have been made a fool of in court. That thought didn't do much to console me. On the other hand, I could begin my practice with writing some wills and getting to know my new community. Building a solid reputation, over time, would bring me other opportunities to become more acquainted with Mrs. Downing, who at any rate would surely be grieving for some time to come over the death of her husband.

Early the next morning, in the street below my window, a man hiked by leading a mule by a halter, and the sandy street lay otherwise empty and ready for business. I washed my face and prepared to go down to breakfast. I would read the morning paper, take a stroll through town and attend Miguel Cordero's arraignment to see what I could learn about working in a courtroom. Actually, I really wanted to see Mrs. Downing one more time before she learned I would not be the lawyer to defend Miguel. Perhaps I would get a chance to speak with her and apologize.

I was the first to arrive, and took a seat in the back row. It looked much like the courtrooms I had visited in Boston, though I didn't recall seeing anything in those Boston courtrooms like the lone chair across from the jury box. In territorial days, the prisoner's dock was surrounded by a thin wooden rail fastened on an iron rod that arose from the floor. At the base of the iron rod was a four-inch iron ring. The man accused sat alone, chained to the iron ring, in judgment before all. My stomach tightened at the image of myself, with no clue what to do or say, facing the courtroom filled with spectators, jurors, lawyers and clerks, the gaunt face of Judge George Davis sternly presiding from the bench. I thanked the stars that the judge had excluded me from the case.

A side door opened and a potbellied little man hurried in, toting a water pitcher. He set the pitcher on one of the attorney tables, and collected three smaller pitchers from the other tables, dumped the water from them out a window, and then began to refill each from the larger pitcher he'd carried in.

Noticing me, he nodded while keeping an eye on his pouring. "Good morning. You're here early."

"Yes. I thought I'd take a look around."

"Around what?"

"The courtroom. I just wanted to see it."

He placed one of the newly filled pitchers on the judge's bench. "Ah. Never seen a courtroom, then? I've seen them too much, or at least this one too much. I'm the bailiff. What are you here for?"

"I'm here for the arraignment."

"Ah. The Cordero case. Well ..." Without finishing his sentence, he turned distractedly and scurried out the side door.

The rear door opened, and I heard whispers in Spanish. Four Mexican men in suits and two women in black dresses made their way past me and slid into the second pew. One of the women was gray-haired and heavy. She leaned on the arm of a wiry, gray-haired man. Miguel's parents, by the look of them. The three younger men appeared to be in their twenties and all bore a strong resemblance to Miguel. The younger of the two women was slender and perhaps twenty. I remember being struck by her intense eyes and the black, thick hair that fell to the middle of her back. I would come to know her as Gabby—Gabriela Cordero. Miguel was her husband.

A man in a starched white shirt and suspenders entered through the side door, carrying a stack of paper, a pen tucked behind one ear. He took a seat at a small table in front, set a black inkwell on his desk, and began arranging his papers on the small desk. More and more people filed in from the back to take seats in the long pews. Carlos Castillo was one, and Mr. Borboa from the meeting with Mrs. Downing. They and others stopped to speak or nod to Miguel's family before finding a seat. I turned to look each time the rear door opened. I had planned the whispered conversation I might have with Mrs. Downing if we spoke before the hearing began—the judge, the problem with my credentials, my missing trunk, all that. The hearing would explain it all, I thought, but I wanted her to hear it from me.

A tall, gangly man in a dark suit rushed in from the back,

set some papers on the prosecution table, and began to spread them around in front of himself as if he were arranging cards. He paused, glanced around the courtroom, and then went back to his papers. I decided he must be the prosecutor.

Hyram Winthrop finally sidled in, then, a thin file in one hand. He paused beside the Mexican family in the second row. The gray-haired man, Miguel's father by the look of him, stood up and shook his hand, nodding respectfully. They spoke in Spanish. Hyram nodded to the younger men, and to Miguel's mother, who did not rise, and then he shook Gabby's hand. His eyes met mine across the gallery, but he gave no other sign of recognition. He moved on to the front of the courtroom, where he nodded to the gangly prosecutor without speaking and took his place at the defense table. He pulled a single sheet of paper from the file, smoothed it out on the table before him, and set a pencil beside it.

The potbellied bailiff came through the side door and stood very still, watching the judge's bench, until at some signal he called out, "All rise!"

The judge entered through a door directly behind the bench and took his seat. The bailiff intoned, "The District Court of the First Judicial District, Territory of Arizona, in and for the County of Pima, is now in session, the Honorable George Davis presiding."

"Be seated," the judge said. There was a half-minute of scuffling and shifting as everyone settled into their seats. When quiet was reestablished, the judge held a piece of paper before him and read aloud, "The District Court is now in session on Docket Number A-1575, Territory of Arizona versus Miguel Cordero." He looked over his glasses at the lawyers. "Present are Mr. Roscoe Dale, for the Territory, and Mr. Hyram Winthrop for the defendant. It is the court's understanding that the defendant is not present this morning because he has refused to be brought to court. Is that correct, Mr. Winthrop?"

Hyram rose to his feet. "Your honor, I have not personally spoken with him this morning. I had expected him to be here."

The judge said, "Then will you waive your client's presence for the purpose of getting this hearing started?"

"Yes. But the law does require that the defendant in a felony case be present at the arraignment, so if he's not here we can't get the arraignment done."

"True enough, Hyram. But yesterday I heard that the defendant was trying to hire a new lawyer, and I also heard that you wish to withdraw from the case. There would be a connection, wouldn't there, between the two events and we should discuss that on the record. Once that's all straightened out, I will have the defendant hauled in here, kicking and screaming if necessary, for his arraignment. That would seem proper, wouldn't it?"

Hyram said, "Well, sir, my client does want a new lawyer. I spoke to him yesterday afternoon after I received the court's message about that. Based on what he said to me when I visited him, I request to be allowed to withdraw as counsel of record. I believe he wants to be represented by a Mr. Bartlett, who claims to be a lawyer from Boston. Harvard Law School graduate, if I'm not mistaken. Came to my office a day or two ago. New in town. Yesterday afternoon, your honor's message said there was a problem with his credentials and that I was still on the case. The defendant's father, who is present here today, wants me to continue the representation, but I don't believe it will be possible for me to work with a client who does not wish me to defend him."

"Well, then, how do you suggest we proceed, Hyram? I talked to Mr. Bartlett. His credentials to practice law are in a trunk somewhere between here and China, so whatever it is the defendant wants, Mr. Bartlett is not going to be his lawyer. On the other

93

hand, the defendant is charged with a capital offense. He could hang if convicted. Wouldn't you agree?"

A gasp came from among the Corderos, and Miguel's mother bent forward.

The judge went on. "I'm not comfortable with having him unrepresented, although the law allows it if he is so inclined. I suppose I could appoint a different lawyer. The court's humble opinion, Hyram, is that he would be better off continuing with your representation. What do you think?"

Hyram shrugged. "My problem is simple, Judge. I wish to withdraw as Miguel Cordero's attorney. After that, you can do what you want with him. I mean no disrespect to my friend seated here, Don Antonio Cordero, or to the Cordero family. I sympathize with them in this tragedy. But there are other lawyers in this town who could help them."

"True, but they don't have your kind of experience." The judge's elbows propped up on his bench, and his index fingers assumed their steeple position. "Mr. Dale, what is your suggestion?"

The prosecutor rose. "Your honor, the defendant is free to choose his own version of due process. If he wishes to act as his own counsel, the law only requires that you inform him he has a right to counsel if he can pay for it. If he's not happy with Mr. Winthrop, and doesn't care to hire another member of the bar, I think the court has fulfilled its legal obligation and we can proceed to arraignment and trial with the defendant representing himself. The bailiff informed me outside the courtroom that a venire of prospective jurors has already been summoned. We could seat a jury this afternoon, and complete the trial tomorrow in time for the weekend."

"Yes." The judge's steepled fingers tapped together, once, twice. "But since the defendant is facing a possible death sentence, I'm still uncomfortable proceeding without defense counsel. Hyram,

I really expected you to be willing to continue on the case. I could order it, you know."

Hyram sat without answering. I could not see his face, but whatever it was doing, the judge chose to change course. "I have another idea." He looked around the courtroom, and his eyes fell on me, seated in the back. "Mr. Bartlett?"

I stood up, smoothing out my coat, my face heated as all eyes turned to me. "Yes, sir?"

"Mr. Bartlett, would you please come up here? You too, Hyram, and Roscoe."

I eased past the knees of the other men in my row, and followed the two lawyers up to the judge's bench.

As we approached, the judge said, "This will be off the record, James." The court stenographer set his pen on the desk and flexed his fingers. We clustered close to the bench and the judge leaned forward to speak quietly. "Gentlemen, we have an interesting problem here, don't we? We have a defendant who wants to get rid of his current counsel. We have another attorney, Mr. Bartlett here, who has indicated a willingness to represent the defendant. From what I gather, the defendant would agree to that. Roscoe, I'm sure you would be happy to try this murder case against a *pro se* defendant, but I'm not comfortable with that, in a capital case. So here's what I propose. The statute allows a defendant in a capital case to be represented by two attorneys. Mr. Bartlett says he's been admitted to practice in Massachusetts, and he's waiting for his papers to arrive. I'm taking him at his word. Hyram, I'm going to ask you to vouch as a member of the bar for Mr. Bartlett, so that I can then allow him to appear *pro hac vice* under Section 398 of the territorial code. I will assign him to represent young Mr. Cordero, and you will be his co-counsel."

Hyram's lip curled. "Judge, no offense, but I have other things to do. Besides, I think the statute allows you to assign a lawyer only if the defendant can't afford to hire one. I happen to know that Don Antonio can afford a lawyer."

"You're right. Hmm. I'll tell you what. Would it be fair to say that without his father's land and money, Miguel Cordero could be considered indigent, and too poor to hire an attorney? Good. That takes care of the law on that, doesn't it?"

He dipped his gavel toward me. "Now, Mr. Bartlett, you will do this case for free, because in the unlikely event you are successful in your defense, you will make a reputation for yourself that will be worth far more than the trouble and time you put into it. If you lose, you will have been paid exactly what you are worth. Hyram, you will keep any money the family has paid you for the case, and you will stay on as co-counsel." He dipped his gavel preemptively in the direction of Hyram's glare. "Don't get disagreeable about this, Hyram. Mr. Bartlett will do all the work, and you have no obligation except to be present in case I need you to step in. Roscoe, as prosecutor, do you have any objections to my proposal?"

Roscoe Dale smiled at me. "Nope. It's fine with me."

"Hyram?"

Hyram leaned one elbow on the judge's bench, and seemed to be scrutinizing the floor for a place to spit. "Fine."

"Done," the judge said. "Mr. Bartlett, this is your big chance. I suggest you take it. The worst that can happen is that your client will be hanged, which is probably what would have happened anyway."

I chewed my lip for a moment, and looked around the courtroom. Mrs. Downing had arrived and was now seated beside her friend Chela in the back of the courtroom, dressed all in black. Her hair was pulled back neatly, and she looked quite elegant. Her eyes met mine.

The judge was right. This was my big chance. Simultaneous waves of exhilaration and dread washed through me as I said, "All right. I'll do it."

At ten-thirty on the dot, Roy and Helen arrive at my door to transport me to the funeral home. Helen's black dress shows off her slight, Audrey Hepburn-ish figure. She has already passed forty, but with her black pillbox hat and her warm smile she could have just stepped out of an airline advertisement in *Life Magazine*. She hugs me, then holds my shoulders and leans back, her eyes searching mine.

I say, "I'm fine." She looks unconvinced.

Roy and I shake hands. He has matured into a paunchy civil service engineer at the air force base. His face looks drawn, as if he hasn't slept, but he otherwise keeps his grief to himself. "Hi Dad. All set?"

"I'm ready." I pull on my suit coat, and take a last look around. This was Eva's home. I feel her presence in every corner and cupboard. Now we're off to say goodbye, and I wonder what I will feel when I return to its emptiness. I clear the catch in my throat and say, "Are the children on their way?"

"They are meeting us at the mortuary. Jimmy wanted to drive. I wish Grandma could see them all dressed up for her. She'd be proud. They look so grown up."

I open the car door for Helen, then climb into the back seat behind her. As Roy starts the engine, I mention that Josue stopped by this morning. "I suppose Carmen sent him to check on me."

Helen says, "Actually, Dad, it was me. I called him and asked him to stop by to see you this morning. I've been worried."

I shrug. "I'm fine. He told me Carmen was at home getting the kids ready. Oh, and Gabby stopped by."

Helen glances at Roy, but says nothing. He has never made a secret of his dislike for Gabby. Over the years I have wondered what he suspects about us.

I tell Helen that Gabby was asking about some earrings Gabby had given to Eva.

"Did she say what they looked like?"

"I wasn't paying that much attention to the details. If she still wants the earrings later, I'll tell her to talk to you."

Through the trees I catch a glimpse of the blue tile dome of the new courthouse. It is nearly thirty years old, now, but to us old codgers it is still the "new courthouse." It was built on the same spot as the Victorian building where I did the trial of Miguel Cordero and where I practiced law for another twenty years, until the second floor warped under the weight of fat law books in the library and they decided to tear the building down. No one was happier than Eva to see that old courthouse go. In the weeks of its demolition, she drove downtown nearly every day, to watch for a few minutes, as if each board pried loose and dropped to the ground represented some painful moment to be hauled away. At the time, I wondered at the ferocity of her obsession. Now I get it. And I understand that the destruction of the courthouse did little to pry loose the worn planks of her own difficult memories.

That morning, after Judge Davis appointed me to represent Miguel, he gave us a recess so I could speak to my new client before the arraignment. In the dark hallway outside the courtroom, Miguel's ankle shackles were connected by a three-foot chain which he held in his fist to keep it from dragging along the floor. The jailer stood a short distance away, pretending not to listen.

"In the meantime," I said after I explained the hearing that had just taken place, "I need to figure out a way to postpone the trial. The judge wants to do it tomorrow."

"Today's court isn't the trial?"

"No, it's the arraignment. I think it will be short." I actually had no idea yet what an arraignment was, and hoped he wouldn't ask.

"And Hyram is going to be with you in the trial?"

"Yes."

"I think Hyram is what will get me convicted. He didn't like what I said about him, did he?"

"He has a tough streak, I'm sure, but losing the trial will make him look bad. He won't want that. I need his experience. *We* need his experience."

"If we lose, he will blame it on you. I will die. He won't care about a Mexican with a rope around his neck."

"I don't agree. I watched him with your family and he was very respectful."

The jailer stepped forward. "Time's up, gentlemen. When the judge says fifteen minutes, he don't mean a second longer." He nodded toward the courtroom door. "He said to drag you in, Cordero, if you don't want to come. Your choice. Walk in or get dragged in."

Miguel stared at the floor for a moment, then stepped clanking toward the door. We entered the courtroom and Miguel, at the jailer's direction, shuffled over to the prisoner's dock. All the courtroom stared. His shackles clanked as the jailer fastened them to the ring in the floor. Don Antonio shook his head slightly, and his wife held a kerchief to her mouth.

Suddenly, Gabby stood up, her eyes on Miguel. A few heads turned.

The bailiff said, "Ma'am, do you need something?"

"I'm standing out of respect for my husband. He didn't kill anyone."

"Well, that's all well and good, but we have our procedures here. If you don't sit down after the judge comes in, he'll have me remove you from the courtroom."

She remained on her feet, eyes on her husband, who sat with elbows on his knees, his eyes on the floor. As I sat down, Hyram abruptly pushed his chair back, and stepped over to the rail, where he spoke quietly to Gabby. She whispered back and he nodded. She remained standing.

At that moment the bailiff intoned, "All rise!" There was a general shuffling as the judge entered and sat down at the bench. "The Honorable Judge George Davis presiding. Territorial Court is again in session."

The judge said, "Be seated."

Everyone sat down but Hyram and Gabby.

The judge said, "Are we ready to proceed?"

Hyram spoke up. "Judge, the defendant's wife is here, and she's upset. May I have a minute to speak to her?"

"What's she upset about?"

She said, "Mr. Judge, my husband did not kill anyone. We should not even be here."

"Well, Mrs. Cordero, we'll have to see about that. The whole point of this proceeding is to present the accusations against your husband. We'll have a trial later, so that a jury can decide if the evidence proves your husband killed Mr. Downing. It's how we do things."

"But it's not fair. He would not ever have killed Stephen, or anyone else for that matter. He looks terrible after being all locked

STEPHEN DOWNING IS DEAD

up and then brought in here in those chains. The jury will think he looks like a murderer." She blinked back her tears.

To his credit, the judge simply watched her without having her removed, listening until she was finished, with his forefingers extended in that little steeple above his other fingers.

"Madam, I trust you will let us all do our jobs. If your husband is as innocent as you say, he will be acquitted." Before she could answer he said, "Hyram, is everything settled with your client?"

Hyram put his hands on the table, bending forward slightly as he spoke. "As you ordered earlier, I'm only here to help. I believe you should check with this fella beside me." With that, he took his seat. Behind us, Gabby hesitated under the judge's gaze, her eyes fierce, and then sat down.

The judge's gaze moved to me. "Very well, Mr. Bartlett. I take it you have explained everything to your client and we can proceed with the arraignment?"

I rose and said, "We are ready, your honor."

"The bailiff will then read the indictment."

The bailiff rose, holding out a single sheet of paper. He intoned, "In the District Court of the First Judicial District, Territory of Arizona, in and for Pima County, the Territory of Arizona, versus Miguel Cordero. Indictment. October term, A.D. 1905.

"Miguel Cordero is accused by the Grand Jury of Pima County, Territory of Arizona, by this Indictment, found on the sixteenth day of October, 1905 of the crime of murder of the first degree, committed as follows. To wit:

"The said Miguel Cordero on or about thirteenth day of October, A.D. 1905, and before the finding of this Indictment at the County of Pima, Territory of Arizona, did unlawfully take away the life of Stephen Downing with malice aforethought, said killing having been committed willfully, deliberately and premeditatedly, contrary to the form, force and effect of the

Statute in such cases made and provided and against the peace and dignity of the Territory of Arizona. Signed, Roscoe Dale, District Attorney."

The bailiff lifted his chin importantly as he finished the reading.

"Very well," the judge said, "does the defendant wish to enter a plea today? Mr. Bartlett?"

I looked to Hyram for direction, but he looked away, out the window. I was on my own. In those days there weren't many crime novels and stories with courtroom scenes. Few people, including me, were familiar with courtroom procedures. I said, "I'm sorry?"

The judge said, "I asked if your client wishes to enter a plea today. Does he wish to plead guilty or not guilty."

"Your honor, why would he plead guilty?"

A flicker of displeasure flashed across the judge's brow. A murmur moved through the courtroom. "The answer to that question is for you and your client to decide, isn't it, Mr. Bartlett? But I take it you wish to enter a plea of not guilty."

I said, "Yes. Mr. Cordero will plead not guilty."

"Thank you, Mr. Bartlett. Very well. A plea of not guilty to the charge of murder of the first degree will be entered. Let's move on, then, to the matter of trial. Are you ready to proceed to trial, Mr. Bartlett?"

"I am not ready."

"You do understand that the court can proceed to trial forthwith?"

"Yes sir. However, at this moment ..." At that moment my mind went blank. Stage fright, I think. I took a deep breath as my mind scrambled to gather itself. "At this moment I have been representing Mr. Cordero for a total of perhaps eighteen minutes. Mr. Winthrop and I have had no opportunity to confer, and I have only had a short time to speak with the defendant."

The judge said, "So noted. On the other hand, your co-counsel

Mr. Winthrop has been involved all along, hasn't he, ever since the defendant was first brought before this court. Mr. Dale, does the prosecution have an opinion as to whether we should proceed immediately to trial?"

The prosecutor rose, holding the ends of his pencil between the index fingers of each hand as if to demonstrate the shortest distance between two points. "Doesn't seem like there's much to prepare for, Judge, so no reason to drag things out. Open and shut sort of thing."

"You would proceed immediately to trial, then?"

"I would."

The judge shuffled the papers before him thoughtfully. Finally, he looked up. "Mr. Bartlett, as I explained to you earlier, off the record, the law allows, but does not require, that we proceed to trial the same day as the arraignment. You may request a day to prepare. The court would be disposed to grant such a request. May we assume you are requesting that the trial be set for tomorrow?"

"No sir."

"No? You are not requesting a day to prepare?"

"No. I am requesting more than one day." I tried to stand a little taller than I felt. "A man's life is at stake. I think due process requires that I have more time to prepare."

The judge's hands came softly together. His fingers interlaced. His forefingers steepled. "Seems to me that while one man's life is at stake, another man's life has been taken, wouldn't you agree? And due process therefore requires that we proceed with justice as expeditiously as possible. Justice delayed is justice denied, as they say."

"With all due respect, your honor, a rush to judgment is not justice if an innocent man is convicted because his counsel did not have time to prepare."

The judge's eyebrows lowered slowly into a scowl. "Let us not

103

bandy aphorisms, Mr. Bartlett. Tomorrow is Friday. I believe that should be sufficient time to prepare."

"Your honor," I said. I needed some excuse—any excuse—for more time. "I believe justice will be served just as well …"

"That's enough. Trial will be tomorrow …"

"Judge," I said, raising my voice above his, "I'd like you to order that an autopsy be done on the body of the victim, to determine the cause of death."

Roscoe Dale jumped to his feet. "Your honor, such a request is outrageous and I strenuously object. For one thing, there is no doubt about the cause of death. The man was lying in the street, having bled so profusely from a gaping knife wound to his neck that his head lay in a two-foot circle of blood soaked into the street. For another thing, digging up a buried man would put his poor widow through the worst pain imaginable. She has already been through enough." Roscoe glared at me. "Mr. Bartlett's request is completely out of order, Judge."

Hyram was now looking up at me with something like a smile fidgeting at the corners of his mouth.

I said, "Judge, may I say something?"

"Go right ahead." The judge's face mirrored the look on Hyram's. Almost a smile, but not quite.

"Sir, I know we are all very sorry for Mrs. Downing's loss. But I can't imagine that an autopsy on her husband's remains would be more painful for her than hearing the graphic description of his murder delivered just now by Mr. Dale, in her presence. While I don't have the extensive experience you gentlemen have, I do know that the Constitution of the United States protects the due process rights of a criminal defendant. It is silent, however, as to the rights of a murder victim's widow."

Mr. Dale was on his tiptoes, his mouth was open, his finger pointed righteously toward heaven.

I headed him off, raising my voice. "Remember that a man is on trial for his life here. He has a right to have *all* the evidence presented. I need a chance to verify that *all* the evidence has been located. And besides," I said, turning to Mr. Dale, "why would you object to an autopsy if it would only help you prove your case?"

His face flamed. "That," he squawked, his finger still pointed heavenward, "that is the most immoral and insensitive argument I have ever heard in a court of law."

The judge's twitchy half-smile finally broke into a grin. "No, it isn't, Roscoe. And Mr. Bartlett has a point, although I am concerned about the feelings of the widow. Mrs. Downing?" He looked past us toward the back of the courtroom. "There you are."

She stood up as necks craned and all eyes turned her way. She looked alone and small. I'm sure I was not the only man in that courtroom who wanted to go back there to protect her.

The judge said, "Mrs. Downing, I don't mean to put you on the spot. But if you don't mind my asking, what would you think of an autopsy? It would, of course, mean that the body of your late husband would have to be exhumed—that is, dug up—and examined, and then reburied."

She hesitated. "I think Mr. Bartlett is right." She paused, as if about to add more, then abruptly sat down.

"Very well," the judge said. He dipped a pen and scribbled out his order, the scratch of his pen the only sound in the courtroom. Miguel stared at the floor. The judge blew on the paper to dry the ink, and then read aloud, "The Territorial Court, Pima County, hereby orders that the body of the late Mr. Stephen Downing be exhumed forthwith and an autopsy be conducted to determine the cause of death. A report shall be presented to the clerk of the court, to be made available to counsel, by Friday, October twentieth, 1905, at three p.m." He looked toward the prosecutor. "Will that work?"

Mr. Dale shook his head. "I object, Judge."

"Objection noted and overruled." The judge waved the paper toward the bailiff. "See that this is delivered to Doc Hinkley by lunchtime. Now obviously, gentlemen, given the autopsy, we won't be able to do the trial before Monday. What does the court calendar look like for Monday?"

The clerk paged through a large book. "Two matters are set for Monday morning, both civil. Monday afternoon is open. Tuesday has one matter in the morning. Civil also, not criminal."

"Very well, have the Tuesday matter rescheduled for later in the week, in case this trial runs over from Monday. Under the law, criminal matters take precedence. Today is the nineteenth. The jury trial in Territory against Miguel Cordero is set for Monday, October twenty-third, 1905, at nine o'clock a.m. We will begin voir dire at that time, and proceed thenceforth with the trial. If necessary, the trial will continue on Tuesday. Mr. Dale, do you expect to call a lot of witnesses?"

"No, your honor. I estimate I will be calling four witnesses. We should easily be finished by Monday afternoon."

"Mr. Bartlett?"

"Sir?"

"Will you be calling any witnesses?"

"I don't know yet, which is why I requested more time."

"Very well, you now have plenty of time. We're adjourned."

After the judge's departure, the jailer unlocked Miguel's manacles from the metal ring at his seat. He shuffled across the floor, chains rattling, with the jailer holding his arm. He glanced toward his family before he exited through the side door.

Hyram, his thin file in hand, said quietly, "You made good arguments this morning, Harvard Boy, but we'll find out next week how well you can keep Miguel off the gallows."

He dropped the file on the table and turned without waiting

for a reply. On his way out of the courtroom, he shook hands with the Cordero family. After he passed, the family turned as one toward me. After a moment, Don Antonio spoke curtly.

"My son is in danger. You will be responsible if he is put to death."

I said, "I understand your concerns. Believe me, I will do the best I can. Mr. Cordero, I know you don't know me, but ..."

"Remember what I said. You will be responsible."

Over the years I would learn to face families who were desperate to pull their sons back from the crushing jaws of justice. That first time, I felt myself blanch at this father's fury. I said, "I understand." Unable to say anything else, I picked up the file. "Please excuse me." I walked past them, out of the courtroom, down the stairs, and out into the bright sunshine.

Across from the courthouse, I found an alley to hide in for a few moments. I leaned against a chinaberry tree, catching my breath. Nausea washed through me in waves and I sat down heavily on a nearby step, my head between my knees as I tried to regain control. I had made such a fool of myself in the courtroom, I was sure. And that autopsy idea! What would the doctor find? What if he discovered bruises, or other marks besides the knife wound in Stephen's neck? What if there was evidence that something different had happened to Stephen, besides just getting stabbed? What Pandora's Box had I opened?

A barefoot boy of five or six came along the alley, holding a thin stick in both hands, and swinging it like a baseball bat. "Woosh!" he said with each swing. "Woosh!" He stopped directly in front of me. "You all right, mister?"

"Yes." I struggled to my feet and dusted off the back of my trousers. "Yes. Yes. I'm all right. Do you live around here?"

He nodded solemnly. "Yessir. Right there. That's my porch where you were sitting."

I stepped aside and he ran into the house as I drew a deep breath. The nausea was passing, and whatever the trouble I had gotten myself into, well, I was into it now. My fingers still clutched the file Hyram had given me. In it were only two pages of scribbled notes, indecipherable except for the name, "Pacheco," beside the word "see."

The sheriff's name was Pacheco. It wasn't much to go on, but I had to start somewhere. I walked back to the courthouse and learned from the bailiff that the sheriff's office was just down the street.

There I found the same burly man I had seen through my hotel window that first morning, the man escorting Mrs. Downing. He was reading a newspaper at a desk. His dark, drooping mustache obscured most of his mouth. Each of his large hands looked powerful enough to pick up a man by the face and shake him with his feet dangling above the ground. The dog I'd seen that first morning, long-haired with a black spot around its eye, now curled up near the foot of the desk, lifted its head briefly as I entered. The man did not glance up from the newspaper. "What can I do for you?"

"Where can I find the sheriff?"

"You're looking at him. Everybody else is at lunch."

"My name is Owen Bartlett. I'm representing Miguel Cordero against the murder charge. I need some information."

His eyes rose to meet mine. "What kind of information?"

"I'd like to see the knife that was taken as evidence from Mr. Cordero's room. I'd also like to ask you some questions about what else you might have found in his room, and what else you might remember from that night."

"I wasn't a witness to anything before the body was found, counselor."

"I understand that. I'm only trying to figure out what happened."

He squinted at the paper another moment. "Ok." He folded the paper, set it aside, and faced me with big hands folded on the desk. "Ask away."

"Well, what made you go to Miguel Cordero's room to investigate the murder? Why did you think of him instead of someone else?"

The sheriff waved toward the three wooden chairs against the wall. "Have a seat. What made me think of Miguel Cordero was what I heard. What I heard was that Miguel Cordero had a pretty good argument with Stephen Downing a few hours before Mr. Downing's body was found."

"What's a 'pretty good argument'?"

"Loud. Threatening. Might have been about money, but the witness couldn't hear."

"Who was the witness?"

"A fellow that works at the hotel. Name of Billsley. Strange fella. Nothing much to say except that the argument was pretty mean-sounding."

"I've met him. And what about the knife? Do you have it here?"

He rose and walked into a back room. The dog watched me until the sheriff returned with a small package, wrapped in brown cloth and tied with a cord. "It's wrapped, and this is my own special knot. That way I know nobody else has messed with it." He untied the cord and unfolded the cloth. The knife was long and slender, with a narrow, polished steel blade and a black wooden handle.

I pressed my finger lightly against the sharp point. It could easily cut through human flesh. "This is the knife you found in Mr. Cordero's room?"

The sheriff nodded.

"What makes you think it's the knife that was used to stab Stephen Downing?"

"I wasn't sure at first. Like I said, I went to talk to Miguel. He admitted the argument with Stephen, when I asked him about it, but he wouldn't say what it was about. I took a look around his room, and there was the knife sitting out on the dressing table. I decided to arrest him, but more to get him out of circulation than anything else. There's been bad blood among some folks who have strong feelings about Mexicans. I'm half Mexican myself, which to some folks makes me a Mexican, so I oughta know. I figured if nothing else came up to connect him to the murder, I'd get his father to come fetch him out of jail and back to the ranch before somebody hurt him."

"What made you think it was a murder?"

"Oh, I don't know, maybe it was the big hole in the dead man's neck where all the blood ran out."

"All right, I'll put it a different way. What made you think it was murder instead of an accident that might have happened in the middle of a fight?"

"That's a better question. There wasn't anything to make it look like a fight. The area in the street around the body was pretty well trampled over by the people who found the body, so I couldn't tell anything from the tracks. A couple of boot scuffs in the street where maybe the deceased was falling. Didn't seem to have any scratches or torn clothes. Maybe a bruise on one cheek, but it's hard to tell after the blood settles. Just mainly a body with a hole in its neck. I realized later that the hole pretty much matched the size of the blade on Miguel's knife, which is what made me decide not to turn Miguel loose after all."

"You measured the cut?"

"As a matter of fact, I did. I got to thinking about it, and I went over to the mortuary and measured the width of the cut to be three-eighths of an inch, give or take. That's the width of the blade on this knife. That's an unusual size, for a knife. Most of the ranchers carry a heavier knife with a wider blade, because it's more useful for ranch work. Anything from whittling to castrating calves. So here I had a knife about the size of the cut in the dead man's neck, and the knife was on the table in the room of the very man who was arguing with the dead man not long before he became dead. If you were sitting on a jury, what would you think?"

"I don't know, Sheriff. I've never sat on a jury."

"Me neither. But I'd sure have to give it some serious thought, and I think most other people would think the same thing I thought. It wasn't a robbery, because the dead man still had his wallet with money in it. Which means the killing had to be about something else, like the argument with Miguel Cordero."

"Was there any blood on the knife?"

"No, but I don't think that says anything. I mean, if you stabbed somebody and didn't want anybody else to know you stabbed somebody, wouldn't you wipe off the knife?"

"I don't know. I've never stabbed anybody."

"Me neither." The sheriff wrapped up the knife and retied the cord. "Any other questions?"

"Did you find blood on anything else?"

"A big patch of it in the street, beside the body. Pretty well dried up and soaked into the dirt by the time I got there."

"No blood on Miguel's clothes? Or on something else he might have used to wipe the knife?"

"Nope."

"The next morning, didn't you escort the widow over to the scene?"

"Sure did."

"Did she say anything, or give you any indication, about whether she had any likely suspects in mind?"

"Nope. When I got there to her house, she was with a Mexican lady who had just told her. News gets around fast. She was crying. Once she calmed down a little, she asked me who I thought did it. She looked surprised when I told her I had arrested Miguel Cordero. She asked if she could see where it happened. I tried to tell her I didn't think that was a good idea, but she wouldn't take no for an answer. She was pretty upset when we got there, but she couldn't say I didn't warn her."

I looked at the cloth bundle containing the knife, feeling terribly unclever. It sure sounded like the sheriff had done everything right, including arresting the right man. "I appreciate your time, Sheriff. Maybe I'll have more questions later. Were any of your men involved in your investigation?"

"Only in the cleanup. I let the deputies do a lot of things, but a big crime like murder, I handle it myself. Jack and me, that is." He reached down to scratch the dog's head. "Jack's a good dog." Jack closed his eyes appreciatively.

Eva and I had been married twenty-four years when she finally confessed the reason she wouldn't have a dog. We were in Paris, and it was 1930. She had talked for years about someday seeing the Latin Quarter and Montparnasse, and rubbing shoulders with famous artists and writers. It was said in those days that in Paris one could meet the most brilliant and creative minds of the age by strolling along an avenue or sitting awhile in one of the cafes. Without telling her, I booked our passage, and presented the plan at dinner on our anniversary. "You'll need clothes," I said.

She laughed. "So will you, sir."

She didn't stop smiling for weeks. Gabby's merchandise didn't run to her taste, so the two of them spent hours at Levy's and Jacome's and Steinfeld's, and even made a trip to Phoenix to shop at Goldwater's and Sons. They bought so much that packing for our trip became a matter of what to leave behind.

As things turned out, we met no one in Paris we could identify as famous or even moderately brilliant, but she was enthralled nonetheless with the exotic atmosphere. If we only got to travel once, she said, Paris was the perfect place. Paris soothed her deeper soul, she said. Which was fine with me. If she felt soothed in Paris, I felt soothed, even though rustic Tucson, with its dust and cactus and small town ambiance, had come to suit me just fine.

One evening in Paris we were taking a walk along some cobblestone street. A half-dozen sidewalk cafes lined a single block, each boisterous with artists and writers—as Eva imagined them to be—waving glasses of red wine and gesticulating argumentatively over—as Eva imagined—issues of philosophy and politics and artistic theory. A small white dog—Eva later thought he might have been some type of terrier, with a pointed nose and long thin tail—navigated pragmatically and quickly among the tables, nose to the ground as he sniffed for scraps. Every waiter tried to kick him away, as did many of the customers, their feet lashing out as he passed. He dodged them all like a broken field runner, with his nose never more than an inch from the sidewalk.

Eva watched him and then bent to put her hands on her knees. She made a little whimpering sound. Instantly he veered toward us. He halted before her, ears perked up, eyes expectant. She laughed and extended her hand in greeting. He sniffed her fingertips, his tail went up, and abruptly he began dancing around her as if they had been best friends since birth. She laughed and clapped for him to follow. Suddenly I was the outsider, tagging

113

behind as she skipped along on the cobblestones and he trotted beside her.

She stopped before one of the next cafes, and as the dog started to go past her into the tables, her hand came out in a gesture for him to stop. He stopped. She spoke to a waiter, making an eating gesture with one hand to her mouth, pointing to the dog with the other. The waiter's chin went up scornfully and he said something to the men at a nearby table. They laughed, but she regained the waiter's attention with a finger poke to his shoulder. She pretended to take a bit of food from the table and hand it to the dog, then pointed toward the kitchen. The waiter shook his head. She nodded insistently and pointed again to the dog. Finally, she pointed to me and rubbed her thumb and fingers together in what must be a universal gesture of money. He shrugged, then, and went inside. She picked up the dog and stroked his head until the waiter came out with a small package wrapped in white paper. He held up two fingers, and she gave me what I call her sweetly look—the flirty face she used to tease me sweetly into doing something. She said, "He needs some money." I pulled out two francs. He nodded and took the money.

Across the street, she put the little fellow down and unwrapped a piece of beef. Squatting down, she held it out to him. He sat without moving, upright and tense. She inched closer, nearly touching his nose with the meat. Suddenly he snatched it from her hand and trotted a dozen feet away. He turned to face her, as if to make sure she wouldn't try to steal it back while he gobbled it down.

She put her arm around my waist as we watched. "Isn't he beautiful?"

I put my arm over her shoulder. "Yes. And so are you. We should get a dog, don't you think? You're very good with them."

"No." She shook her head slowly. "I don't think it would be good for me."

She squatted down with the little dog as he finished his meal, watching as he licked at the cobblestones to make sure he hadn't missed anything. She said, "If we got a dog, it would be horrible. It would all come back."

I had no idea what she meant, but I knew she would eventually get around to making her point. The little white terrier let her pet his head, and then he turned and trotted away down the cobblestones without looking back.

A block or two later, she added, "The morning they found Stephen in the street, when the sheriff came to my house to tell me, he brought Jack with him. Jack, his dog. The sheriff stood there, inside my front door, and he told me what had happened. He held his hat in his hands, and I remember he wore that look a man gets when a woman is crying, like he wished he could be anywhere else. But Jack came over and lay down at my feet, and licked my bare toes while I was sitting there. I know he would have hugged me if he could."

I held her waist a little tighter, but she pulled away. "Everything would come back if we had a dog. It would all come back."

W e returned from France on the RMS Aquitania. After sightseeing in New York, we took a train to Boston and booked ourselves into the Copley Plaza. It all felt like home, though by that time I'd been gone for almost three decades. Eva liked history, and I showed her the site of the Boston massacre and Paul Revere's house, and we crossed to Charlestown to see Bunker Hill. We spent a morning at the new public library, where she fell in love with the great marble staircase and the French murals. I described the nooks in the old building, now gone, where Mother and I spent Saturday afternoons. We strolled around Back Bay, and I pointed out Mr. Norman's house where, perhaps even then in his dotage, he might be peering out a window. I took her to see my alma mater—the YMCA where I attended law classes. The big old building itself had burned years before, but my law program had evolved into Northeastern University, with a real campus.

Our last day before boarding the train back to Tucson, we walked to Roxbury to see the house on Bard Avenue where I had grown up. It, too, was gone, replaced by an apartment building. I stood on the street and pictured for her exactly where it had stood. In my mind's eye, Mother still busied herself in her kitchen, scolding me for coming home late to dinner "one time too many, young man," her sandy brown hair tucked behind her ears and her hands busily drying themselves on her apron. Mrs. Schwartz's house was still there, white now, not green, with white shutters as before. Even today I can hear her German accent as she burst forth every time our baseball banged into her door. She would scowl and scold, pointing at windows she always insisted our ball had narrowly missed. She would carefully examine the door for damage. Then, like clockwork, a few minutes later she would re-appear with a tray of marzipan in the shapes of cats and dogs and other less distinguishable animals. We thought ourselves so clever, sneaking up and lobbing the ball against her door to draw her out, not realizing she probably watched us coming and enjoyed the game as much as we did. I don't recall ever seeing anyone else come to see her.

In front of other houses, tall trees marked the passage of decades, where before there had been only a lawn or a small hedge. On the corner, where we used to torture a certain strong sapling into a catapult for firing rocks and sticks, there now stood an oak, thirty feet tall with a spread that reached nearly across the street.

I ran my hand across its rough bark, my fingers tracing a peculiar twist to the trunk that could have been the legacy of those fine summers.

The City Hospital still stood, a few blocks away, where my mother had gone to work as a volunteer. Gossipy neighbors had stirred up suspicions over how she and I never seemed to lack for anything, even though she had no job and no man in her life. How could this be, they asked. Something fishy must be going on. Or worse, immoral. As I got older, Mother fended off the criticism by volunteering at the hospital and pretending in the neighborhood that she had taken a job. She left the house each morning after I went off to school and arrived home in time to make dinner. She loved it, her "job." It made her feel important.

I described how, after a few years, Mother was caught in a sudden confluence of diphtheria and measles that swept through the hospital. She died as I sat on a wooden bench outside the contagion ward, my fingers digging hard into the seat, unable to pass beyond the locked door to hold her hand and pull her back into this life, my life. Immediately upon her death they sealed her into a coffin in an attempt to contain the diseases, and put her in the ground, allowing me to watch from the other side of the cemetery wall. Fourteen other people died the same month, all buried hurriedly and unceremoniously.

Eva and I held hands all the way back to the hotel. I told her about the man who arrived at my door the day after Mother's funeral. I was seventeen, then, and I remember he wore a flat-brimmed straw boater hat, the height of style at the time, which he did not remove when he invited himself in. His appraising eyes swept over every item in the small parlor, and never looked directly into mine. He represented, he said, a certain landlord who had a commitment from a certain gentleman to maintain the property as a rental paid for by the certain gentleman, for so long as my mother lived. Since my mother had now passed away—God rest her soul—that commitment was no longer in effect.

He paused, his gaze taking in a corner table covered with my mother's collection of small, carved wooden cats. He picked one up and looked at it closely. "So you will have to leave," he said.

I removed the wooden cat from his fingers and returned it to its place on the table. I asked if his employer had spoken with the gentleman to see if an eviction this precipitous was what the gentleman really had in mind. "Precipitous" was a word I knew from all my years in the library. His lips played silently with it, and I could tell he had no idea what it meant. No matter, he said. The bargain was the bargain, and it was time for me to go.

He was cocky and broad shouldered, and though he looked quick, I knew I could have him down in a flash, bloodied on the floor. But this was still my mother's floor, and I would not dishonor her. I asked where I should go. He shrugged, his eyes moving to the somewhat threadbare sofa. "You'll simply have to leave. You have family, I suppose?" Without waiting for a response, he turned for the door. His hand on the doorknob, he added, "And I suppose, if you must find a place, I can be generous. I'll give you a full week. A week should be sufficient. Oh yes, and I'm supposed to give you this. It's from a fund." He pulled a sealed brown envelope from his coat pocket and handed it to me. At the door again, he pinched the fabric of the window curtain. "Hmm," he said to himself, as if surprised by the feel of it. Then he was gone.

I showed Eva the building on Camden Street where, using some of the money I found in the envelope, I rented a second-floor apartment, moving as much as I could of our belongings from my mother's house, giving the rest away to the neighbors. My friends, now young men themselves, offered to throw a party for me. I said no thanks, and shook hands with each one. Friends forever, we promised.

Eva held my hand tightly until we arrived back at the hotel. After dinner, as she dressed for bed, she said, "Do you think your mother would have liked me?"

"My mother would have loved you."

"Why do you think so?"

"Because you are my wife. You have to understand what being a wife meant to her. In her world, it was the acme of what a woman could be, and she never got to be one. She would have admired you and she would have been proud of me for catching you and marrying you. God help me if I should ever think of leaving you."

"Would you ever leave me?"

"Never. I love you. Besides, Mother would tan my hide in heaven for all eternity."

"I see." Eva smiled as she got into bed. She crooked her finger at me. "Come here, then, young man."

B illsley was at the front desk when I arrived back at the hotel after speaking with the sheriff. He stiffened as I approached. "Billsley, I'd like to talk to you about an argument you witnessed a week or so ago. I got your name from the sheriff."

His eyes grew even more cautious. "Sheriff?"

"I've heard there was an argument between a man named Stephen Downing and one of your hotel guests, Miguel Cordero. It was here in the hotel one evening. Sheriff Pacheco told me you witnessed the argument."

"He told you that?"

"Yes. Do you know what I'm talking about?"

"This is about the fellow who was murdered?"

"He was found stabbed."

Billsley looked off toward the other side of the lobby for a moment. "I don't think I want to talk to you about it."

"A man's life is at stake. I'd like to know what you remember about the argument."

"Sheriff Pacheco said the same thing, after I told him what happened. That a man's life is at stake."

"What did you hear, when you heard the argument? I mean, why did you think it was an argument?"

He sighed and rolled his eyes petulantly. "All right. Well, I was here, and they were over there, by the window."

"So you were close enough to hear what they were saying?"

"No sir. Not really. Just, you know, the tone. They didn't get real loud. Might have been about money. The American fellow was standing like he was about to throw a punch. You know, with his shoulder cocked back. His face was red and his eyes were, you know, if you ask me, a little crazy. It's part of my job, not to pay much attention to other folks' business, if you know what I mean. But another part is to watch for trouble. He was looking for trouble."

"And the other man? The Mexican man?"

"He just stood there. He had that kind of look like he wasn't worried about getting hit, like he could handle a fight if he had to."

"Could you hear anything they were saying? The sheriff said it was a loud argument."

His eyes looked in every direction except toward mine. "No, like I was saying. Mainly the tone. It wasn't really the loudness of it. The tone stood out."

I couldn't tell whether to believe him. "Billsley, you do understand that a man's life is at risk in this, don't you?"

"Don't I know it. That poor fellow who was stabbed, I keep thinking about him. Right out behind the hotel, too, where he died."

A man in a large white hat approached the counter, so I backed away. With a furtive glance in my direction, Billsley hoisted his chin toward the man. "May I be of some help, sir?"

The man wanted a room, and Billsley happily turned his back to me as he began what sounded to be a long soliloquy about the history of the Santa Rita Hotel and its famed hospitality. Long enough to make me go away.

The big Irish jailer on duty stood by the bars of the cell, shouting orders for the inmates to stand off to the side, and for a man he called Jericho to come forward. Jericho, a tall, heavy man with blood at the corner of his mouth, yelled from the center. "Why me?" He pointed back toward the other inmates. "What about them? That sonofagoat over there is the one that pissed on me. What about him?"

The jailer shouted back. "I don't care what he did! Do you hear? When I tell you to do something, you do it. My job is to keep order, and by golly we'll have order or I'll piss on the lot of you myself. Now come over here, Jericho! I mean it! I'll deal with Johnson later."

The jailer's scowl cracked into a grin when he saw me. "Evening! You caught me when the animals are acting up. Give me a minute, here." The grin vanished and he glared at Jericho. "Hands behind your head."

Jericho flapped his arms. "But ..."

"I said hands behind your head or I'll put you out cold. That's it. The rest of you, get over in the far corner." He unlocked the door as the dozen other inmates, Miguel Cordero among them, congregated at the far end of the cell. He pulled Jericho out by the back of his shirt and relocked the cell door. "Over here!" He pushed Jericho toward a cage in the corner of the room. "You'll spend the night in there and see how you like it." He shoved the big man into the four-by-four cage and locked the door.

Jericho stood looking out through the bars. "How am I supposed to sleep in here? This isn't even big enough for a boy. I can't lie down."

"Not my problem. You're not supposed to sleep. You're supposed to appreciate how good you had it in the big cell with the grown-ups. Maybe tomorrow you'll decide to be a grownup and behave yourself."

That drew catcalls from some of his former cellmates.

"Quiet!" There was an instant quiet. "That's good. If you all behaved yourselves in the first place we wouldn't be doing this." The jailer nodded in my direction. "Who you here for?"

I said, "Miguel Cordero."

"What's your business?"

"I'm his attorney."

"Ah. I remember you. Cordero! Over here."

Miguel stepped forward and came to the bars. Despite the ruckus, his hair was combed and his face was clean.

From the disciplinary cage, Jericho growled out, "You better step careful, Cordero. We ain't safe with you around. Watch your back!"

Miguel rolled his eyes as I leaned against the bars, my face inches from his so we could speak quietly. "Are you all right?"

Miguel looked back at his cellmates and then over at Jericho. "Are you going to be able to help me? When we were in court I wasn't too sure."

"I tried to tell you that I have no experience like this."

"You are a lawyer, right?"

"Yes. So is Mr. Winthrop, and he will be helping me."

Miguel shook his head. "It doesn't look good, does it?"

"Who knows? Perhaps we'll get something good from the

autopsy. Perhaps it will turn out there were other factors in the death of Mr. Downing. Or perhaps I'll find some other information that will help." I tried to gauge his look. He was sturdy, and frustrated, and I could picture him stabbing Stephen Downing. "Can you think of anything I've missed?"

"No."

"Is there anyone who could testify that you were in your room all night?"

"No."

"I hear you had an argument with Stephen the night he was killed."

He frowned. "Where did you hear that?"

"From the sheriff, who heard it from the desk clerk who was on duty at the hotel that night. The desk clerk said he saw you and Stephen having words in the lobby of the hotel. The sheriff said you admitted the argument when he asked. The desk clerk at the hotel said it looked like a pretty fierce argument."

He stared at the floor for a moment. "We did talk, Stephen and me. He brought me an assay report, but it was for the place he wanted to dig a mineshaft. I didn't even know he had sent in a sample for an assay. My father didn't want nothing to do with a mineshaft until we had money coming in from the water lines we were going to bring down from the mountain. Stephen left, but then he came back that night. I saw him in the lobby. It was late. He asked me if I was talking to his wife."

"Talking to his wife? What did that mean?"

"I don't know." He glanced around as if to make sure no one else was nearby. "I told him I didn't have any idea what he was talking about. I don't think he believed me. He stood right in front of me like he wanted to fight. He said he had reason to believe she was seeing me. I told him he was crazy, because it was a crazy thing to say. Then he asked me about the mine, whether she said anything about the mine. He wanted to know what she said about the assay report. I told him I didn't see her, and I wasn't interested in the assay report until we got everything worked out about the water lines."

He rubbed his chin. "I didn't want to tell you because I thought it would make her look bad. She's a nice lady. This kind of thing could ruin her reputation."

"So he was jealous? Suspicious?"

"He seemed like it. But the next morning he was dead."

I let the jealousy idea sink in. It could be a reason for a bad fight between Stephen and Miguel. The prosecutor would jump on it, if he found out. "Did Stephen have a reason to be jealous?"

"Not from me. You saw my wife in court. Standing up for me the way she did. I feel the same way about her as she feels about me."

"The hotel desk clerk was of the opinion that the argument might have been about money. But an argument about jealousy would look even worse for you."

"It's all bad, Mr. Bartlett. This is a bad place, and the longer I'm here, the more I think they will hang me no matter what. I hope you can help me."

The jailer tapped me on the shoulder. "Sorry. Have to break this up pretty soon, counselor. Supper is an hour late, and if I don't get some food in here pretty soon there will be a worse fight than before."

I said, "Give me a minute." He moved off, and I whispered to Miguel, "How did the argument end?"

"He was too mad, so I walked away and went back to my room. That was the last time I saw him. The next morning he was dead."

"All right." I kept my voice very low. "I'm sure I don't need to advise you not to talk about this with anybody else."

The jailer broke in again. "Time's up, gentlemen. Cordero, back away. Food cart's coming in."

There was no food cart in sight, but I nodded to Miguel. "I'll be back."

He did not back away. He was still leaning against the bars when I glanced back from the door.

A little while later, I was sitting at the writing desk in my hotel room, making notes about Miguel, when someone knocked at my door. I opened it to find Josue, who said, "Please. To cahm, me. Please." He made a beckoning motion with his hand. "To cahm, me. Please."

"Where are we going?"

He pointed to himself. "No English. You cahm, me. Please."

I hesitated, and then grabbed my coat from the back of the chair. "All right. Where are we going? Never mind. Lead the way."

He led me out of the hotel and down the street.

Realizing our direction, I asked, "Are we going to Mrs. Downing's house?"

He gave no sign he'd heard, and ignored me when I asked again after a half-dozen blocks more. We passed the block where Eva lived, and continued on toward Signal Peak and the Santa Cruz Wash. We passed a small field of wheat near the wash, and came to a stable with dozens of pens and corrals. I followed him between the rows until I rounded a corner and came upon Eva brushing a white horse. Her straw hat was cocked back on her head, and her eyes were red and looked tired. Nonetheless she smiled at my arrival, and dug some coins from her skirt pocket to offer to Josue, who refused politely with a shake of his head. She spoke to him in Spanish, but he grinned and said no.

She said, "He told me the other day he wants to be a businessman, but now he refuses to be paid. I'm telling him he'll never succeed that way, but he won't hear of it. Did he speak to you in English?"

"Sort of."

"What did he say?"

"It was something like, 'You come with me. Cahm,' he said. And he said 'please.'"

"Good. We practiced it before he went for you. He doesn't get much chance to practice English with his family at the mortuary. They all speak English well because they have been here in Arizona for generations, but within the family they use only Spanish. He arrived from Mexico a few weeks ago." She set the brush in a basket, and picked up a hand tool with a dull-pointed metal tip. She lifted one of the horse's hooves and dug at the bottom, prying out dirt stuck under the hoof. "This is Molly. She's my baby. My thousand-pound baby. I named her after a famous racehorse, but she's not a racer. People around here think it's odd that I make such a pet of a work animal, but I don't mind. Stephen and I rode a lot, especially up into the mountains. His horse is that big bay gelding over there. He's already sold." There were a number of horses in the direction she nodded, and I couldn't tell which one she meant.

Her fingers were slender, but there was strength in the way she worked the tool around the hoof. She finished with one hoof and let it down, moving easily to the next, taking hold of the horse's leg above the hoof and gently tugging upward until the horse allowed it to come off the ground. She balanced the hoof in one hand as she worked the tool with the other, and it didn't seem to occur to her that this thousand-pound baby could easily kick her across the stall. She was in command.

Without breaking the rhythm of her hoof work, she said, "I wanted to talk to you about the case. Is there some way I could help?"

I thought about what Miguel had said to me. "I'm not sure how to answer. Sometimes one finds out things about other people that could be uncomfortable or embarrassing. But there might be something useful in it."

She nodded as if she knew what I meant. "Mr. Bartlett, having one's husband die under these very public circumstances is as difficult as life can get. I think I can bear about anything at this point. I want to help."

I decided to take her at her word. "I've heard that Miguel and your husband were seen arguing at the hotel shortly before your husband was stabbed."

She set the hoof down and dropped the metal tool into the basket, then picked up a brush and began working at the tangles in the horse's mane. "I don't know what happened between them that night. All I know is that Miguel would not have killed Stephen."

"Could your husband have provoked a fight?"

She worked the long hairs of the mane. "They had some business disagreements, now and then. I don't know if that's what the argument was over."

"What were the business disagreements about?"

"Usually something about setting up the mine. I think the whole Cordero family was uncomfortable with Stephen's ambitiousness. He wanted to move too fast. But people have disagreements all the time without killing each other."

"Why are you so sure Miguel didn't do it?"

She tugged the brush through a knot in the mane. "He didn't. That's all. For one thing, he's not that type of man."

"Miguel told me that your husband wanted to know if you were with him that night. With Miguel. Were you with Miguel that night?"

She tugged hard suddenly at the mane with her brush, and the horse shifted its weight uneasily. "I suppose what you really want to know is why my husband would ask him that."

"I'm sorry. I have to ask. I'm having trouble putting together what happened. I must ask questions."

She rested both hands on the horse's back and looked me in the eye. "I understand that. But no." She went back to brushing the horse's mane. "Stephen and I had our disagreements over the last few months, but I would never ..." She pulled hard enough at the mane that the horse shook its head. "Shh. I'm sorry. I'm sorry, girl."

"Stephen apparently didn't understand your faithfulness."

Her jaw tightened as she worked. "Apparently not."

"And now we'll never know from him why he thought it." I raised my hands immediately and added, "I'm sorry. I didn't mean ..."

"Don't worry, Mr. Bartlett. I don't wear my grief on my sleeve, and I'm not going to burst out in tears."

"I'm sure you don't have anything to hide. At any rate, since you brought up your grief, may I apologize for requesting an autopsy? I'm sure that was a painful moment for you in the court. Before Jose came to get me at the hotel, I was thinking of speaking to you about it."

"Josue. His name is Josue, not Jose. Pronounced hose-sway. And I'm not upset. I'm not going to be there when the doctor does the autopsy. And afterwards, they'll put Stephen back in the ground. I don't want to be there for that. But I don't think an autopsy will help very much. I saw all the dried blood in the street. I'm sure he didn't die of a heart attack."

Josue leaned against a fencepost nearby, listening to us. I wondered what we sounded like to him, chattering away in English.

Sunset was approaching and the air was pleasantly warm. I said, "I was wondering about something else. Why did you assume so quickly that I would be a good lawyer for Miguel?"

"I just knew."

"You seem to do that a lot."

"What do I do a lot?"

"You 'just know.' But how did you 'just know' about me?"

She shrugged. "I can't really explain. I took one look at you and just knew you would be perfect."

"Well, I 'just know' it was probably foolish of me to say yes to taking the case."

"Which is why you'll be perfect. You won't take anything for granted. Stephen took things for granted. A lot of people do that. I think Hyram Winthrop would take Miguel's case for granted, and he wouldn't fight hard enough. To a lot of people around here, Miguel is just another Mexican, even though his family has a big ranch, and even though they've been here for generations. I knew you would not assume he is guilty because he's Mexican. I knew you would find a way to help him."

"I'm not sure I agree with you about Hyram. I get the impression he dislikes people in general, equally, whether they're Mexican or not. It's odd that people here in the west see race mainly as white and Mexican. In Boston they blame everything on the Irish, or the Italians. My mother was part Irish and she had a difficult life. Back east, or at least in New England, everything isn't a matter of skin color. There is plenty of prejudice to go around even for white people among white people."

"I didn't know that, but I just knew you would see things differently than some other people do here. That is why I wanted you to be Miguel's lawyer."

"What if I told you it's hard not to believe Miguel is guilty, when one looks at the evidence? If I told you that, would you think you've made a mistake about whether I should represent him?"

"You don't believe that. And I haven't made a mistake."

"But what if you're wrong?"

"I'm not wrong." She turned back to the horse, fumbling with the straps around its big head. "I don't care about the autopsy. They won't find anything except a knife wound. But Miguel didn't make that knife wound, and I can't watch an innocent man, an innocent *good* man, be sent to prison, or worse. I watched you in court. I think you'll do a good job."

She spoke to Josue in Spanish, and he picked up the dangling reins and walked off with Molly toward a stall. Eva turned around to face me, and abruptly our faces were hardly a foot apart. "Mr. Bartlett," she said, moving back a step, "being a lawyer is a special thing. Not many of us have the opportunity to help people this way. Maybe you are new at it, and I'm sure you have a lot to learn. That's why Miguel has an advantage. You'll care. If you don't care about Miguel, at least you'll care about doing a good job. You'll care about it as a matter of pride. When I looked at you at my husband's funeral, I didn't know you were an attorney, but I knew I was looking at a decent man. That's all this case needs. A decent man who can figure things out and fight for what is right."

I could smell the sweetness of her breath. "Well, thank you," I said. "I hope I can justify your confidence in me."

Walking away, I knew, I just knew, she was watching me.

That night I dozed off in my chair with papers strewn around me, and she taunted me in my dreams. Smiling, she opened her blouse slowly and moved to press herself against my bare chest, but then she was on the other side of her horse, gazing naked across at me. I chased her around the white horse. She moved easily ahead, beyond my reach. Her hand stroked the horse's white flank as she passed and the horse's body became my body. Her hand moved like white fire across my thigh and abruptly I sat up in a sweat. Surrounded by papers. After a minute, I shook off the dream and picked up a pen.

The case of Territory of Arizona against Miguel Cordero.

Fact: Stephen Downing had been stabbed in the neck outside the Hotel Santa Rita.

Fact: Miguel Cordero was nearby when it happened.

Fact: Stephen and Miguel had an argument only a short time before the stabbing.

Fact: A certain knife of certain dimensions was found in Miguel's room.

The prosecutor would weave those facts into the story of how Miguel had killed Stephen Downing. I needed a different way to put the story together. Somehow I needed to convince a jury of twelve men that something different had happened that night.

What if Miguel really had killed Stephen Downing, as the evidence suggested? Perhaps, in a fit of jealous rage, Stephen had attacked Miguel, and Miguel stabbed him in self-defense? Or perhaps they fought over something else—money, or the development of the mine, say—and Miguel reacted in self-defense. Or perhaps the whole thing was an accident.

Each of these scenarios would require me to know more about what really happened. And what if it turned out that Miguel was guilty as charged? How could I defend a man I knew was guilty? A tough question. I knew what the textbook answer must be. The textbook would say that a defendant is innocent until his guilt is proven beyond a reasonable doubt, and it was the prosecutor's job to provide that proof. My job, as the defense attorney, was to question and test the proof. If the proof was weak, my job was to call attention to that weakness, no matter what I privately knew about Miguel's innocence or guilt. My job, in other words, was to defend my client. That was the textbook answer. In reality, I had no idea what the real answer should be.

131

I decided to focus on the defense, and leave the philosophy for some other time. Perhaps if I could learn more about what had passed between Miguel and Stephen, I might be able to show that the argument was inconsequential, the sort of thing friends engage in without getting angry enough to kill each other. Only two people—Miguel and Stephen—knew what the argument was about. One of them was dead. The other said nothing about the argument until I confronted him.

And Eva? I began to have a sense that she might be hiding something. How could she be so certain Miguel was innocent, so certain that she would jump in to help defend him? The evidence against Miguel was bad, yet she was convinced of his innocence. I wanted to know why.

I arrived at her door a little before sunrise and knocked softly. I waited, looking around, then knocked again, slightly louder. After a minute, the door opened an inch. "Yes? Owen. It's you. What's wrong?"

I could not see her through the narrow opening. I whispered, "I'm sorry to bother you like this. I need to talk to you. I don't have much time before the trial. I didn't know another way to contact you."

After a long pause, she said, "Meet me at the stables in half an hour." The door closed, and I hurried away, toward the conical shape of Signal Peak that was forming now in the early light. At the stable, I strolled up and down the rows of stalls. The horses watched me sleepily as I passed. Two men carried bundles of hay from a small adobe barn to horses at the other side of the complex of stables. When I found Eva's stall, Molly approached me and sniffed at my hand. I rubbed lightly above her nose until she pulled her head back. "Sorry girl," I said. "I didn't bring breakfast. We're both waiting, I suppose."

When Eva appeared on the far side of the stable, she was striding purposefully, dressed out in a feathered hat and white kerchief, a dark skirt and black riding boots. Perhaps she would invite me to go riding, or perhaps she would simply want to talk with me as she prepared to go off by herself. Her hair was pulled up. She made her way between the stalls and walked directly up to me, her eyes meeting mine fiercely.

"How dare you!" she said quietly. "How dare you!"

"How dare, what?" I stepped back against her advance.

Her eyes were fierce. "Were you raised on Mars, Mr. Bartlett? I thought someone from Boston would have more sense. What were you thinking?"

"What was I thinking about what?"

"What were you thinking as you pounded on my door at dawn for all the world to see? My God, do you think people don't talk, especially now, with all that is going on? Did you think I would simply invite you in for tea at dawn, with all the neighbors watching?"

"I wasn't thinking about that. I was ..."

"That much is very clear, sir." She whirled on her heel and started toward the barn. "And what were you doing up so early, anyway? You should have been at your hotel asleep."

"You don't understand." I started after her.

"I understand very well, Mr. Bartlett. You are completely caught up in your own concerns, and you have no interest in the concerns of other people."

"That's not true. I tried to be very quiet, you see."

"Quiet? Are you joking? This is not Boston. Every sound carries, especially early in the morning."

She entered the barn and came back out almost immediately, nearly crashing into me in the doorway, her arms wrapped around a bundle of hay. She stopped. "Are you joking?" Without waiting for my response, she moved around me and stomped back to the stall.

The sweet smell of the hay did nothing to soften the sting of her anger. "I'm sorry. You're right. It was thoughtless of me."

Molly waited, head over the fence, ears perked forward as Eva approached. Eva reached the hay between the rails and dropped it in a corner of the stall. She put her hands on her hips without facing me. "What was it that you wanted, Mr. Bartlett?"

"I was up all night, thinking about the case. I need to know some things. I wanted to ask you again about the relationship between Miguel Cordero and your husband."

"What about it?"

"I need to know more about what they were arguing about on the night your husband was killed."

She started back toward the barn. "I told you. I don't know. I wasn't aware of an argument until you told me about it."

"Well, that may be true, but …"

She whirled about. "*May* be true?"

"You're missing my point, Mrs. Downing."

"Which is?"

"Which is that if I can show in court that the argument was about something minor, the jury might believe the argument had nothing to do with your husband's death."

She turned back toward the barn. "It didn't have to do with Stephen's death. I'm certain of it."

"Well, tell me how you can be so certain."

"I just am."

"Wouldn't you like the jury to be just as certain?"

"Of course."

"Then tell me what you know about the argument."

"I told you. I didn't know there was an argument. But if there was, it had nothing to do with Stephen's death. Miguel did not kill Stephen. Miguel isn't that kind of man."

"How do you know?"

"It doesn't fit what I know about Miguel. Ask Gabby, his wife. Ask his family. He isn't that kind of man."

"All right, fair enough. Did Stephen and Miguel get along?"

"They got along well enough. They spent a lot of time together in the mountains."

"Did your husband ever talk to you about the plans for the mine, or about what he thought about Miguel, or about whether he was getting along with the Cordero family?" I followed her into the barn, where she picked a rope halter from among others on the wall and started back out, nearly bumping into me again.

"My husband was not the most communicative man. And don't follow so closely."

"But that doesn't answer my question, Mrs. Downing. It doesn't seem likely that he told you nothing at all. There must have been some detail you picked up which suggested that perhaps things weren't going well with the mining project. Or that perhaps he and Miguel didn't like each other. Or, anything at all. Were you completely in the dark?"

She stopped and turned again. "No." Her voice was softer. "I wasn't completely in the dark. I knew they were planning a mining project. I knew that sometimes Stephen seemed exasperated by how slowly it was going. But Miguel was—is—a nice man, a quiet man. If they didn't get along, it was because Stephen was so impatient. I saw and heard nothing from Miguel—or from Stephen—to suggest that Miguel was upset with the project. After all, he was in complete control. He was coordinating the financial resources from the group that was putting together the money. The mine and everything else was on his father's property. Miguel controlled the pace of the project. He controlled everything. It was all in his hands. That's what made Stephen crazy. He liked to be the one in control."

I smiled. "So you see, Mrs. Downing, you do know something after all."

She smiled too, as she looked down at the halter in her hand. "Yes. I do. But I don't exactly know why they were arguing that night."

"Tell me about the group that was putting the money together."

"It was some men from the Alianza." She hung the halter from a fencepost next to where Molly was concentrating on the hay pile on the ground. "A group of Mexicans, mostly business people. I don't know much more than that. You met two of them when you came to Chela's for lunch the other day. Mr. Castillo and Mr. Borboa."

"Could it be that someone in that Alianza would know something?"

"Stephen didn't talk about it much, except to say he thought they were too slow at making decisions. He thought they were too cautious."

"Then maybe the next step is to see Mr. Castillo again."

She disappeared inside the barn and came back out, a bridle draped across her shoulders and lugging a saddle and blanket, which she swung up onto a crossbeam near the horse. She hung the bridle next to the halter. "I'll have Josue take you to the shop." She waited for the horse to polish off the last of the hay, then slipped on the halter and tied it loosely to the fence. With a brush, she smoothed and cleaned the horse's back and sides, moving surely from one side to the other. I watched her thoughts play across her face like slight ripples crossing a pond. She glanced in my direction once or twice. Without saying anything, she laid the blanket across the horse's back. Grasping the saddle with both hands, she pulled it from the crossbeam and swung it up onto Molly's back, shifting it into place on the blanket, and began hooking up the straps under the horse's belly.

I watched as she pulled a strap tight. Without really thinking, I said, "Perhaps you could teach me to ride sometime?" Instantly I regretted the question. "I'm sorry. I know this is a terrible time for you."

"Don't worry," she said. She took the bridle from the fence post, fitted the metal piece into the horse's mouth and then pulled the straps over the horse's ears. She smoothed out the long hairs of the mane. She said, "This is the West, Mr. Bartlett. Rules are different. I'll teach you to ride if you can get Miguel out of jail. Unless," she added with a slight smile, "you embarrass me again by showing up at dawn on my doorstep."

The Castillo Saddle Shop smelled deeply of new leather. Josue and I stood at the counter dividing the customer section from the working area. Rows of cowhide hung from high rafters, and several men worked at tables, tapping with hammers. A young man behind the counter spoke to Josue in Spanish. Josue answered with a gesture toward me.

I said, "I'd like to see Mr. Castillo. My name is Owen Bartlett."

The man whistled softly to a figure working at a bench in the far back of the long shop, then called out, "Carlos!"

The figure in back looked up, and set whatever was in his hands on the bench. He strode to the front wiping his hands on a cloth. "Mr. Bartlett, what brings you to my shop? I would have thought you'd be hard at work preparing for Miguel's trial."

"As a matter of fact, Miguel's trial is why I'm here. I need some information."

"I see. And young Josue, here, he is your interpreter?"

"Of course."

"Of course." Carlos winked at Josue, and raised the countertop so we could pass through to the back. He led the way to the back corner of the building, to a table stacked with papers. Pulling up a couple of wooden crates, he motioned for us to sit. He took the chair. "What kind of information do you need?"

"I'm trying to find out more about the relationship between Miguel and Stephen Downing."

Carlos nodded, and waited.

I said, "No one is telling me much."

"Who have you seen?"

"I've talked to Miguel. I've met his parents, and his wife, but we didn't have time to talk about much in the courtroom. I've talked to Stephen Downing's widow. I've talked to the sheriff, and I talked to Hyram Winthrop."

"I'll bet that was entertaining. Mr. Winthrop, I mean."

"I keep telling people he's a better lawyer than I am. Anyway, I got to thinking about what you'd said, that you were a close friend of Miguel's. I was hoping perhaps he talked to you, or confided in you. I'm running out of people to ask."

"And you are here because you hope I'll tell you about what was going on between Miguel and Stephen."

I spread my hands. "As I said, I'm running out of people to turn to."

Carlos pursed his lips for a moment. "What sort of things are you looking for?"

"That's the problem. I don't know, except that I heard there was a big argument between them the night Stephen was killed. I don't know what it was about."

"I see." Something caught Carlos's eye across the room and he jumped up. "Jaime! No!" He held up a hand to me and said, "Excuse me." He scooted out from his chair, moving quickly over to where a man was hoisting a large saddle from one rack onto another. Carlos corrected whatever it was the man was doing wrong, pointing to another area of the shop. When he resumed his seat, he said, "This is a little difficult, I guess, because law is not my business and I don't know what kind of information you might find helpful."

"What have you heard, Mr. Castillo? If I may be blunt."

Carlos smiled. He said something to Josue in Spanish that had the ring of an inside joke. He said, "I think we all want to protect our friend."

"Then protect him by giving his lawyer some information to work with."

"All right. There are two rumors that I know of. One of them is not true. I know. But the other, maybe, maybe not."

I waited.

"The one that is not true is that Miguel might have been having an affair with Mrs. Downing."

"How do you know it is not true?"

"Because I know Miguel. Mrs. Downing is a beautiful woman. She is, maybe, a little more independent than some people around here are used to. People say sometimes she doesn't act like a married woman. She goes out riding alone, she is seen speaking to men."

"How do people connect that to thinking she was having an affair with Miguel?"

"Stephen got jealous easily. He didn't try to hide it. I was there once when his wife was saying something to Miguel and Stephen told Miguel to leave. He said he wanted to speak to his own wife alone. Like that. Like he thought Miguel needed to be reminded of whose wife she was."

"Did you ask Miguel about it? About these rumors?"

"Yes."

"And?"

"He got mad when I asked him. He said there was nothing between him and Mrs. Downing. Nothing at all."

"You know Miguel very well, don't you?"

"He is like my little brother. My father worked for Don Antonio and I grew up on the ranch. That is why I came to you at the hotel, before I knew you were a lawyer, to see if you heard anything or saw anything when Stephen was killed. I wanted to help my little brother."

"Do you think he would lie to you?"

"Mr. Bartlett, we all lie a little bit, even to our best friends. Or maybe especially to our best friends, sometimes. But I think I would have been able to tell if there was something between Miguel and Mrs. Downing. There was nothing. Miguel loves his own wife. That is all."

"What was the other rumor, the one that might be true or might not?"

"The other rumor was that Miguel found out Stephen was cheating him on the mining project."

"How could he be cheating if they hadn't even started digging it yet, or constructing it, or whatever you do with a mine?"

"I don't know. I've heard that Miguel paid him some money, but Stephen didn't use the money the way he said he would. Miguel and his father had this idea that they could run a pipe from high up the mountain, to bring water down to where the placer mining was going on. That's ..."

"What's placer mining?"

"Placer mining is where they put scoops of dirt and gravel in a big pan, and then wash it to bring out the gold. Some people call it panning for gold. It takes a lot of water to do that, and Miguel wanted to bring water down from the top of the mountain. Don Antonio, Miguel's father, thought the pipe idea was worth investing in, and it would be a lot less expensive than what Stephen wanted. What I heard was that Miguel gave Stephen some money to order a bunch of pipes from back east, and Stephen maybe used it to order lode mining equipment instead. Don Antonio was very upset when he heard about it. Somebody else I know thought maybe Stephen lied about the assay reports."

"In what way?"

"I don't know. Stories spread around and you don't know where they come from." He rose to his feet and held out his hand. "I'm sorry, but I have to get back to work." He shook hands with us and said something to Josue in Spanish, then added "Understand?"

Josue responded in English. "Little bit."

"Whoa!" Carlos said, slapping Josue's shoulder. "Señor English speaker! Pretty soon this *abogado* can hire you. I heard you want to be his secretary."

I said, "After this trial, nobody will ever hire me again as a lawyer. Josue and I can come to work in your shop."

"Ah," Carlos said, "you'll do better as a lawyer. A saddle shop is no way to get rich. You know those automobile machines you see running up and down the streets? Someday they will be everywhere, and there won't be any more use for a saddle shop. People don't believe it yet, but you just watch."

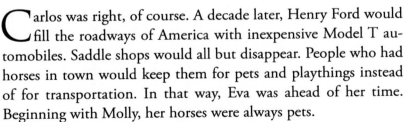

Carlos was right, of course. A decade later, Henry Ford would fill the roadways of America with inexpensive Model T automobiles. Saddle shops would all but disappear. People who had horses in town would keep them for pets and playthings instead of for transportation. In that way, Eva was ahead of her time. Beginning with Molly, her horses were always pets.

She taught Roy to ride when he was four or five, and he was her favorite riding partner until she was well into her sixties and had to stop riding because of back pain. Molly died suddenly of colic when Roy was about seven, and she was so devastated she couldn't get out of bed for nearly a week, rising only to send Roy off to school. It was curious, I thought, that she grieved so much more dramatically for Molly than for Stephen, but I said nothing. Some blows to the soul wound so deeply that years can pass, or more, before grief makes its way to the surface. Roy and I plied her with flowers and the grilled cheese sandwiches she had taught him to make, but nothing worked until she had done enough crying. After that, he pestered her daily until she finally took him around to all the local stables to find a new horse. They fell in love with a chocolate quarter horse mare Roy named Lightning because of the white marking on her forehead. They bought Lightning, along with a paint mare he named Patches. Before long they were out riding every Saturday again. The streets were becoming unsafe for horses on account of Henry Ford's Model T automobiles, so they would go trail riding along the Santa Cruz Wash, or out through the desert to the foothills of the Catalina mountains. She was good with Roy.

I never got the hang of playing the way she could. Having never had a father around when I was growing up, I kept up the stern-father-disciplinarian-breadwinner role I believed I was supposed to play in their lives. Once or twice Roy and I tried to play catch, but he lost interest when, he said, I kept throwing the ball too hard. With his mother, on the other hand, he was curious about everything, and his questions were endless. Why was cholla called jumping cactus? And why did we pronounce it *choya* instead of *chola*? Why was the horse's back sweaty under the saddle even if they only went for a slow ride? Why did lizards' tails come off when you caught them?

He grew quieter and more reserved in adolescence. Eva said he was becoming much more like his father. I think she missed his childhood dependence on her, and their closeness. She even got a bit jealous of the girls in his life. Approaching graduation from Tucson High, his dinner talk was all about football and girls and college. He played halfback on the football team, and he got his share of female attention. Eva wanted to know about every girl who spoke to him, and her ears would perk up when she heard that this one or that one liked to ride horses. When Roy asked to be allowed to take a certain girl riding on Lightning and Patches, Eva had him invite the girl to ride first with her. If the girl could show she knew what she was doing with a horse, Eva would trust her with Lightning.

The girl later complained to Roy that his mother kept bringing the conversation around to Stanford University, where he had been accepted into college, and where, she repeatedly pointed out, he would be meeting a whole new crop of girls. After Roy furiously took her to task at the dinner table, and after he endured my equally furious reminder that he was not entitled to address his mother in that manner, Roy did not invite any more girls horseback riding.

M y stomach tightens as soon as I see the church coming up. Roy pulls the car smoothly into the large parking lot and sets the hand brake. A black hearse is off to one side, behind the building, and ours is the only other car in the lot. Helen turns to me from the front seat, with a sympathetic smile and her eyes moist, as Roy opens first my door, and then hers.

I'm not ready to go in there, but I don't want to cause a fuss and I swing my feet out onto the pavement. Helen takes my arm and together we make the slow walk toward the big wooden church door. My feet feel as if they are encased in concrete. Roy swings the door open and we enter. A heavy perfume of flowers fills the air as our eyes adjust to the dim light. There, in the silence within, is her casket. A half-dozen lit candles make yellow points of light.

Roy stands awkwardly with his hands in his pockets. Helen grips my forearm.

There must be a dozen or more bouquets and wreaths. I'm sure Helen will take care of getting the names and writing thank you notes. I'm glad people knew Eva, but my first impulse is to say that, although she loved flowers, she preferred to enjoy them on growing plants rather than in bouquets and cut arrangements. She would spend hours in her garden, coaxing out the last blooms of the season before the brute heat of summer arrived, or the chill of winter. Spring was her favorite time, with blooming cactus and desert wildflowers. She often told me the names of the wildflowers as we drove through the desert or walked in the hills, but the flower names never stuck with me. What mattered was the way the colors cheered her and brought color to her cheeks.

The door from the church nave opens and a short, round woman in a dark dress comes in. She smiles professionally and greets Helen like a friend. Helen introduces us. Margaret, she says, is the person who keeps everything running smoothly here at the church.

Margaret shakes hands with Roy, and takes my hand in both of hers. Her eyes are kind with sympathy. "I'm so sorry for your loss, Mr. Bartlett. I have no doubt that your wife is happily with our Lord, but those of us left behind have a heavy burden, don't we?"

I agree, awkwardly. This is a conversation I don't want to have, so I get right to my point. There isn't a lot of time. I wonder aloud if the casket might be opened and if I might have a few minutes alone with Eva before everyone else arrives.

Margaret's warm hands tighten briefly on mine. "Yes, of course," she says. "We anticipated that." She expertly flips a latch and opens the lid of the casket, adjusting something in back to hold it open. "Here you are." She steps aside, and adds, "She looks lovely. Your friend, Mrs. Cordero, stopped by a little bit ago. She wanted to see the makeup. I think she was pleased."

Helen and Roy pause for a quiet moment by the open casket, and then they go out with Margaret into the nave of the church to take their seats. I stand still, waiting behind the casket until they go, before I move around to the front to be alone this one last time with Eva.

Her cheeks have settled back, just a little but noticeably, giving the effect that she is relaxed. She appears not quite as if she were napping. They've given her a permanent that matches the way she wore her hair in the last few years. She would have liked the do, I think, after the miserable dishevelment of her hair those last few days at the hospital. They have dressed her in her favorite white shoes, and a green skirt I don't recall. A matching green jacket is buttoned over a white blouse, which is buttoned up to her throat, just as she would have chosen to wear it. The collar is a white lace ruffle. Her hands are folded on her stomach. Everything is still.

I rest my hands on the side of the casket and try to memorize it all, a large, deep bubble of sorrow rising painfully from inside my chest. I want to say something to her, but no sounds will come up. My throat clogs, my nose fills, my eyes get misty. I touch my forehead to the fabric of her green jacket. And then I am crying, gripping the side of the casket to keep my balance. There are things to be said about a life, and things to be said about a life lived together. Questions to be asked and answered. Was I good enough? Was she? Were we good enough together? It is easier to measure the weight of a life at its end, rather than in the middle, but right now, there is only her absence. I miss her. I kiss her forehead. I step back to blow my nose and wipe my eyes. I reach into my jacket pocket and take out the letter opener wrapped in the white handkerchief. I slide my hand between her shoulder and the casket lining, to make sure there's a space for it.

Just then the front door opens, sunshine fills the room, and I slip the letter opener back inside my jacket pocket. Gabby walks in. Her black hat anchors a black lace veil that drops down to her cheeks. She sees me, and looks around.

"Owen, are you here alone? You should not be alone."

I tell her that Helen and Roy are in the church. "I was having a moment alone with Eva."

"Oh, I'm so sorry. I didn't mean to interrupt." But she slides her hand around my upper arm and looks down at Eva. "Doesn't she look nice? Except for the makeup. I came earlier, and that woman only let me have a quick peek before she closed the lid. I told her I brought Eva's favorite shade of lipstick, but she … well, I didn't want to make a scene. You should come sit down. Come." She tugs at my arm and leads me into the large nave of the church. Roy is seated all the way in the front, watching as Helen and Margaret do some last minute arranging of flowers along the altar rail. The entire railing is filled with flowers. So many flowers.

Helen hurries toward us, beckoning for Roy to follow. "Hello, Gabby. Roy, honey, would you mind staying in the vestibule with your mom, so she's not alone while all the people come in. Make sure everyone signs the guestbook. Gabby, you'll be sitting right over here, in the second row, behind the family."

Gabby looks up at me, as if for an invitation into the front row with family, but I pretend not to notice. This is not the time. "Of course," she says to Helen. "By the way, did you see her makeup? I think they used the wrong color for her cheeks."

Helen shakes her head. "That was her own makeup that they used. I'm not worried about it, but thank you for noticing, Gabby. Owen? You don't look well, and I think you need to sit down."

She leads me to my place. "Do you want the kneeler down?"

I tell her I'll be fine, and then I tell her that, after everyone has arrived and is seated, I want one more moment alone with Eva before they close the casket. Helen pats my hand. "We can do anything you like," she says, and then hurries off.

From the pew behind me, Gabby says, "So many flowers. Eva would have liked plants better, but these are beautiful."

"Yes." I answer without looking back. "It is all beautiful." I touch the pocket of my jacket and feel the letter opener inside.

The clerk of the court was settling down at his desk when I knocked at the open office door. "How are you, sir," I said. "My name is Owen Bartlett."

"Yes?" He peered over the top of his glasses. "Ah. You are a lawyer, am I right?"

"Yes. I'm representing Miguel Cordero."

"I see. I do recall that."

His starched white shirt was wrinkled at the shoulders by his dark suspenders. I said, "I believe you sent me a note about an autopsy report?"

The clerk brightened. "Ah. So I did." He rose and went to a wooden box on a shelf behind his desk. He fumbled through a stack of papers. "Here. Autopsy report, deceased name of Mr. Stephen Downing." He handed me a white envelope.

I slipped it into my coat pocket. "Thanks."

"Aren't you going to open it?"

"No, sir," I said. "But thanks."

Outside, I stood at the bottom of the courthouse steps reading the report. It was brief, and, unlike so many documents at the time, written on a typewriter. It described the body of the deceased: "Partially decomposed white man, about five feet eight inches tall, one hundred and forty-five pounds more or less. Hairline fracture of the maxilla. Puncture wound at the right anterior neck, approximately an inch below the jaw. Said puncture wound is difficult to measure precisely, given the evident state of decomposition of the body, but it is approximately half an inch wide, traversing inward at approximately forty-five degree angle upward to the spinal column itself, partially severing the carotid artery. This puncture wound is the manifest cause of death. There are no other remarkable traumas marks to the body which would account for a sudden demise."

There was no mention of an examination of the organs, no mention of any chemical tests which might have found poison in the body, no signs of a heart attack or disease. The doctor had presumed that the cause of death was the knife wound, and had written the report to justify his presumption.

"Problems, counselor?"

I looked up to find Hyram Winthrop standing beside me, grinning. He spat into the street. "How's that practice of law going?"

I stared for a moment, a dozen thoughts racing through my mind. "The practice of law is interesting, as I'm sure you know. How's the practice of law for you, Mr. Winthrop?"

His wry grin broadened. "It's a thrill, I tell you. Nothing like it in the world."

I tried to gauge his eyes. "Mr. Winthrop, no one knows more than you do that I need some help."

His eyes narrowed, and his grin softened almost imperceptibly. "Help? For a Harvard man like yourself? What kind of help?"

"You've done many trials in your career."

"True."

"I'm doing my first trial on Monday."

"True."

"My very first."

"Yes."

"I need some help. You know it as well as I do."

He spat again at the dirt, and stared hard into my eyes for what must have been four or five seconds.

I returned the stare. "Well?"

"I'll give you a half hour, counselor. Then I got other things to do." He wheeled and started down the street.

I watched him move away. "Now?"

He stopped and put his pocket watch up to his ear. "Still ticking. Half hour isn't much."

I hurried after him, across the street, up the steps and into his office. I closed the door behind me and handed him the autopsy report.

He read it and then peered at me over the top of his glasses. "What's the problem?"

"The problem is that it doesn't say anything."

"Doc Hinckley is just a country doctor. The report says Stephen Downing is dead, with a hole in his neck big enough to kill him. What did you think a country doc would say?"

"I was hoping he would examine the body more thoroughly so that, if the knife wound really killed him, it would be clear. Perhaps there were bruises or broken bones. Ruling out other causes, in other words."

He spat downward, presumably into his spittoon, then wiped his lower lip with his forefinger. He gazed at the forefinger thoughtfully. "You know what? I'm starting to think you have the instincts of a good trial lawyer. You don't back down from the judge and you don't take crap from the prosecutor, as long as you can figure out what's going on. As for this report, you are hoping you can generate some reasonable doubt from what it says there. Am I right?"

"Correct."

"But think about it again, counselor. You don't really believe that fella Downing was struck by lightning or called to his Maker on account of some kind of sudden kidney failure, do you?"

I shrugged. "There are too many things about this case that I don't know. Starting with the cause of death."

He leaned toward me. "I know I said this before, but your problem is that you went to law school. At Harvard, to boot. That would twist up any man's mind."

"I keep telling you I didn't go to Harvard. And I don't see why going to law school is a problem."

"I'm sure you don't. But you're about to try a case to a jury of the defendant's peers in Tucson. Way out here in the desert among the gila monsters."

"What's a heela monster?"

"It's a lizard, big and kind of pinkish. You're out here among a bunch of big pink lizards. You aren't even technically in the United States, just in one of its territories. And even after Arizona becomes a state, you'll never find a jury around here that thinks like a law professor thinks. Reasonable doubt? Are you kidding? You've got a knife hole in a man's neck, and you've got another man who looks like he had a reason to kill him. For any jury around here, that's all it takes."

"What reason to kill?" I straightened in my chair. "What reason, Mr. Winthrop? What do you know that I don't know? There was an argument between the two men that night in the hotel. The hotel desk clerk will testify that he saw them arguing, but he doesn't know what it was all about. You strike me as a man who has a dozen arguments a day, and nobody gets killed afterward. So what do you know that I can't find out from anybody else? How does an argument about God-knows-what turn into a motive for murder?"

Hyram leaned back. I think he was enjoying my discomfort. "Because the prosecutor is going to turn it into a motive for murder.

That's his job. Argument, then killing. *Post hoc ergo propter hoc.* After this, therefore because of this. It's just that simple, for a jury. Downing died after the argument, therefore he died because of it. The line of reasoning is older than Aristotle, because it works. The jury isn't going to care what the argument was about. They'll care that it occurred right before the killing. What does Cordero say? Miguel Cordero. What does he say?"

"He admits there was an argument, but won't go into it."

"Exactly. Look at it this way. A jury around here doesn't need to know what the argument was about. The prosecutor is going to give 'em a dead white man with a stab wound in the neck, and a live Mexican man with the right kind of knife who had an argument with said dead white man shortly before the murder."

He held up the autopsy report and flapped it at me. "The jury isn't going to believe the dead man might have died of tuberculosis while he was lying there in the street with a hole in his neck. They're going to be remembering that a few days ago there was another white man who was killed by a couple of Mexicans, up by Silver Bell. Comes a time when a town has to put its foot down. Doesn't really matter if the foot comes down on the wrong Mexican. What the town cares about is whether they can vote guilty quick enough to get home for dinner. You'll have to pull a pretty big rabbit out of your hat to get anything else."

"But that's not justice. Where's the presumption of innocence? Where's the requirement for proof beyond a reasonable doubt?"

He sagged for a moment—his whole body at once. He drew a breath, then released it. "I ought to laugh, mister, but I won't. Let me give you some solid advice. Don't take these folks for simple country rubes." He paused to lean over and spit, and then went on. "They're just folks with a little bit of common sense and not much education. Think about it. If you see the sheriff walking by with a fella in handcuffs, what's your first thought? I guarantee you it isn't 'Why, there goes an innocent man in handcuffs!' No sir. Your first thought is 'I wonder what that poor fool did.' That's a presumption of guilt, and that's the way people think. They presume the man is in handcuffs because he committed a crime.

"If you want to practice law down here with the common folk, you'd better learn how common folk think. Your jury is going to walk in the door thinking your client is guilty. They're going to take one look at Miguel Cordero and know this is a case about a Mexican killing a white man. There's no way they're going to let that Mexican free again in the community. *Punto*. You lose, before you open your mouth to defend your client."

I chewed the edge of a fingernail for a moment. "So what would you do in my position?"

Hyram grinned. "I'd forget about legal theories. That's for sure. Do the trial the best you can, don't put up with any crap from the prosecutor, and hope for the best."

"All right. I can do that. Now, here's a question you probably don't expect. Tell me what happens in a jury trial."

"What happens? What do you mean, what happens?"

"I believe I mentioned that I've never done a jury trial before. I've never even seen one. What should I expect?"

His grin widened. "You got yourself a set of *cajones*, counselor, doing this trial, and that's the truth."

"Is that good?"

"Depends. All right, the judge will start off with preliminary motions. You know what motions are?"

"I do know what motions are."

"Good. Don't bother with motions. He'll deny them anyway, just to remind everybody he's the boss. Then he'll tell the bailiff to bring in the group of jurors. The group is called a venire, and it'll be a couple dozen men the sheriff dug up off the streets. You and the prosecutor will ask them questions about themselves, and then pick the ones you want to get rid of. Process of elimination. You don't really pick a jury. You just get rid of the worst ones, and the ones who are left get to be the jury. For better or worse."

"What kind of questions should I ask?"

"Don't ask any, if you can't think of anything good. The idea is to get these men to reveal things about themselves they won't tell their own mothers, so you can figure out their prejudices. But they'll probably all be white and most of them will be prejudiced against Mexicans, and the judge will think that's natural and won't let you strike them for admitting they think white people are better than brown people. Sit quiet and let the prosecutor do all the work. By keeping your mouth shut, you'll look more intelligent.

"Once you've got the jury picked, you and the prosecutor will each make an opening statement. A little speech about the case. Prosecutor first, then you. Then the judge will tell the prosecutor to call his first witness. He'll call whoever found the dead body. Then, since you insisted on an autopsy, he'll call Doc Hinkley to testify about the cause of death. Then he'll call the sheriff to talk about the investigation, and why he arrested Miguel Cordero. He'll for sure call that hotel fella, the desk clerk, to testify about the argument."

"When do I get to ask questions?"

"They didn't teach you much in that law school, did you? Did they talk about cross-examination? For each witness, you can ask questions after the prosecutor asks questions. Like I said about everything else, if you can't think of anything good, don't ask anything at all. This is a small town, and every person in the courtroom is going to know that this is your first case and your first jury trial. If you go shooting in the dark, you'll only make a fool of yourself. When you are doing cross, ask leading questions. That's the one time you get to do that."

"What do you mean by leading questions?"

He leaned over and dropped a wad of greenish-brown spit into the spittoon by his chair. "Look at it this way. The joke is that cross-examination is lawyer's chance to testify and have the witness verify his testimony. Leading questions go like this: You came here to talk to me, didn't you?"

"Yes."

"You were hoping I would tell you something helpful, right?"

"Yes."

"Because if you don't get something helpful from me, your client will hang, or at least he'll go to prison for a real long time, right?"

"Right."

"See? Those are leading questions. You make a statement to the witness, and then you have the witness say yes or no. That's what leading questions are, and that's what you do in cross-examination."

"All right. So I sit tight and ask leading questions and don't make a fool out of myself. And that's my trial strategy?"

"That's it. Then come closing arguments. The prosecutor will stand up and make a speech about why the evidence shows your client is guilty. You'll stand up and make a speech about why the evidence shows your client must be not guilty. Then the prosecutor'll stand up again and talk about why of course your client is guilty. The judge will give the jury its charge about justice and looking at the evidence with a keen eye. Proof beyond a reasonable doubt. All that horse crap. The jury'll go off for a few minutes while you sit there in the courtroom and stew in your juices. Then the bailiff will come out and tell the court the jury has a verdict, and then he'll bring the jury back in. The judge will listen to the verdict of guilty and then set a sentencing date for a week or two later, and then everybody will go home. And that's it. As predictable as rain in July."

"It rains here in July?"

"Buckets. You don't know much, do you? Now, about your defense. You don't have a prayer of proving Miguel didn't do it. I don't mean he really did do it, but no matter what you try, the jury is going to believe he killed Stephen Downing. *Punto*."

"So what is my defense, if I don't have a defense the jury will believe?"

"Your defense is in the mens rea, the state of the defendant's mind when he stabbed the victim. Your goal is to convince the jury that there is no evidence of malice aforethought, which is what the prosecutor has to prove if he wants to get a first degree murder conviction."

"Meaning?"

"Meaning you want the jury to believe there was no evidence that Miguel willfully intended to take Downing's life, and no evidence that he planned it. The prosecutor may try to prove that the killing shows Miguel had what's called an abandoned and malignant heart, because he overreacted to the argument by killing Downing. That or malice aforethought would be first degree murder.

"So your real goal is to show that, by the prosecutor's own evidence, the killing could just as easily have been an accident, that maybe they got into a fight and Miguel stabbed him during the fight. If the jury believes you, they'll go with murder of the second degree or maybe even manslaughter, which means Miguel will get ten years instead of life, or instead of hanging."

A chill ran down my spine at what I was up against. "I have another idea."

"Yeah?"

"How about if you do the trial and I'll assist you."

Hyram laughed. "I could almost get to like you, Bartlett. The answer is no. It's your baby. I'll sit beside you, but that's it. You can't win this trial, but then again, I don't think I could win it either."

Hyram did almost get to like me, but not during the Miguel Cordero trial. The conversation we had that day in his office was the last civil dialogue we would have for years. As those years passed, we opposed each other in court on several occasions. He was an unpleasant negotiator and a tough trial attorney. I had to work twice as hard to beat him as I did against other lawyers on similar cases. In other words, he made me a better lawyer. I tried to return the favor. I don't know that he noticed, but he did eventually begin to show me more respect than he showed other lawyers, meaning that he snarled less, and listened when I made an argument.

The turning point seemed to come about because of a case involving Gabby, around the time the whole town was getting excited about the war—now we call it World War I. For some reason that had to do with the war effort, most women were wearing long, dull-colored fabrics. Gabby marched into my office in a bright red skirt that exposed most of her calves and made herself comfortable on the small sofa across from my desk. "Good morning. *Como estás?* How is Eva? I haven't talked to her in a month."

I put my pen down. "She's doing all right, I suppose. The doctor says she needs to rest."

She leaned forward. "*Pobrecita.* What is wrong?"

"She's been in bed. Depressed ..."

"What is she depressed about? Are you being mean to her?"

"You know how she gets, once in a while. For weeks she can barely get out of bed. She just lies there. She doesn't move, doesn't eat. She keeps the drapes closed and the house dark. She hasn't been this bad in a long time. She's out of bed now, at least, and she seems to be getting better. It's just that sometimes, I don't know, something gets her down."

"Maybe I should bring some *caldo* over. *Caldo con pollo*. Or I can have Maria Teresa bring it over. Everybody needs some chicken soup. That's what I'll do. I'll have Teresa make it but I'll bring it myself. I haven't seen my Eva in so long. I've been so busy, Owen, you wouldn't believe. I need to open another store. That's why I'm here. They can't take my property like that."

"Who can't?"

"My in-laws. Don Antonio."

"You mean your former in-laws?"

"You know how I feel. My Miguel has been dead for twelve years, but I will be married to him forever. So they are still my in-laws. To me. Maybe they think I am not part of the family anymore, but to me they are family. Even if I can't stand them. Anyway, I want to sue them for taking all those cattle that should have been mine."

"What cattle are you talking about?"

"The cattle Miguel and I owned. They were mixed in with Don Antonio's herd on the ranch. We had over five hundred head."

"You never said anything about them before."

"Miguel had them mixed in with the rest of the family herd. I have always thought that they were still mine. Now I want them, or I want the money for them."

"I see. Have you talked to Don Antonio?"

She shook her head. "He won't have anything to do with me. I wrote him three letters asking for some of the money from the cattle and he never wrote back. I didn't hear anything. Then Nina Aguilera told me that Don Antonio doesn't think I deserve to make any money from those cattle because of the way I treated the family. He also said I owe the family money because they took care of the cattle so long. He said he will keep the cattle to pay the debt. So I want to sue."

"Why didn't you try to get your money before? It has been eight or ten years now."

"I've been so busy, and for a long time I couldn't even think about going back there to the ranch, even just to talk to them. I can't believe that Don Antonio would cheat me like this."

I tapped my pencil on the desk for a moment. "I'll tell you what. I want you to go home and write down everything you can remember about the cattle—where were they kept, whether they were with other cattle, whether they were branded separately as far as you know, and so forth. Write down everything you can remember about conversations you remember with Don Antonio, or Alonso, or anybody else. Look through your old records to see if you can find anything about the cattle. Meanwhile, I'll get together with Hyram Winthrop, because I'm sure Don Antonio would retain Hyram for this, if we decided to sue. Hyram might have an idea of some way to approach Don Antonio. How about that?"

She pouted. "Will this take very long? I was thinking we could just sue Don Antonio and I'd get my money so I can open the other store."

"This isn't like a criminal case. Miguel's trial moved very fast, if you remember. A lawsuit takes time to put together, and if we don't put it together right, the judge will throw it out of court. That's why your notes will be important."

She picked up her purse and stood. "Do you remember I brought a big trunk to your house from the ranch? I have never been able to look in it, because it has a lot of Miguel's things in it, and his business records. He kept very good records of everything, just like he taught me. I tried to look through it when I first moved into my own house, after I lived with you and Eva, but it made me cry and cry. I was so sad. Maybe there is something in the trunk that will help us."

"Excellent. See what you can find about the cattle and I'll tell you then whether there's any point in going forward. Meanwhile, I'll talk to Hyram."

After she left, I had my secretary put a call through to Hyram's office. Angela was my first female secretary. It seems silly now, but in those days I had my doubts about whether a woman could really do a secretary's job. She turned out to be the best I would ever have. A dark-haired, 5'2" package of Italian intelligence and energy, if she had been a man with a man's opportunities she'd have been a millionaire by thirty-five. Her ambition drove her west, away from her New Jersey family, and somehow into my office one Monday afternoon just after I fired my most disastrous secretary of all time, Robert, who had come to work reeking of yet another weekend drinking binge. When Angela walked in looking for a job, I was rummaging through the file drawers searching for the file I needed in court in ten minutes. We both looked at the half-empty whisky bottle in my hand, which I'd just pulled from between two files, and I'm sure she thought I'd been drinking from it. I informed her I'd just fired the man it belonged to, and to replace him I was looking for a qualified man, not some girl who would be carried off by the first offer of marriage. Besides, I said, I was due in court and didn't have time to talk.

She said, "That's fine. Why don't I wait here? I can answer your phone if it rings. I'm qualified to do that, at least, and you can find a man for the job later."

When I returned an hour later, she was ensconced at Robert's desk as though she had owned it for years, and was in the middle of reorganizing all the office files. There were three liquor bottles in the trashcan. I let her stay, in part because a lot of the local men were enlisting to drive the Kaiser's army out of France. She lasted only two years, until the end of the war, before heading off to California one afternoon with two hours' notice, but I spent the rest of my career searching for her match as a secretary.

Dealing with Hyram was probably the toughest part of her job. She grimaced as she waited for the call to go through.

"Hyram," I said when she got him on my line, "how are you?"

"Who is this?" he shouted back. In those days, it was still necessary to raise your voice to be heard through the telephone, but Hyram thought that meant he should shout.

"It's Owen Bartlett, Hyram. I want to come down and talk to you about something. Are you free?"

"What do you want to talk about?"

"I'll tell you when I get there. Are you are free at the moment?"

He hung up abruptly, which was his way of saying there was nothing else to say.

When I arrived at his office a few minutes later, he was moving a heavy box of files out into the hall. I offered to help, but he either didn't hear me or he ignored me. Finally he straightened up stiffly and hitched up his trousers. His face was flushed. Age was beginning to wear him down. "Well?"

I stuck out my hand, but he waved it off and gestured toward his office door. I took a seat across from him. I said, "How are you, Hyram?" Civility was always wasted on him, but out of respect I usually tried.

"What do you want?" he said. "I asked you that on the telephone. Isn't that the point of those things? So you wouldn't have to come all the way over here?"

"My office is only two blocks from yours, Hyram. Anyway, I have a client who wants to sue one of your regular clients."

"Who's that?"

"Gabby Cordero. Gabriela. You remember her, I'm sure. She was Miguel Cordero's wife."

"'Course I remember her. Pretty thing. Why would she want me to be her lawyer?"

"She doesn't. She wants to hire me to sue Don Antonio."

"Why would she want to sue him?"

"Well, she thinks Don Antonio and the family have converted

a bunch of cattle that rightfully were hers. The don won't talk to her about it, and she wants her money."

Hyram leaned back in his leather chair and pulled a tin of snuff from his pocket. He tapped it on the heel of his hand and pulled the lid off before holding it out to offer me a pinch. I shook my head. I had once taken him up on the offer, and nearly gagged, much to his delight. Now he never missed a chance to offer me more.

I said, "I'm assuming Don Antonio would retain you to defend him. You know him pretty well, so tell me what you think it would take to work this out quickly."

He tucked a plug of tobacco inside his lower lip and shrugged. "What do you suggest?"

"I have no idea. Gabby seems pretty certain of her ownership of the cattle, as community property from her marriage to Miguel. She says the family assured her they were keeping records, and she has only just found out they weren't."

"Did she make any arrangements for the upkeep of the cattle? How many head we talking about?"

"I don't know. She's supposed to put together the information for me. I was wondering if maybe you could talk to Don Antonio and see if he's willing to buy out whatever remains of her interest. Otherwise this could get complicated. We're talking about more than a decade of cattle ranching to sort out. Calves born, attrition, steers slaughtered for beef, herds interbred. And there's no statute of limitations issue if she just recently found out her cattle aren't her cattle anymore. She isn't going to back down on this, and I think we both know the court would award her something if we go to trial. Maybe not as much as she wants, but enough to make a lawsuit worth her while. You might suggest to Don Antonio that he should settle this cattle thing."

Hyram leaned over to the side and let drop a wad of spit, I

presumed into a spittoon. "I think you're pissing up a rope on that, but just the same, I'll speak to Don Antonio. I need to spend a week or two at my ranch anyway. The place is falling apart, and I wouldn't be surprised if some of my cattle have wandered over onto Don Antonio's spread."

Two days later, a wagon pulled up to my office. Two men carried a large trunk into my reception room and handed a note to Angela that this was a delivery from Gabby. Angela read me the note when I returned to the office from court.

"Dear Owen," she read. "Here is the trunk I told you about. I still cannot bear to look in it. Please go through it for me. *Mucho cariño*, Gabby."

Angela's raised eyebrow communicated her disapproval, but I laughed it off. "Gabby is like that. I'll do it. Maybe tomorrow." When the eyebrow went slightly higher, I added, "Don't worry. We can always charge her for the time I spend going through the papers."

Angela shook her head. "As long as we charge her, then. That's a big trunk."

But Eva immediately quashed that idea, when I told her the story as we prepared for bed that night. "No. You can't charge Gabby a cent. Not ever. We owe her too much." She was brushing her hair at her dressing table.

I watched her hand guide the brush through her long, coffee-color hair. I was still as attracted to her as a moth is attracted to a light bulb, and she knew it. Her slender fingers wrapped lightly around the brush as it moved down, pulling the long strands of hair away from her back, letting them fall.

Her eyes met mine in the mirror. "You can't charge her."

"Why do we owe her anything? She stayed with us, we helped her out. I don't think we owe her anything. Not that I feel like I have to charge her. But we don't owe her, that's for sure."

She set the brush down and turned to face me. "Maybe I feel like I owe Gabby something."

"For what?"

Her answer was to come to me on the bed. She pulled the straps of her nightgown down from her shoulders, exposing the intimate skin of her breasts. There was a distance in her eyes as she leaned over me to kiss me on my neck and on my chest and on down my belly.

As I sorted through the contents of the trunk over the next few days, I realized that Miguel had been a careful businessman. A number of the documents were in Spanish, but by then I understood enough of the language to be able to see his meticulous care. He kept detailed inventories of cattle, of trades and sales. One ledger seemed to be a record of breeding. Another detailed purchases of supplies for the ranch. Another was a record of supplies he had purchased for the mining project, along with some notes that seemed to be about land investments. I recognized some of the names he mentioned as having been Alianza members.

I also came across several letters to Miguel from Stephen about the mining project. In each of them, Stephen urged Miguel to encourage the Alianza investors and tell them how quickly the lode mine could be up and running if only they would be willing to put up the capital soon enough. Stephen seemed frustrated that Miguel and his father were mainly interested in running the water collection pipes from high altitudes down to the placer mining down below. From what the letters said, Miguel thought the best path to success was to sell water to placer miners who were panning for gold, in return for a percentage of the gold they found. Such a return, Miguel thought, could be reinvested in the lode mining operation that Stephen wanted. The final letter from Stephen, dated only a week before he died, asked Miguel to come to town as soon as possible to see proof that they should focus their efforts on developing the lode mine.

Near the bottom of the trunk I found an assay report from Joseph Bros. Assay Company, San Francisco, California. Stephen Downing was listed as the person requesting the assay. There were some numbers, and some references to tonnage. I didn't know what the numbers meant, and I couldn't tell whether it was a good report or a bad report. A smudge caught my eye on one of the numbers. A certain number seven looked altered, or perhaps a one had been turned into a seven. I held the report up to the window and found several other numbers that appeared to have been altered, either by smudging or by being transformed with a slightly different ink. I remembered how Carlos Castillo had once told me of rumors in the Alianza that Stephen had lied about the assay reports. These smudges might bear out those rumors, but those issues no longer mattered, after all the years that had passed.

I finished with the trunk and sent a note to Gabby that the records were insufficient to establish an exact number of cattle she might have owned on the Cordero ranch, but there was good documentation to show that the number of cattle had been substantial. When Hyram returned to town from his ranch, a few days later, I told him the same thing. To my surprise, he almost immediately quoted me a settlement figure he'd been authorized to offer, a number higher than I'd expected. On an impulse, I said, "Double it, and we've got a deal."

Hyram's eyes narrowed. "I'll cut it in half, if you want to play games, counselor."

"Ok. I'll write up the agreement."

"One more thing. Don Antonio wants a contingency, and this is why he's doing it. Gabriela Cordero must agree that she will never again seek out any contact with the family. If she does contact them, even if she accidently sees them on the street and doesn't go the other way, she agrees to return all the money. Don Antonio wants nothing more to do with her. If she doesn't agree, we're going to trial."

"You think an agreement like that would be enforceable?"

"It's what he wants. Take it or leave it."

"Ok, then, I'll write it up and talk to my client."

As it turned out, Gabby had no problem with the contingency. Or at least, she tried to act as if she didn't. In my office, she read the agreement carefully and signed it without hesitating. She looked up, anger shining in her eyes. "I can't believe my husband came from such a family. He would never have let them treat me like this."

I decided not to mention that I had discovered the forged report. It must have been among Miguel's belongings from the hotel room after his arrest.

I worked very late the night before the trial began, trying to come up with something I could argue besides Miguel's lack of malice aforethought. I pushed aside the curtain and stared out the window into the darkness. Right there, it had happened. What had Stephen been doing out there, that night? Why was he *behind* the hotel?

Later, I lay in bed, and shut my eyes tight, willing myself to sleep. Or trying. It must have worked, because I awoke with a start in morning light, momentarily panicked that I had slept through the trial. But it was just after sunrise and my watch said I had two and a half hours to get ready. I hurriedly straightened out my papers, washed up and dressed. Too nervous to eat, I sat in my room, tapping my feet, defenseless against every wild thought winging its way through my brain, until the moment came to walk over to the courthouse.

A vague mustiness hung in the courtroom air when I showed up and put my papers on the defense table. Only days had passed, but they felt like months. A floor plank squeaked under me as I paced. The jury box was narrow and long, set with two rows of wooden chairs that looked even less comfortable than the wooden pews in the gallery. I tried to picture the jurors. Who would they be? What would they look like? What would they think?

"Members of the jury," I intoned, my voice hollow and too high. I tried again, my voice deeper. "Members of the jury, the issue before us is justice. What does justice mean, when one man lies dead and buried in the ground, and another sits before us accused of causing that death ... I mean, and another man sits ... accused of ..."

A bilious wave rose from the pit of my belly. What if I made no sense at all? Would they laugh? Would the judge stop me mid-sentence and order me sit to down, as my Latin teacher had once done when I lost my place in the middle of a Latin recitation from Julius Caesar? Would Miguel Cordero change his mind, point at me and demand a chance to find a new lawyer? Or what if I did make sense, but boring sense, and no one could remember a thing I said? What if nothing I said made any difference at all? What if Hyram was right and I had no idea how to influence the frontier townsmen who would sit on this jury?

I bent slowly over at the waist until my head nearly touched my knees. I drew in a deep breath. The nausea passed. So be it. I would do my best. I would listen closely to the evidence. I would argue it as well and thoughtfully as I could. Then I would go back to my hotel room and bang my head against the wall for being such an idiot.

It would be like the times in contracts class, in law school, when the professor had chosen to focus only on me, and engage me in front of the whole group in Socratic dialogue, to the exclusion of the other students. We all had to take our turns, squirming this way as the professor poked holes in our arguments before our classmates, for twenty or thirty minutes at a session. I did fine, as long as I stayed focused on the professor and what he was saying. The moment I allowed myself to be aware of the other students watching me, my mind would go white with stage fright.

I gazed out the long, high windows, lost in my thoughts, until I was startled by the sound of the back door opening. The bailiff came in carrying his large water pitcher.

"Good afternoon, sir," he said, resting the pitcher on his protruding belly with one hand as he reached back to close the door behind him. "You are Mr. ...?"

"Bartlett. I'm representing the defendant."

"Yes, that's right." He shuffled the large pitcher over to a small table beside the jury box. "Bartlett. Fred Barnhill, here. We met, when was it, two weeks ago?"

"Last week. You're the bailiff."

"Correct. Can I get you anything, Mr. Bartlett? I'll have some water on your table in a few moments."

"I'm doing fine."

"You're one of those who likes to come early and get the lay of the land, I take it."

"For the moment. I'm enjoying the quiet and gathering my thoughts."

He took the hint. "Don't let me bother you, sir. I'm just doing my job." He waved and left again through the back door.

I shuffled through my notes back at the defense table. I had written out the order of the trial, as Hyram described it. Jury selection. Then some instructions to the jury by the judge. Then opening statements by the attorneys. I had no idea what to say in my opening statement, but I would listen to the prosecutor and respond to that with just a few words of my own. After that, the testimony by witnesses would begin.

The door behind me opened. The bailiff again, bringing four small pitchers. "Pay no attention to me," he said. With the large pitcher he'd brought in earlier, he filled each of the smaller ones, and set them out, one each on the defense and prosecution tables, one at the jury box, and one on the judge's bench.

At the table I pushed my notes together, my stomach now set in a hard, painful knot. Soon the first of the spectators would arrive. No doubt Mr. and Mrs. Cordero would arrive early. Perhaps Eva would come. Others. I had no idea how many others. The drama would begin. The knot drew tighter.

When I heard the door again, I half expected to see the Corderos. I wasn't looking forward to Don Antonio's glare. Instead, Josue entered. He wore a tie and a starched white shirt that fit him well. He glanced around shyly as he approached. "Good luck for you today, señor."

"Thanks. You've been working on your English."

He nodded again. "*Sí.* Good luck." As he slid into the rear bench in the gallery, the bailiff came through the door near the judge's bench. Spotting Josue, he waved his arm as if he were shooing away a puppy. "You'll have to leave, boy." He waved his arm. "Out."

I said, "Why does he have to leave?"

The bailiff continued to flap his hand at Josue. "He's Mexican, and anyway it's too early for people to come in. I don't have the courtroom ready."

"This town is full of Mexicans. I'm sure they're allowed to observe public trials."

"The point being, it's simply too early. Is he with you?"

"Yes. I may need him to help me with something."

"Well, it's too early for everyone else. They'll have to wait five more minutes. And if you don't mind, now that you are in, you're in until I unlock the door." He bolted the door, and without another word, clomped pointedly across the courtroom and departed through the door beside the judge's bench.

Josue grinned and shrugged. I smiled back and wondered how much he had understood.

I decided that my office—when I got an office—would be the place where I could sit quietly and prepare for court. No distractions. Better to be able to make a good entrance when the courtroom was already filled. A grand entrance.

The bailiff returned scarcely two minutes later. "All set. Let the show begin." He unlocked the back door and glanced out. The first person to enter was, indeed, Don Antonio. His eyes were sunken and bloodshot, as if he hadn't slept, but his suit was pressed and elegant. Mrs. Cordero was all in black, with a lace scarf draped across her shoulders. I rose to greet them, and gestured to the front bench of the gallery, directly behind the defense table. "Perhaps you'd like to sit up here?"

Don Antonio nodded and led his wife to the front row. She sat quietly for a moment, then whispered something to him. He patted her knee, and did not look my way. Gabby—Mrs. Miguel Cordero—also all in black, took the next seat, followed by Miguel's brothers. Another family came in and took seats immediately beside Miguel's parents. There were hugs and handshakes all around, and whispers in Spanish.

Other people arrived, most of them white. The whites filled the prosecution side of the gallery, and then spilled over into the defense side, which was nearly empty. I recognized no one except Miguel's family until Father Arnold arrived. He nodded to me and sat down in the exact center of the gallery. The Mexicans nodded to him in recognition. Two or three of the whites spoke to him, as well, as the gallery filled to the last seat and men began standing along the walls.

The more crowded the courtroom got, the tighter my stomach knotted. At five minutes to nine, Mr. Dale, the prosecutor, hustled through the door, arms loaded with papers and files. Behind him, more calmly, came Sheriff Pacheco and Jack the dog. Mr. Dale nodded to me as he dropped his papers on the prosecution table, and immediately began organizing them. The sheriff took the second chair at the prosecution table, as Jack settled in under the table. There was no sign yet of Hyram. I was not surprised he was late, but the sudden possibility that he might not come knotted my stomach even more painfully.

Once Mr. Dale and the sheriff were seated, the bailiff stepped forward and called out, "Would all who have been called to serve as prospective jurors please raise their hands."

Three-quarters of the whites raised their hands. No Mexicans.

The bailiff announced, "All prospective jurors are now requested to exit the courtroom and to assemble at the end of the hall immediately beyond. I will meet you all in a few moments. I will call the roll, and will give you your instructions on how you are to proceed and behave. Now please, all of you go out into the hall."

There was a grumbling of voices and scuffing of shoes on the wooden floor, as the crowd of prospective jurors rose and disentangled itself from everyone else and made its way, one man at a time, out through the door and into the hallway. A few might have been ranchers and cowboys who had been drafted in the middle of chores, some appeared to be businessmen. They looked to be mostly between twenty and forty. I waited. Where was Miguel?

Surely the trial would not begin without the defendant present. And where was Hyram?

The bailiff pushed the last of the group out the door and closed the door. He turned and marched back to the front. Placing his hands on his hips, he began again, loudly enough for all to hear. "Now, each of you remaining is going to have to stand and move to the back of the courtroom, along the wall. We will need the seats for the jury venire. Once they are seated, you may take any seats still available. After the jury is chosen, there will be plenty of places for you to sit."

No one moved.

He raised his voice a notch. "I said please stand and move to the back of the courtroom, as I directed. Unless any of you wants to speak to the judge."

They all looked at one another, and then rose to move to the back. The elder Mrs. Cordero pressed close to her husband's side against the wall.

A jailer came through the side door, glanced around, and then brought in Miguel Cordero. His heavy ankle chain rattled across the floor as he shuffled to the prisoner's dock. He was shaven and his hair was clean, but his red, bleary eyes revealed his exhaustion. Once he was seated in the dock and the jailer had locked the ankle chain to the ring in the floor, the courtroom settled down. The bailiff entered and intoned, "All rise! The District Court for the Territory of Arizona is now in session, the Honorable George Russel Davis presiding." The judge entered and took his seat at the bench.

"Be seated," the judge said. He picked up a paper from the bench. "The District Court of the Arizona Territory is now in session on Docket Number A-1575, Territory of Arizona versus Miguel Cordero. Present is Mr. Roscoe Dale, for the Territory, and Mr. ... Is it Owen?"

"Yes, your honor."

"Mr. Owen Bartlett for the defendant. I believe we are missing Mr. Winthrop." The oddly amused look in his eyes gave me pause. Was he expecting Hyram to miss the trial?

I rose and glanced toward the back door. "Judge, I wonder if it would be possible to wait a few minutes. I'm sure Mr. Winthrop will be here shortly."

The judge said, "It is now ten minutes after nine. Nine o'clock is the designated time for this trial. Are the parties ready to proceed?"

Mr. Dale rose again. "Yes, your honor."

I said, "We are waiting for Mr. Winthrop."

The judge turned to the bailiff. "Let us proceed. Mr. Barnhill?"

Still trying to buy some time, I remained standing. "There's one more thing, your honor."

"What is that?"

"The defendant's chains. I don't believe it is appropriate for the jury to see him in chains."

"Good point, Mr. Bartlett. What is the territory's position on the chains, Mr. Dale?"

"Your honor, the Territory objects to the removal of the chains. Any prejudice that might result from having the jury see the chains would be outweighed by the fact that the defendant is facing a murder charge. If we remove the chains, he might flee. If he were successful in an escape, he would be a danger to the community of Tucson."

The judge nodded. "Another good point. How do you respond to that, Mr. Bartlett?"

Still no Hyram. "Mr. Cordero was escorted into the court-room by a guard. The guard could remain nearby to prevent any problems. And if I understand the law correctly, Mr. Cordero is presumed not to be a murderer or a danger to the community unless and until he is convicted."

The judge paused, then said, "I'll deny your request, Mr. Bartlett." He looked at the bailiff. "Mr. Barnhill, please proceed."

The bailiff marched through the courtroom to the back door. He held it open and called out, "Come in, gentlemen." The line of men shuffled into the courtroom. The bailiff directed the first fourteen to the jury box, which filled the seats there, and herded the remainder into the first four rows of the gallery. Once all were seated and finally quiet, he allowed spectators to take the few remaining seats. There was a rush that left Don Antonio and his family standing. He held his wife's arm, his chin high. Carlos Castillo rose to offer his seat, and at that, several other people offered theirs to the Corderos as well. Mrs. Cordero motioned that everyone squeeze in together, and ultimately, the courtroom came to rest with everyone seated in a pew.

At that, the bailiff took his seat, and the judge said, "For those of you in the venire, which is to say those of you who are prospective jurors, you will all be asked a number of questions. Some of the questions will sound personal, but the questions are necessary to find out whether each of you can be fair and impartial to the defendant. At the end of the process, those of you who remain will have their names placed into a box. From that box will be drawn the names of the twelve men who will serve as jurors. Is this clear?"

A leathery-faced man of about forty in the back row of the jury box raised his hand. "Your honor, I'm in the middle of moving about a hunderd fifty head of cattle up the ridge from the Rillito Wash. I got only my two boys to help me, and that isn't enough, specially with me gone. Them cattle're gonna be all over the valley before two days have gone by. How long's it gonna be 'til we can get this Mexican hanged and I can get back to work?"

The courtroom erupted in boisterous laughter, as Mr. Dale and I rose simultaneously to our feet to object to such talk. In the din, the judge's face darkened. He waited about half a minute, until the laughter had crested and begun to subside. Then, without a word, he held up a hand. Silence fell instantly.

"What's your name, mister?" the judge said.

The man's smirk faded at the look on the judge's face, and he glanced around for support. "Ephram McGarvey. Your honor."

"Mr. McGarvey, do you see this man sitting over here?" The judge wagged a finger toward the bailiff. "This is Mr. Fred Barnhill. He is my bailiff. I want you to get up and walk over to Mr. Barnhill's desk."

Mr. McGarvey's face reddened as he shuffled over to the bailiff's desk. Once there, he looked again at the judge. "Yes sir?"

"Do you have anything in your pockets, Mr. McGarvey?"

"Yes sir."

"Take whatever it is out of your pockets and put it on Mr. Barnhill's desk."

"Yes sir." McGarvey dug his hands deep in his pockets. He pulled out a Barlow knife and some coins and something brown and furry that looked like a rabbit's foot. "Yes sir?"

"Now turn around."

McGarvey turned around.

"Mr. Barnhill," the judge said to the bailiff. "I believe you know what to do."

Mr. Barnhill nodded. He reached into a drawer and pulled out handcuffs. He said, "Put your hands behind your back."

McGarvey's eyes grew wide and he began to turn back around. "But your honor, this isn't … You don't need to …"

The judge half rose in his seat and said fiercely, "Do as you are told, sir."

Mr. McGarvey wilted and turned around. His suddenly moist eyes looked toward the ceiling as Barnhill handcuffed him.

"Now," the judge said, "Mr. McGarvey, you will not be part of this jury …"

McGarvey burst into a sob. "Oh, thank you, sir," he bellowed.

"I wasn't finished, Mr. McGarvey. You won't be part of this jury because you will spend the length of this trial in jail. I find you in contempt of court. And," he added, his eyes sweeping the courtroom, "anybody else who treats my court, or this trial, or anything else within my hearing or sight, with the slightest disrespect, will join Mr. McGarvey in a jail cell until the end of the trial. Do I make myself clear?"

McGarvey blubbered. "A second chance, your honor? A chance?"

The judge waved a hand dismissively. "Mr. Barnhill, we need to proceed." He thumbed through the papers before him as the door closed behind the two men. The courtroom remained silent, with every eye on the judge, who continued to look through the papers on his bench until the door finally opened again and the bailiff emerged.

The judge said, "Now, as I was saying, we are going to be asking all of you some questions."

Picking a jury in the territorial days of Arizona meant asking questions of each man in the venire to decide whether he could be fair and impartial during the trial, and whether he could render a verdict in accordance with the law. Mr. McGarvey turned out to be an example of one kind of man, the kind who could easily sound off with his opinion. Over the years, I would learn to trust people like McGarvey on my juries, because they were predictable and honest about what they thought and believed.

There is another kind of juror, the poker player type, who injects a secret ice into the veins of a trial, killing the possibility of real due process and real justice, the kind of person who sits quietly and gives only terse answers, and is holding back for some agenda of his own. This is the person you can't trust, the kind you want to strike from the jury. On the Miguel Cordero jury, William Harshaw Jackson was an example of that kind of juror. I tried hard to strike Mr. Jackson.

I remember that his shoes didn't match. On his left foot was a black riding boot. On his right was a black oxford. The cuffs of his pant legs were frayed. He was an older man, roughed out by years in the desert.

I said, "You've been hearing what the charge is in this case. When Mr. Dale was asking you questions, you told us that your wife was killed in an Apache raid."

"Yes. My first wife. She was."

"You found her body?"

"Yes."

"I'm sure that was a difficult experience."

"It was." His face was inscrutable, his gaze bruising.

"Sir, you will no doubt hear testimony about what Stephen Downing's body looked like when it was found. You will hear that there was blood. I'm sure that what you hear will remind you of your experience with your wife."

He shrugged.

I tried again. "Let me put it this way. You were probably very angry with the Apache warriors who hurt your wife, were you not?"

"'Angry' isn't the right word."

"How about hatred? Is that a better word? Did you hate them?"

"Sure did. Still do."

"Don't you think you will feel that same sort of thing again when you hear about what happened to Stephen Downing?"

"No. No sir. That was different. And with my wife, that was a long time ago. Thirty-some-odd years. I've put it behind me."

"Can you really put something like that behind you?"

The prosecutor rose to his feet. "Judge, Mr. Jackson has answered the question. I object to further questioning along this line."

The judge looked up at the clock. "I'll allow a couple more questions."

I said, "So, Mr. Jackson, you don't think you will feel angry at the defendant here, because of what happened to your wife?"

"Only if I think he done it. And like I said, that was a different thing. This fellow here has nothing to do with it."

I watched his eyes as he spoke, trying to read him. I said, "Sir, we hear a lot of talk about white skin and skin that is not white. I'm sure you've noticed that the defendant is not white. He is browner than you or I. So were the Apaches who attacked your wife. Don't you think the defendant's darker skin will affect the way you see him? Don't you think you'll associate him in your mind with those who attacked your wife?"

His eyes narrowed, and there it was, that ice-in-the-veins something. "No sir," he said. "I don't think I'll associate this fella, the way you say, with them as killed my wife."

The judge spoke up. "I take it then, Mr. Jackson, that you believe you can be a fair and impartial juror in this case?"

Jackson nodded. "I believe I can, Judge."

The judge wagged the gavel at me. "Let's move on, Mr. Bartlett."

I said, "Your honor, I move to strike Mr. Jackson from the jury."

"Denied. Move on."

Jackson looked away, as if to dismiss me, as Mr. Dale rose to question the next juror. I sat down to make notes. I had no doubt Jackson intended to see Miguel hang.

H yram arrived after we finished with jury selection, and at the end of a fifteen minute recess. I had spent the recess staring at the notes for my opening statement, my mind totally blank, and I breathed a long sigh of relief at seeing him.

"All rise," the bailiff intoned just then.

The judge took his seat and said, "Are we ready to proceed, counsel? Mr. Winthrop, nice of you to come."

Mr. Winthrop rose. "Thank you, your honor. I apologize for my absence. I was detained by an unrelated matter. I'm sure this young fella here did fine."

The judge said, "Apology accepted. The bailiff will bring in the jury."

As the jury filed in to take their seats, I leaned over to Hyram and whispered, "I hope you'll offer suggestions as we proceed."

He shook his head and whispered back, "You're on your own."

"Good morning, again," the judge said. "The trial of Territory against Miguel Cordero commences in earnest. We will all be here at least for the remainder of the day. Perhaps we will continue to tomorrow as well. We will begin with a reading of the indictment."

The bailiff rose, and in the same self-important way he'd adopted to read the indictment at the arraignment, he intoned the legal words accusing Miguel Cordero of the murder of Stephen Downing. After he was finished, the judge said, "Let's get on with business. Members of the jury, the lawyers are going to stand up and tell you about the case of Territory against Miguel Cordero. Mr. Dale, representing the Territory of Arizona, will go first. Then Mr. Bartlett, representing the accused, Miguel Cordero, will take his turn. Mr. Dale?"

All eyes shifted to Mr. Dale as he pushed his chair back and rose to his feet. His hands rose to grasp the lapels of his coat, hanging there, fingers splayed. His eyes watched the floor as he strolled slowly and meditatively toward the center of the space between the judge and the attorney tables. When he reached his spot, he paused. He said, "May it please the court, and counsel." Then he turned slowly to face the jury. He said, "Stephen Downing is dead." His eyes moved from face to face as he repeated, "Stephen Downing is dead." His hand rose like the hand of death, and he pointed its long index finger at Miguel. "And the evidence will show that Miguel Cordero killed him.

"This case is as simple as that, members of the jury. We believe the evidence will show that on the night of October 13, 1905, Miguel Cordero got into a serious argument with Stephen Downing. You will hear from one, possibly two witnesses about that argument. Mr. Cordero and Mr. Downing were business partners in the development of a mining project. You will hear about that business, that project.

"Like most business partners, they spent a lot of time together. And as happens with some business partners, they grew to dislike and distrust each other, until finally one of them, Miguel Cordero, had enough of his partner, Stephen Downing. You will hear that, on the night of October 13, after the argument, Miguel Cordero went out into the darkness. There, Miguel Cordero pulled out a knife, and there, Miguel Cordero used that knife to stab Stephen Downing in the neck.

"You will hear that Stephen Downing lay in the darkness, in a pool of his own blood, staring up into the night sky as he bled to death.

"Because there were no witnesses to the actual moment of the murder, you will have to ask yourself how we know that Miguel was the one who did it. Well, the answers to the question are quite clear. First, there was the argument. There will be no doubt in your mind that Miguel Cordero was angry enough, as a result of the argument, to kill Stephen Downing.

"Second, there is the knife. You will hear testimony by Dr.

Hinkley that the wound was about three-quarters of an inch wide. You will hear testimony from Sheriff Pacheco that a knife with a blade three-quarters of an inch wide was found in the hotel room of Miguel Cordero, and you will hear that it had been wiped clean as a whistle, just as it would have been if Miguel Cordero were trying to cover up evidence of his involvement in the crime.

"After you hear all the evidence, members of the jury, you will find beyond a reasonable doubt that Miguel Cordero is guilty of murdering Stephen Downing." He held himself erect and motionless for a full ten seconds after he stopped speaking, his eyes meeting the eyes of the jurors, one after another, as if to seal his covenant with them. Then he turned to me, nodded, and returned to his table.

The judge nodded to me. "Mr. Bartlett?"

I f I live to be a thousand, I will never forget that moment of pure white fear when I rose to give my first opening statement to a jury. All the blood in my body sank to my ankles. I looked in the judge's direction and could see only a blank whiteness. The jury was lost in the same white blur. I rested my hands on the defense table and bent forward over my notes, as if to check something I'd written there, trying to regain my balance. I mumbled something like, "If I may have a moment, your honor?" I heard the judge respond, but had no idea what he said. Hyram was a blur beside me. I thumbed through the pages of my notes, but could not read them. I fought back the hot panic rising in my belly. I waited for what was probably only a few seconds, and gradually the words on the papers sharpened into focus. I nodded, trying to look thoughtful as I pretended to study them. I tested my knees, flexing them slightly to see if they would hold me up if I let go of the table. Stand up straight, I told myself. I stood up straight. Look at the jury, I told myself. Look them in the eye. Let go of the edge of the table. Concentrate.

I heard the judge say, "Mr. Bartlett, may I presume you are standing because you intend to make an opening statement to the jury?"

A collective chuckle fluttered through the courtroom. They knew. Everyone knew, I was sure. Twelve faces watched me from the jury box. I focused on one, then another, trying to recollect what each man had said about himself during jury selection. This one was a rancher. This one looked barely old enough to shave, had a wife and child, worked in a store. This one had lost three fingers in a mining accident. The bearded old man in the corner had, as a boy of fifteen, passed through Tucson fifty years before, traveling back to the family farm in Indiana because he and his father had gone bust in the California gold rush. When he married at eighteen, his wife refused for decades to come to this desert place to live. Now that she was gone, he had come alone, and found the warm desert weather the perfect salve for his aching bones.

And there was Jackson, at the far end of the jury, who had survived all my efforts to keep him off the jury, the man who had found his wife with her throat cut after an Apache attack. His arms were folded across his chest, and the smirk on his face betrayed his enjoyment of my discomfort.

These twelve men were nothing to be feared. They needed me to tell them what to think. I opened my mouth, and said the first word that came to my mind.

"Friday," I said.

The jurors looked at each other, then at the judge.

"Friday. It was a Friday night, that night." I paused again to let the next thought come, hoping one would come. Tell them a story, I told myself. Any story, but hold their attention. Tell them what to believe. "It was not a hot Friday night, the way a night can be, here, in the summer. It was a cool night in the middle of October. It was the thirteenth."

That was it.

"Friday the thirteenth. It was a bad luck night, for Stephen Downing. Because that was the night he died. That was the night he was viciously attacked and stabbed, so he lay there in the street behind the Santa Rita Hotel, and bled to death with no one to help him. What happened to Stephen Downing was a crime. Without a doubt. It was a crime."

I paused again. A story. Tell them a story and sit down.

"What happened next makes perfect sense. Someone found him, someone went for the sheriff. Or perhaps they even called the sheriff with one of those telephone gadgets in the hotel."

That was good, I told myself. Some of the jurors had probably never yet encountered a telephone.

"If you've never seen one, it's a big wooden box, connected by a black cord to a hard black tube. If you put the hard black tube up to your ear, you can hear someone talking through it. It's true, I swear. And there's a kind of black trumpet that sticks out of the middle of the wooden box. If you shout into the black trumpet, the sound travels through the wires all the way to another telephone perhaps miles away. The person on that other telephone can actually hear what you are saying by putting the black tube on his telephone up to his ear. It's amazing."

The bearded old man frowned. He didn't believe me. The boy with the young wife was staring at the floor. I was losing their attention. "Anyway," I said, raising my voice to bring them back, "somehow the sheriff was notified, and he came. He talked to some people, did an investigation, tried to find the man who killed Stephen Downing. He found a likely suspect. He found Miguel Cordero.

STEPHEN DOWNING IS DEAD

"But there were no witnesses to the killing, as far as anybody here knows. There were witnesses to other things, of course. You are going to hear from them. These witnesses may tell you the very things Mr. Dale has said they will say. Witnesses to an argument. Witnesses to the finding of the body. Witnesses to this, and to that. As you listen to these witnesses, ask yourself whether their testimony really does point to the guilt of Miguel Cordero. There was a knife, the one that was used to stab Stephen Downing. Mr. Dale is going to present a knife to you, and the sheriff will tell you he found that knife in Miguel Cordero's hotel room. When you look at it, that knife, ask yourself how many other knives you've seen like that. Ask yourself how many other knives with blades like that could have been nearby, within a five minute walk, on the night of the killing."

I was running out of ideas, though now I wanted to go on. My stage fear was gone and I wanted to talk. I had a job to do. I pointed to Miguel. "Miguel Cordero did not kill Stephen Downing. That's what the evidence will show, members of the jury. At the end of the trial, you will realize you don't know the true story of what happened to Stephen Downing. And because you won't know the true story, you will vote to acquit Miguel Cordero."

Jackson shifted in his seat and shook his head. I gazed at him until our eyes met. He glared back. I held his glare for an instant, and then walked back to the defense table. I was now quite focused.

❦

"Thank you, Mr. Bartlett," the judge said. "Mr. Dale, you may proceed."

Mr. Dale rose to his feet. "Your honor," he said, "the Territory calls Joaquin Montano."

A small man with skin like beef jerky made his way forward from the back of the courtroom. The bailiff met him at the bar and walked him to the court clerk, who stood up at his desk, holding out a Bible.

"Place your hand on the book, sir," the clerk said. "Do you swear to tell the truth, the whole truth and nothing but the truth, so help you God?"

"I do," Mr. Montano said. The bailiff pointed him to the witness stand, and he settled into the seat quickly, his eyes on Mr. Dale.

"Please state your name, sir," Mr. Dale said.

"My name is Joaquin Montano."

"Where do you live?"

"I live over at the Scott Boarding House. It's on Scott Street." His voice was rough, and he squinted toward the prosecutor each time Mr. Dale spoke, as if to hear the questions better.

"Isn't the Santa Rita Hotel also on Scott Street?"

"Yes sir. It's about a block away."

"Do you go to the Santa Rita Hotel?"

"For what?"

"To eat, or to rent a room?"

"No sir."

"Why not?"

"Costs too much. And it's too big, for my blood. I heard it has two hundred rooms."

"Do you ever pass by the Santa Rita Hotel?"

"Yes sir."

"Did you happen to pass by the Santa Rita early on the morning of October 13?"

"No sir."

Mr. Dale glanced up from his notes. "You didn't?"

"No sir. Not in the morning. It was still night."

"I see. So it was still dark outside?"

"Yes sir. I was walking down the street. On my way to work. At the railroad."

"Do you normally work on Saturdays?"

"Yes sir. Without fail."

"Did something unusual happen to you, in the dark?"

"Yes sir. I tripped over a dead body in the street. It was just lying there. That's pretty unusual, I'd say." A grin flitted across his face and then was gone.

"Do you recall what time that was?"

"No sir. It was still dark, maybe first light. It probably was about five thirty, because that's about the time I'm going to work. But I don't remember exactly."

"Do you remember what you did, after you tripped over the dead body?"

"Well, I wasn't sure what to do. If I was to be late to work, I might get fired. But a dead body is, you know, something different. I didn't want to leave it alone in the street. I finally figured out I could get somebody at the hotel to go for the police, and I'd go to work. So I went into the hotel. There was a man there, and I told him."

"What did he do?"

"Well, he said he couldn't leave the hotel, and I should go to the sheriff's."

Mr. Dale glanced my way, and said, "Did he tell you to use the telephone?"

"No sir. I wouldn't know how anyways."

"I see. So, did you go to the sheriff's?"

"No sir."

"What did you do?"

"I went to work."

"Do you know if the man at the hotel went for the sheriff, or called on the telephone?"

"I'm pretty sure he didn't. I don't think he really believed me."

"What makes you so sure he didn't go for the law?"

"Because when I got to work, I told the foreman what I tripped over, and he set me to work along with some other fellows. Then he went off to the maintenance shed. They have one of those telephones there."

"Did the sheriff come to talk to you later?"

"Yes. Yes sir, I mean."

"Did you tell him about what happened? About your tripping over a dead man?"

I had been listening to the testimony, trying to figure out whether I was supposed to be objecting. I didn't want to look like a potted plant sitting there. Now I stood up and said, "Your honor, I object."

"To what, Mr. Bartlett?"

"Hearsay," I said. "The question calls for hearsay."

The judge looked at the jury, then at his notes. "Are you objecting?"

"Yes, your honor."

"On the basis of hearsay?"

"Yes."

The judge squinted at me. "I believe the question was whether the witness told the sheriff what happened. It's a yes or no question. A yes or no question doesn't call for hearsay. He can say yes or no. Objection overruled. Answer the question, Mr. Montano. Did you tell the sheriff what happened?"

I felt my face redden and I sat down quickly.

Mr. Montano said, "Yes sir."

Beside me, Hyram had his elbows propped on the table as he stared off out the window.

Mr. Dale said, "What did the sheriff do after you told him?"

"He told me I shouldn't ..."

I stood again. "Objection. Hearsay."

The judge smiled. "That's good, Mr. Bartlett. Now you understand the concept of hearsay. Objection sustained."

Mr. Dale ignored the exchange. "Did you see the sheriff do anything else after you told him what happened?"

"No. We talked, and then he left. He said …"

Mr. Dale held up a hand. "Thank you. No further questions."

The judge said, "Mr. Bartlett? Cross-examination."

I stood up again. I'd been thinking all night about what Hyram had told me about cross-examination and leading questions. This witness hadn't really said anything harmful to Miguel's case. In fact, perhaps he had been helpful. I decided to reinforce the point he had been helpful about.

I said, "Mr. Montano, you didn't happen upon the body of Mr. Downing until about five thirty in the morning. Isn't that correct?"

"Yes sir. That's right."

"No further questions."

The judge said, "Anything else, Mr. Dale?"

Mr. Dale hesitated, then asked. "Mr. Montano, when you found the body, could you tell how long it had been there?"

"No sir."

"Nothing further, your honor."

"You may step down, Mr. Montano," the judge said. "Mr. Dale, your next witness?"

"Call Sheriff Pacheco."

The sheriff's powerful presence captured the room as he made his way to the front and was sworn in. With his dog Jack walking confidently beside him, he took his seat as if it were his second home. He nodded to the jurors. Both Jackson and the old man nodded back. I tried to think of some reason to object to the dog's distracting presence, but decided to let it go, since everyone, including the judge, seemed to think the dog belonged at the sheriff's side.

Mr. Dale's tone became almost theatrically respectful as he

walked the sheriff through a recitation of his background for being sheriff. Dale nodded and looked at the jury each time the sheriff answered a question. I couldn't think of an objection to the prosecutor's performance, and I found myself unwillingly drawn into the sense he was building of the sheriff's authority and competence. I was surprised to learn that the sheriff had been an army officer before coming back to Tucson, where he had grown up. He had participated in the last of the Indian wars, including the final chapter of the capture of Geronimo. He had been Pima County Sheriff now, he said, for nearly eight years. Yes, he said, he had been sheriff on the morning of October fourteenth last.

Mr. Dale said, "Do you remember an incident involving a body that was found behind the Santa Rita Hotel?"

"Yes, I received a report of a body behind the Santa Rita Hotel. So I went over there. There was a body on the south side of the hotel, in the street. A large pool of blood around it."

"Would you please describe the position of the body as you found it?"

"It was a man, a male, in his mid-twenties. I found out later his name was ..."

I had to do something to interrupt. The sheriff's decision to arrest Miguel was going to be very important to the jury. Somehow I needed to make him look a little less competent. "Objection," I said, jumping up.

The judge's eyebrows rose. "Yes?"

"He's not answering the question, your honor. The question was about the position of the body."

The judge's eyebrows lowered into a scowl. "Mr. Dale, you keep your witness on track. Mr. Bartlett, save your objections for issues that count. Am I being clear? Good. Objection sustained. Ask your question again, Mr. Dale."

Mr. Dale said, "Sheriff, let's take this one point at a time. Was the body you found in the street the body of a man?"

"Yes."

"Did you later learn the name of the deceased."

"Yes. It was Stephen Downing."

"Good. Sheriff, describe the position of the body as you found it?"

"He was lying sort of on his back, but slightly twisted at the waist, with one knee bent. One hand, I believe it was his right hand, was on his neck, over the cut that was there, and the fingers were bloody. His other arm was stretched out straight from the shoulder."

"Pointing upward?"

"No, just stretched out, lying stretched out on the street."

"Did the body appear to have been interfered with?"

"What's that?"

"Did it appear that someone had moved the body or changed its position?"

"I don't think so."

"Then you think the body was lying in the same position in which the man fell, or at least in the same position as when he died?"

"Yes. Probably."

"After you found the body, what did you do, Sheriff?"

I listened closely to the details, hoping for some gap I could work with, but the sheriff was thorough. He had enlisted the aid of a couple of passersby to keep gawkers away. Since the dead man appeared to have a stab wound, the sheriff looked all around for a knife that might have been dropped or thrown away. When the doctor arrived at the scene, the sheriff watched as the doctor checked over the body and declared the man dead, and then the sheriff helped lift the body onto a hearse for transport to the mortuary. One of the horses drawing the hearse seemed a little skittish, the sheriff remembered.

He had gone to inform Mrs. Downing of her husband's passing, and she had asked to see the place where it had happened. Reluctantly, the sheriff said, he had taken her to the spot, and then escorted her home.

I glanced toward the back of the courtroom. Eva was not present.

Mr. Dale said, "Was she terribly upset?"

"You bet. She said she'd been crying all night when her husband didn't come home. I told her I didn't really think it was a good idea for her to go to where it happened, but she insisted. When we got there, to the Santa Rita Hotel, the boys were just getting around to cleaning up the street, and there was still a big patch of dried blood. I'm sorry she saw that. She didn't take it too well."

"As one might expect. So you escorted her back to her home?"

"Yes. She cried the whole way. When we got there, some of the Mexican neighbor ladies were gathered by her door. I guess they had heard the news. I left her with them. I went back to make sure the boys completed the cleanup. Then I went to the undertaker. I made sure Mr. Dominguez knew how to get hold of the widow about the arrangements, and then I continued my investigation."

"Mr. Dominguez?"

"The undertaker. He handles most of the funerals for the Mexicans."

"But the late Mr. Downing was not Mexican, was he?"

"No, but Dominguez was the one who sent a hearse, and later, Mrs. Downing approved having the body at the Dominguez mortuary. Dominguez doesn't only bury Mexicans."

Mr. Dale reviewed his notes for a moment. "That's a dirt street, isn't it? Where the body was found?"

The sheriff grinned at the jurors. "Is there any other kind around here?"

The judge scowled when some of the jurors chuckled. "Save the humor, Sheriff. This is a murder trial. Answer the question."

"Sorry, your honor. It is a dirt street. Yes."

"Did you see any distinguishable footprints around the spot where Mr. Downing was found?"

"There were several clear footprints."

"Did you ... let's see, you later arrested Mr. Miguel Cordero, didn't you?"

"Yes."

"Was he wearing boots?"

"No sir. Not when I found him in his room."

"Did he put boots on when you took him to the jail?"

"No sir. He walked barefoot."

Mr. Dale looked perplexed for a moment, and shuffled through his notes. Finally, apparently not finding what he was looking for, he said, "In the street, in the area where Mr. Downing's body was found, did you find any marks indicating there had been a struggle right there?"

"Yes. There were some deep scuff marks. They looked the way it would look if someone had dug his heels in and pushed or pulled."

"Based on that, Sheriff, can you say whether those marks were made by either Mr. Downing or someone else in a struggle?"

"Yes sir. They could have been made that way. In a struggle."

"Did you match any of the footprints to the boots or shoes worn by Mr. Downing, the deceased?"

"There were a couple of footprints that could have been his. One of them kind of slid over, like he was falling, maybe."

"Did you try to match the footprints to the boots worn by the defendant, Miguel Cordero?"

"Like I said, Miguel wasn't wearing anything on his feet when he walked to the jail. But I did take a look at his boots later, after

I came back to the hotel from the jail. They didn't match any of the prints."

I made a note of that, as Mr. Dale looked again through the papers on his table. "Tell the jury what led you to arrest this defendant."

"Well, since the killing happened outside the Santa Rita, my first thought was to see if anyone there had noticed anything or reported anything to the desk. I talked to the desk clerk, Mr. Billsley, and he said he had heard there was a ..."

"Objection," I said, jumping up. "Hearsay."

"Sustained."

Mr. Dale said, "Did you receive information from Mr. Billsley that might connect the deceased and a hotel guest?"

"Objection," I said, again.

"Overruled."

"It's hearsay, your honor."

"Overruled, counsel. It's a yes or no question. The witness will answer."

The sheriff said, "Yes, he told me he heard ..."

"Objection," I said.

This time the judge agreed with me. "Sustained," he said. He leaned toward the witness. "Sheriff, the question was whether you received information connecting the deceased and someone staying at the hotel. It's a yes or no question."

The sheriff said, "Yes. I received that information."

Mr. Dale said, "And what did you do with that information?

"I asked for the room number of the guest who was connected to the deceased. I went to his room. The guest's room."

"Was the guest there, in his room?"

"Yes."

"Please tell the jury the name of the guest."

"Miguel Cordero."

"And the gentleman sitting in the prisoner's dock, is he the same Miguel Cordero?"

"Yes he is."

"May the record reflect that the witness has identified the defendant, your honor?"

The judge said, "The record shall so reflect."

"Did you talk to Mr. Cordero that morning?"

"Yes. I asked him if he knew the deceased. He said yes. He said ..."

I stood up again. "Objection. Hearsay."

"Overruled," the judge said. "Mr. Bartlett, I'm sure you were instructed in your law school that the statements of a party are not hearsay. They are admissions. Your client, as the defendant, is a party. Therefore his out-of-court statements are not hearsay. Need I instruct you further?"

I remained on my feet. "Your honor, I was instructed in law school that a defendant's statements are only admissions if they tend to go against him. To define as an admission everything he said would be absurd. With all due respect to the court, your honor."

The judge said, "Counsel approach the bench."

The jurors leaned forward in their wooden seats as we rounded our tables and walked up to the bench. The stenographer stood up to join us with his notepad.

At the bench, the judge leaned toward us and whispered, "Mr. Bartlett, let us get something straight. You will never again, ever, refer to a ruling of this court as absurd. This court, in return, will not put you in jail for contempt."

My face burned as I met his fierce gaze. "I apologize, your honor. My words were not well chosen."

"I'll say."

"On the other hand," I went on, "with all due respect, I must advocate for my client. Doesn't that include arguing matters of law?"

193

"I agree. But if your advocacy blurs into contempt, you'll be spending a night or two in the hoosegow with your client. Now, I believe your argument is that your client's statements are only admissions to the extent that they tend to show guilt. Is that correct?"

"Yes."

"Then, I will admit only those statements of his that tend to show his guilt. Anything else he said will be considered hearsay, and the jury will not hear it. Understood?"

Mr. Dale grinned. "Understood, your honor."

Too late, I realized my tactical error. By being too clever, I had made sure the sheriff could not testify that Miguel had denied committing the murder. Very well. I'd have to think of a way around that one.

That moment was the real beginning of my life as a trial lawyer. I liked this game. I smiled back at Mr. Dale as I said, "Understood, your honor."

When we were back at our tables, the judge said, "Objection overruled. The witness will answer."

The sheriff looked at Mr. Dale. "What was the question?"

Mr. Dale glanced at his notes. "Did you question Mr. Cordero?"

"Yes."

"Did anything he said lead you to believe he might have been involved with the killing?"

"Yes. Mr. Cordero said he knew the deceased. He said they were business partners. He didn't say anything when I asked him about the argument in the lobby."

"What argument?"

The sheriff glanced at the judge. "The argument I'm not supposed to say I heard about from the hotel clerk."

I jumped to my feet again. "Objection." Every man on the jury was now listening carefully, eyes alert. "Hearsay," I said quietly. The cat was out of the bag. When I had made my hearsay objection, I had prevented the sheriff from talking about the argument he had heard about from Billsley. Now it had slipped out anyway.

The judge said, "Sustained. The jury will disregard what the witness just said. Ask your next question, Mr. Dale."

"Your honor, they can't ..."

"I said the objection was sustained. Mr. Dale, ask your next question."

The jury was sitting up straight again, their eyes registering the effort of figuring out what they weren't supposed to be thinking about.

Mr. Dale said, "Sheriff, anything else the defendant said that made you inclined to arrest him?"

"Not really. I told him Mr. Downing had been killed outside in the street, and I asked if I could look around the room."

"Did you find anything?"

"Yes, I found a knife beside the bed on the nightstand."

Mr. Dale walked over to the clerk's table and picked up a long object wrapped in a cloth. He glanced at the tag dangling from a string around the cloth. "Territory's exhibit number 1," he said, holding the object up toward me so that I could see it, and then walking slowly to the sheriff, holding it up for the jury the whole way. "Sheriff, do you recognize this package?"

"Yes. I brought this over from my office this morning."

"How long has it been in your office?"

"Since the morning of October 14th."

"Did you place this cloth over what is inside the cloth?"

"Yes."

"Has anyone else handled this package since you put it in your office?"

"The defense attorney. He came over one day and asked to see it."

195

"And after he saw it, did you yourself rewrap it and store it in a secure place?"

"Yes."

"Without showing it to the jury, will you open the package and see if you recognize what is inside?"

The sheriff held it close to his lap, unwrapped the string, and lifted a corner of the cloth. "I recognize it. It's the knife I found in Mr. Cordero's hotel room."

"Your honor, I move to admit Territory's exhibit number one."

The judge looked over at me. "Counsel?"

I looked to Hyram. He ignored me, his eyes on the sheriff.

The judge said, "Mr. Bartlett, do you object to admission of Territory's number one?"

I stood. "Yes, your honor."

"On what grounds?"

"Relevance." It was a shot in the dark.

A slight smile tugged upward at the corners of the judge's mouth. "Counsel, are you arguing that a knife is not relevant to a crime involving a stabbing?"

I kept myself from wincing. "Yes. The prosecutor has not yet established that this particular knife had anything to do with this particular stabbing. I object to its admission into evidence."

"Isn't the question of whether this particular knife was used in this particular stabbing a question for the jury to decide?"

He had me again. I nodded.

"Is that a yes, Counsel?"

"Yes."

The judge leaned back in his seat. "Objection overruled. The knife is admitted. Proceed, Mr. Dale."

"Thank you, your honor," Mr. Dale said. "May I publish to the jury?"

"Of course."

Mr. Dale handed the knife in its wrapping cloth to the juror seated at the end. The man opened the cloth, glanced at the knife, and handed it to the next juror. The courtroom was quiet. Mr. Dale stood motionless before the jury box until the knife made its way around. It was an important lesson for me in how to use a courtroom as theater. Mr. Dale remained as still as a statue, and all attention was focused on that knife.

After the last juror had handled it, Mr. Dale took the knife and placed it back on the clerk's desk. "Sheriff, after you found the knife in Mr. Cordero's room, did you find anything else?"

"No sir. Not anything I thought might have to do with the killing?"

"No papers, no signs of trouble?"

"No sir."

"What did you do then?"

"Well, since I'd found the knife, and since I had heard about the trouble between Miguel and the deceased, I decided to arrest Miguel. So I did."

"You arrested him right then? Why?"

"I figured he'd be heading back home to the Cordero family ranch. That's pretty big country, and a man can get lost. Disappear. I figured it would be better if I kept him here in Tucson in custody."

"Did he resist? Or try to resist?"

"Objection," I said. "Relevance."

Mr. Dale said, "The question goes to the defendant's state of mind, your honor."

"Overruled. You may answer, Sheriff."

"No, he didn't resist. Not physically, that is."

Mr. Dale paused and looked at the jury. "What do you mean, not physically?"

"He went along with it. He kept saying he didn't do anything. He kept turning around and saying that. He ..."

Mr. Dale held up a hand to make the sheriff stop speaking, as I hid my grin behind my hand. The prosecutor had let the witness get ahead of him, and now the jury knew Miguel had denied committing the murder. I made a note to follow up on that when I cross-examined the sheriff.

Mr. Dale sat down and thumbed through his notes. "A moment, your honor." He flipped through some papers. "No further questions, your honor."

The judge looked at me. "Mr. Bartlett?"

"Thank you, Judge." I could feel the eyes on me.

"Knives. You were talking about knives. You testified that you found a knife?"

"I sure did. I believe you were sitting right there the whole time, just like the jury."

The judge's hand slapped hard on his bench. "Sir! I believe you were sitting right over there when I put a man in jail for his feeble attempts at humor in my courtroom."

The sheriff's face darkened and his eyes narrowed. "Yes, your honor. I apologize."

The judge glared around the courtroom. "Is there anybody else here who thinks he can't make it through the day without a smart-alecky comment? No? Proceed, Mr. Bartlett."

The jurors were on the edges of their seats. I didn't want to lose their attention. "Sheriff, you found a knife in Miguel's hotel room. Correct?"

"Correct."

"You testified that the knife we saw earlier was the knife you found in Miguel's room?"

"That's right."

"You didn't measure the exact width of the blade against the exact width of the cut in Mr. Downing's neck, did you?"

"No sir, I did not. Not exactly. But they looked close."

"You did not stop to check whether the cut in Mr. Downing's neck was made by a double-edged blade, did you?"

"No sir, I did not."

"Did you notice whether the knife you found in Miguel's room was single edge or double edge?"

"No sir. But it's a single edge."

"How do you know?"

"Because I was looking at it just now."

I had been hoping he wouldn't have noticed. "But knowing that today, you still agree that you didn't check to see whether this knife matched the cut in Mr. Downing's neck?"

"That's true. I didn't check."

"And because you neglected to check, the jury is missing an important clue about whether Miguel's knife actually made the cut in Mr. Downing's neck. Correct?"

"Correct." The sheriff's lips pursed, as if he were considering something to add.

I didn't give him the chance to say it. "How many people would you say live in or somewhere near Tucson?"

He shrugged. "I have no idea."

"Ten thousand?"

"Maybe."

"Or maybe even more?"

"Like I said, I have no idea."

"But you are sure, at least, that there could be at least ten thousand people. Right?"

"Pretty sure. Yeah. I think the 1900 census was ten or twelve thousand. That was five years ago."

"Any idea how many of those ten or twelve thousand people carry knives?"

"No idea at all."

"Would it be fair to say that one in ten carries a knife? Two in ten? Three in ten?"

Mr. Dale rose to his feet. "I object, your honor. The witness has testified that he has no idea how many people carry knives."

"Sustained."

I said, "Sheriff, rather than guessing at numbers, wouldn't it be fair to say that you see a lot of knives around town?"

"I suppose. Depends on what you mean by a lot. But there's a fair number."

"And when you investigated the killing of Stephen Downing, you didn't walk around looking to see how many of the knives in town had narrow blades, like the one you found in Miguel's hotel room?"

"No sir, I did not."

"You simply grabbed the first knife you found, correct?"

"That's true, sir. I grabbed the first one that went with a person who was having a fight with the deceased the night before the deceased died. Yes."

A stir went through the courtroom at that. "Good point, Sheriff," I said. "Now, you testified that you looked all through Mr. Cordero's hotel room. Correct?"

"That's correct."

"You examined his clothing?"

"For what?"

"Did you examine his clothing at all, for any reason?"

"I don't know as I particularly examined his clothes. I looked around for anything unusual, and I was looking to see if he had a knife."

"Looking for something unusual? Would it have been unusual to find bloody clothing in a hotel room?"

"Bloody clothes would have been pretty unusual, yes. I'm sure I would have noticed that."

"But you didn't notice any bloody clothing, did you?"

"I did not."

"Thank you." I glanced at my notes again. "You said earlier that you matched a couple of the footprints in the street to Mr. Downing. To the deceased."

"Yes. I said that."

"You said that there were other footprints in the area of the body."

"Yes."

"Any idea how many?"

The sheriff shifted in his seat. "No idea at all. I guess you could say there were layers. One footprint covers up another."

"So you couldn't really tell how many other footprints there were around the body."

"No sir. I couldn't."

"Were you able to match up any of the footprints to any other person in Tucson, other than the deceased?"

"Nope. That's what I already said."

"Yes. I'm trying to make sure I understand. The footprints around the body could have been from anyone in the Tucson. Is that right?"

"Yup."

"So, the only other boots or shoes you did try to match up to the footprints were the boots you found in Miguel Cordero's room on the morning after the killing."

"That's right."

"You mentioned that you searched his hotel room."

"Yes."

"Did you find any other boots or shoes in his hotel room, besides the ones you mentioned, the ones you tried to match to the footprints in the streets?"

"No sir. Just the one pair. That's all I found."

"And you can positively say that the one pair you found did not match the footprints near the body. Is that correct?"

"That is correct."

I paused, looking at the jury the way I had seen the prosecutor do it for dramatic effect. "Then, wouldn't it also be correct, sheriff, to say that the only person you eliminated as a possible attacker, based on the footprints, was this defendant, Miguel Cordero."

The sheriff's face jerked back as if he'd been slapped. His eyes narrowed. "That isn't what I said. You're twisting it around." His eyes flitted toward the jurors, who leaned forward. Even Mr. Jackson.

"Sheriff," I said, "I'm not trying to say you didn't do your job. I'm only asking about what you found. And between the footprints that were clear, and the footprints that were scuffed, none matched Miguel's boots. Correct?"

The sheriff's hands were on the arm of the chair, as if he wanted to jump up. "That's right, but …"

I said, "No further questions, your honor."

The judge said, "Any redirect, Mr. Dale?"

Mr. Dale stood motionless at the prosecutor's table for fully thirty seconds, until the courtroom had grown quiet again. Then, quietly, he said, "Sheriff, did you find any footprints near the body to indicate that someone else, besides Miguel Cordero, may have committed the murder, besides the defendant?"

"No sir."

"Thank you. No further questions for this witness, your honor."

A stir went through the gallery. I turned to catch Don Antonio's eye. He smiled slightly, and nodded. Gabby was beaming. Hyram sat beside me with his arms folded across his chest, staring thoughtfully at the floor.

Of course, Don Antonio's smile at that moment did not mean we would become friends. We never did, and I think it was his animosity that kept me from getting Mexicans as clients over the next few years. His bitterness came to a head around the time Arizona was admitted to the Union. That would have been in 1912, seven years after the trial. It had to do with Gabby.

I was home for lunch that day, and about to leave because I was late for a meeting. I had taken a couple of hours off to help out at home because baby Roy was sick with some kind of infection, and Eva was not feeling well either. Leaving, I opened the front door to find Gabby standing there. She was alone. In front of the house was a ranch wagon harnessed to a draft horse. In the back of the wagon were two travel trunks.

She said, "I'm sorry, Mr. Bartlett. I would like to speak to your wife."

"Mrs. Bartlett isn't feeling well," I said. "Is there something I can do?"

I heard the clatter of hoofs from down the street. Two men on horseback cantered up to the house and stopped. I recognized them as Miguel Cordero's younger brothers, now grown into handsome young men who strongly resembled Miguel.

They recognized me, as well. They dismounted, and the taller one nodded as he approached. He said, "*Buenas tardes*," and spoke to Gabby in Spanish that was too quick for me to follow.

She listened, fists clenched, then turned toward me. "No!"

I said, "What is going on?"

"They want to take me back. I won't go."

"Back where?"

"To the ranch."

I looked again at the brothers. "It's none of my business, of course, but is there a reason you want to take her against her will?"

The taller one nodded. "Señor, she took one of the family wagons without permission, and must return it. My father insists."

"Well, if she is part of the family, wouldn't she then have permission to borrow the wagon?"

He shook his head. "Everything belongs to our parents. If they don't give their permission, there is no permission."

Gabby stepped toward me. "I needed the wagon and Don Antonio wouldn't give permission for me to move into town. I don't need his permission. *Abogado*, isn't there a law that says I can do that, move into town? And I'm not going back."

The shorter brother casually hitched his horse to the back of the wagon. I said, "Wait. This doesn't make any sense. She doesn't have to go with you if she doesn't want to."

The taller brother said something in Spanish that caused Gabby to shake her head violently. I recognized the word *viuda* for widow. "Listen," I said. "*La viuda* needs to make up her own mind. She has that right. Let's unload the trunks. You can have your wagon, and she can make up her own mind."

The brothers glared. The shorter one jerked the trunks, one by one, from the wagon onto the ground. Boarding the wagon, he snapped the reins and the draft horse started off. Eva and Gabby greeted each other with warm hugs as I dragged the heavy trunks into the house, one by one. When I left to go back to the office, Gabby was holding baby Roy on her lap as she explained to Eva the story of her coming.

That evening, Gabby retold some of the story for my benefit. "It got to be like a prison," she said. "*La doña*, Miguel's mother, was so kind at first, but then she started accusing me of wanting to be with the ranch hands. She accused me of stealing her silverware. I think she was getting a little *cochiti*. Losing her mind. She got to the point where I had to be there with her in the room, and if she couldn't see me she would start screaming like she was being attacked.

"Don Antonio always listened to her, and the boys thought I was mistreating their mother. A couple of years ago, I started saying I wanted to leave, that I wanted to have my own life and not be a shut-in *viuda*. They told me I wanted to ruin the family name and be a disgrace. Every time I went outside the house, even to wash clothes, someone would be there to keep an eye on me, even if it was a ranch hand. One of those guys was so horrible. He would grin at me and say things. I was afraid. When I told Don Antonio he just shrugged. When I told *la doña* she screamed at me that I was a slut."

Eva said, "This doesn't even sound like the same family I knew. They were all so kind when Stephen and I would go to visit."

"They changed, after Miguel. It is bitter there. So bitter."

That night, Eva and I had only the briefest of conversations about whether to let Gabby move in with us for a while. Eva was seated at her dressing table. We had moved Roy's crib into our room for the night, and fixed up a makeshift bed for Gabby in Roy's room.

Eva said, "I want her here. I owe her so much."

"What in the world could you owe her?"

She avoided the question. "And I could use some help, too. We can help her get on her feet."

"All right. Where shall we put her?"

"We can leave Roy's crib in our room for now, and she can use Roy's room. We'll buy her a bed. Not that I mean she'll stay forever, but maybe this is the time to think about adding that extra bedroom. After she leaves, you can use it for a study."

And just like that, Gabby became part of our lives. Eva included her in every family discussion, and for a while, Roy seemed to have two mothers. When I came home, they would be laughing in the kitchen, talking about working in the yard together, or shopping, or about nothing at all. Some days they would load Roy into his pram and head off to the stables, taking turns riding Molly and playing with Roy. They drew up the plans for a third bedroom, and arranged for a carpenter to come in and do it. All I had to do was pay for the project. This was a pivotal time for Eva. She had been fading for a long time. Gabby's arrival brought her back to life.

When we were first married I understood Eva had not finished her time of mourning. I hoped that my taking care of her would smooth her way, offering my love and the security I could bring to our home. For a while, it seemed to be working. We busied ourselves with our new life, our new house, gardening. I went riding with her, though I never enjoyed it the way she did. I had rented a small office for my law practice, and she helped me with secretarial tasks until I had enough clients to justify hiring a fulltime secretary. I can't say we laughed and danced our way through those early times. We had both been traumatized in our own ways by what happened. For a long while after Miguel's trial, I would wake up in the night, shivering from nightmares. Eva had her own bad dreams, dreams that would awaken her or make her thrash in the bed. She would never discuss what the dreams were about. But in the daylight we held hands and for a time we both seemed to be coming to peace with what had happened. Something—and only now do I understand that the something was her heavy sense of guilt—began to bring her down again. Her smile lost its sparkle. She moved a little more slowly. She spoke less. The changes weren't immediately obvious, but as time went by, I noticed and began to worry. Roy came into our lives, perking her up for awhile, but even he wasn't enough to buoy her against the weight her soul carried. I thought it was just her grief, but I was wrong. Then Gabby arrived, turning the table for us all.

Almost as soon as Gabby arrived, though, she was nearly driven away again by the circumstances of her own life. A couple of Sundays after her arrival, she and Eva were in the kitchen, where Gabby was demonstrating how to prepare the masa for tamales. There came a heavy knock at the door and I opened it to find Don Antonio. His wife and sons waited in the wagon out front. His face had become etched with deep angry angles.

I invited him in, but he insisted on speaking with Gabriela. I called her from the kitchen, and she came out wiping her hands cautiously on a cloth.

He said to me, "I would like to speak with *la viuda* alone, please."

Gabby shook her head. "I have no secrets from Mr. and Mrs. Bartlett. Stay, Owen."

Eva came in and watched as Don Antonio and Gabby had a brief, bitter exchange. The Spanish was too quick for me to follow, but Gabby's words flew against his contemptuous gestures. Then it was over. She wheeled about and left the room. His glare moved my way. I shifted my balance carefully, half-expecting him to swing at me and knowing I would have to take on his sons as well, but he turned and walked back out to the wagon. Without a glance my way, he giddaped the two horses and the wagon rolled away.

Gabby had retreated into her room. I went into my study. A minute later, Eva knocked and let herself in, closing the door behind her. I sat at my desk. I picked up the newspaper, then let it drop again, my deliberate, deep breaths trying to slow my racing pulse.

When Eva emerged, she sat down on the sofa. "We have to be careful."

"Why? If I understand correctly, Don Antonio demanded that Gabby return to the ranch, and she refused. Am I right?"

"Yes. But I'm afraid she wants to leave. She is embarrassed, and doesn't want us to be caught up in this."

"In what? We are simply helping her out."

"I know. But Don Antonio says she is disgracing the family by her behavior. By Mexican custom, as a widow she is supposed to remain in mourning in the home for the rest of her life, or at least until they find her another husband."

"What if she went home to her own family in Mexico?"

Gabby spoke up, at the door of her room. "In Mexico I would be restricted even more. Here it is not so bad, because there is a mix of customs." She took a seat beside Eva on the sofa. "At the ranch I found a way to slip out, and I was able to get away. In Mexico I would have no way to do that. They would find me and drag me back. I don't want to live the life of *la viuda*. I don't want someone to find another husband for me. I am Miguel's wife. Forever. What I really want is to start a business so that I can be independent and I can live my own life."

She looked to Eva. "Am I a crazy Mexican woman?"

Eva laughed and they hugged on the couch. "Of course not," Eva said, patting her gently on the back. "You are probably the only sane person here. Except for Owen, of course. He is the most sane person I know."

For some reason they both laughed as if that was the funniest thing they had ever heard. I waited uncomfortably until they stopped. I said, "If starting a business is what you want to do, we will help you."

"Yes," Eva said. "We will. But not too fast. I am enjoying having you here for company and for helping with Roy."

They hugged again, and then went back into the kitchen to work on the masa project. At my desk, I thought about businesses that might be appropriate for Gabby. I assumed, since I was a lawyer and had come to know many of the business people in town, she might look to me for direction. She probably didn't know much about numbers and bookkeeping, so I figured she wouldn't be very good at running a store or a shop of some kind. I considered a cleaning service, or perhaps a babysitting business, but those didn't have much of a future. I realized the project would take quite a bit of thought, and some looking around to see what other women were doing.

It would turn out, of course, that she had no interest at all in my opinion of her qualifications. One evening, in the middle of practicing cross stitching with Eva, she announced that she had decided to start a clothing shop. She smiled as my eyebrows rose. "You don't think that is a good idea, do you?"

I tried to be diplomatic. "Well, I'm sure you could do it. But what do you know about that kind of business? There are records to be kept, inventory to be bought and maintained. Pricing. Of course you would be very good with the customers. I'm not trying to be negative, but what do you know about running a retail business?"

Eva said, "She can learn. Some of the men who run shops in this town aren't nearly as bright as she is. She could pick it up in no time."

In the face of their laughing enthusiasm, I kept my doubts to myself—wisely, as it turned out. Eva convinced me to lend Gabby the money she needed to start the business. The two of them, with little Roy in tow, spent the next several months finding a shop to rent, discovering how to find suppliers, learning the basics of bookkeeping. There was a man in Nogales willing to supply her with a few fashionable dresses from Mexico, to go along with the American inventory she ordered from a catalog out of Chicago.

Eight months after our first conversation about it, "Gaby's" opened for business, using the Spanish spelling of Gabby's nickname. It opened and it promptly failed. She had chosen a location on the south side of town, an area where a lot of Mexicans lived. She had chosen dresses she thought girls in that area would like, stylish without looking too American. She decorated the store in an interesting mix of bright and pale colors, reflecting both Mexican and American motifs. In those days all the stores used counter service. A customer asked for what she wanted at the counter, and the clerk would fetch the requested items from shelves and hangers behind the counter. Gabby and Eva sat up nights plotting ways to make the waiting area more inviting. They painted the ceiling. They installed two or three comfortable chairs for customers awaiting their turns. They went over and over every detail to make sure everything—every dress, every fabric, every detail—would be just right. But that first day, not a single customer came into the store. Eva and Gabby sat by the counter all day, as Roy toddled among the shelves in back. People walked by the door without so much as turning their heads to look inside.

Anyone else might have felt discouraged. Gabby was merely furious. "It is those *aliancistas*! I know it is. Don Antonio talked to all his little friends in the Alianza about me, and they spread the word—"No one goes to Gaby's." I know that is what it is. They think I am not a good Mexican woman because I won't wear black and stay in the house all day like a good *viuda*. Well, I'll show them. If they want to treat a woman like that, I will show them how a woman should be treated."

The next morning, she used the last of the money she had borrowed from us to pay a young neighborhood woman to work in the store for two weeks. She packed a few dresses into a basket and set out into the neighborhoods around her store. For days, she knocked on doors and showed her wares to the ladies who came to the door. She smiled and cajoled and invited any who would listen to come into her shop to see what else they might like. But she was right. She had been blackballed by the *aliancistas*.

No matter. She persisted, smiling all the while. And her magic began to work. Someone told a neighbor about one of the dresses, and next time Gabby came around, the neighbor wanted to see it. The women felt the fabrics, held a dress up to see how it would look. Now and then, someone even tried a dress on. No one was buying but the ice began to thaw, the word began to spread. She returned to all the doors that had closed in her face, and a few days later, she returned again. Each time, she encountered fewer scowling faces, and more open doors.

Each evening she had to clean handprints and smudges from the dresses, left by hands in the middle of housework when she arrived. She didn't mind. The more the ladies touched, she told Eva, the more they would remember the feel of her dresses. Finally, at the end of the two weeks, out of money and refusing to borrow more, she let her employee go, and she waited.

Curiosity saved her. Someone, noticing that she no longer carried her basket through the streets, came into the shop late one morning to see if she was all right. An hour later, the same woman came back with two friends to look at dresses. Gabby made her first sale on her eighteenth day in business. Then she made another, and another. After two more months, the little store was the most popular clothing shop on the south side, and Gabby had to hire her employee back. That employee became her first store manager when Gabby opened her second shop.

Gabby paid me back every dime she had borrowed, and insisted on paying interest on the loan. She also insisted on paying back rent for the bedroom she had been using, and before long she rented a tiny house a few doors from her store.

Her departure left an awkward vacuum at first. Much as I enjoyed having Gabby and Eva together, I looked forward to a bit more quiet around the house. But reading together in the evening,

I would catch Eva looking at me quizzically, as if she were seeing something in our life she hadn't seen before. If I asked, she would smile and say it was nothing. It was not nothing, of course.

The next several years saw Gabby at our house for dinner almost every Sunday. She and Eva would meet at the church for the noon mass, and then she would spend the afternoon with us. After I bought our first car—a 1915 Hudson Super Six Phaeton—we drove to pick up Gabby for church. Afterwards at the house, we would laugh and play with Roy, and if I excused myself to get some work done, Eva would tug at my sleeve and ask me to stay a little longer, since Gabby was there. In nice weather, we would sit out in the yard under the chinaberry tree and sip tea. Eva would make some excuse to go back inside, leaving Gabby and me together, and sometimes it seemed she took a very long time to rejoin us.

One evening at dinner, when it was just Eva and me, she wiped crumbs from the corner of Roy's mouth and said, "Owen, I can't tell you how grateful I am that we had this time with Gabby, and that we could help her get started with her shop." There were tears at the corners of her eyes.

Surprised at the tears, I said, "Grateful?"

"Yes. Grateful. I just feel I owe her so much, and this was a chance to give her something. She has been through so much. She misses Miguel. And she misses, well, you know what I mean she misses."

"We all miss that sometimes, don't you think? You decided you did not want more children, which is fine, but it means we must exercise a certain discipline. That's just the way life is."

She reached across the table and laid her hand on mine. "You're a good husband, Owen. I hope you think I'm a good wife. Some men might not think so."

"I'm not some men, am I? I'm not complaining."

She smiled. "Of course not. Anyway, as much as we can, anything she needs, we help her out. Do you know what I mean? It's what I want to do. It's important." As an afterthought, she added, "Poor Gabby. The doctor told her she could never have children. She and Miguel could have, you know, kept going forever."

A Sunday or two later, Gabby stayed until after dark because Roy was sick. He was about five at the time and he had thrown up during dinner. Eva rushed him off to get cleaned up. Gabby and I picked up the dishes, and she insisted on cleaning up the kitchen without my help, so I retired to my study, as I usually did after dinner. I could hear their voices as I worked. Roy continued to cry on and off, and after a while, Eva came in to ask if I would mind driving Gabby home by myself.

On the way, Gabby asked if we couldn't drive a little further south to a spot she liked near the Santa Cruz Wash. It was too far to walk at night from her house, she said, and she wanted to see what it looked like under the full moon. We drove to a quiet wheat field near the wash and sat for a few minutes, taking in the moonlight and the cool night air.

"Owen," she said, "I've wanted to thank you for a long time for the help you have given me. I know it wasn't easy, with two women in the house all the time and you trying to get your work done in the evenings, but there is something ... I don't know. There is something between Eva and me. I don't know what it is. I wanted to thank you." She turned to me and our faces were only inches apart.

Her perfume hung between us like an invisible flame. There was a moment of hesitation, and then like magnets suddenly brought too close, our lips met and our bodies locked together. There were no words, only soft moans as we touched each other and pulled at our clothing. She shifted and leaned back into the narrow seat, and then I was inside her. Her hands gripped the seat

213

as she pushed back against my thrusts. The coolness of the night vanished in our heat.

It didn't take long, for either of us. She held my head against her breasts as our breathing slowed. When I sat upright and looked at her, she touched my nose with her finger, and smiled.

I said, "Are you all right?"

She nodded, and whispered, "*Sí*. I miss my Miguel, but he would understand. My body gets hungry, once in a while."

"What about Eva?"

She smiled in the moonlight. "I think I should be asking that question. Eva is my best friend, but she is your wife. I know you and Eva have not done this in a long time. At least not much."

"How do you know that? Girl talk?"

She began to adjust her dress. "Women know these things about each other. I lived in your house for a year and a half. The nights were very quiet. But there is something else. I have a feeling she would not mind that we did this. I can't say why. Something in the air."

Whatever was in the air, sour guilt washed up inside me as I drove into our driveway. I undressed quietly and got into bed beside Eva just as I realized that I still carried the scent of Gabby's perfume. I stared up at the dark ceiling, listening to Eva's breath and knowing she was listening to me.

The next morning, I awoke to the sounds of her moving around in Roy's bedroom.

"Good morning," she said, cheerily, as I walked past the door.

I pretended to be groggier than I felt. "Morning," I mumbled, heading for the kitchen.

She came in as I downed a glass of water. She said, "I assume you got Gabby home safely last night?"

"Oh, yes. She seemed fine. A little bit worried about Roy."

She smiled and went back into the bedroom. I felt puzzled

at her smile. Surely she suspected something. I offered a piece of bread to little Roy, but he shook his head. I found a basket of a half-dozen brown eggs on the counter, and lit the coal in the kitchen stove.

As that day worn on, and the next, Eva was very sweet, and I made up my mind to avoid being alone with Gabby. Watching Eva, feeling her touch on my shoulder as she walked by, I could not understand then that for her, what had happened between Gabby and me was a kind of restitution payment, a way of making up for her guilt. For me, I had enough to make up for in my life, and didn't need any more guilt to carry around. Not enough years had passed since Stephen's death, and Miguel's trial, and all that happened afterwards.

After the sheriff finished testifying, Mr. Dale, the prosecutor, said, "For the next witness, the territory calls John Billsley."

The bailiff rose and held the gate open as Billsley glided toward the witness stand, head erect, arms nearly motionless at his sides. The court clerk stopped him with a gesture and swore him in. After Billsley slid into the witness seat, Mr. Dale said, "Sir, please state your name."

Billsley's chin went up slightly. "John H. Billsley."

"Mr. Billsley, what do you do for a living?"

"I'm a desk clerk at the Santa Rita Hotel."

"A desk clerk? What's that?"

"I work at the lobby desk, sir. The guests come to me for assistance."

"Been there long?"

"Over a year. Since the hotel opened. I was hired by Mr. Iager himself. The owner of the Santa Rita Hotel."

"Would you please describe your duties as desk clerk?"

Billsley's chin went up another inch as he spoke of keeping an eye on the hotel guests, catering to their needs, ensuring that the details of their lives at the hotel were managed. "Once in a while," he said, "a guest may be a little trouble." He glanced toward me as he spoke, then closed his eyes. "Usually it's somebody new, from a large city in the east who finds Tucson rather under-civilized. But I manage to keep nearly everyone happy, most of the time. Except for those few."

Mr. Dale said, "Do you recall the evening of October thirteenth of this year?"

"Yes sir. I surely do."

"What do you recall about it?"

"That was the night Mr. Downing was murdered. I'll not forget it."

"Were you working that evening?"

"I worked until about eleven. It was a double shift, starting in the morning, because the man, the man who was supposed to work the evening shift, was a little under the weather. I worked until eleven, and then I came in the next morning at seven for my regular shift. I remember there was a bad argument between Mr. Downing and …"

I jumped to my feet. "Objection, Judge. The witness is not answering the question. The question was whether he was working the evening Mr. Downing was killed, not about any supposed argument."

"Sustained. The witness will confine his answers to the questions asked."

Billsley's eyelids drooped to half-mast as he glared at me. "Yes sir. Sorry."

Mr. Dale said, "You were there at the hotel until eleven p.m., then?"

"Yes sir."

"The front desk where you work," Dale said, "is that situated where you can observe what happens in the lobby of the hotel?"

"Yes. From where I stand, I can see almost everything. Yes."

"Did you, sir, happen to observe an encounter on the evening Mr. Downing died, between Mr. Downing and Miguel Cordero?"

"I did."

"How far were you from where the encounter took place?"

"Not far. Maybe from me to that door over there." Billsley pointed to the back door of the courtroom. "No farther than that."

Mr. Dale surveyed the distance. "That's about forty feet?"

"I suppose."

"By the way, Mr. Billsley, do you recognize Miguel Cordero in the courtroom today?"

Billsley turned his head, barely, toward Miguel. "He's that fellow there."

"Your honor, may the record reflect that the witness had indicated the defendant?"

The judge said, "It may."

"Well, Mr. Billsley, from that distance of about forty feet, were you able to hear what was said?"

"Every word of it. They were loud, and I couldn't help but hear it."

I jumped up again. "Objection."

"Yes?" the judge said. "On what ground?"

"He couldn't. He couldn't possibly have heard, your honor."

"Oh?" The judge leaned forward. "I take it you wish to testify in your own case, Mr. Bartlett?"

"Well, no judge. It's that …" I looked over at Dale. "May we approach the bench, your honor?"

The judge opened and closed his hand beckoningly. "By all means, Mr. Bartlett."

Mr. Dale followed me to the bench. The judge leaned forward and whispered, "What is the problem, Mr. Bartlett?"

I whispered back, "Judge, he told me the other day that he didn't hear anything. He only heard the tone of their voices, nothing else. That's what he said."

"Ah," the judge whispered. "Wouldn't cross-examination be a better moment for you to mount your attack on what he has to say today? Unless, as I said, you wish to make yourself a witness. In which case I'll have to declare a mistrial and give your client a chance to find another lawyer. You can't be your own witness, you know. So how do you wish to proceed?"

I leaned toward Mr. Dale and whispered, "I'll withdraw my objection. But your witness is lying through his teeth."

Dale shrugged. "Says you. Is that it, Judge?"

The judge waved us away and we returned to our tables. Miguel caught my eye and raised his eyebrows. I shook my head. The jurors were watching me, and to hide my irritation I picked up a pen and pretended to be scribbling a note.

Mr. Dale said, "Mr. Billsley, I'll repeat. Were you able to hear what was being said in the argument between the deceased and the defendant?"

"Yes sir. I was." Billsley glanced at me. "I heard everything."

"Tell us what you heard, then."

"Objection," I said again, without rising. "Foundation."

"Foundation?" the judge said. "How are we lacking foundation?"

"We don't know when or where the argument took place that the witness is testifying about."

The judge frowned. "I believe the witness testified that the argument took place the night Mr. Downing died. What other foundation could be missing?"

Dale waved his hand dismissively. "Never mind, your honor. I'll lay the foundation. Mr. Billsley …"

218

I stood up, deciding to make this as difficult as possible. "Your honor, I don't think you ruled on my objection."

"Objection overruled."

I remained standing as Mr. Dale nodded and went on. "You testified that you heard an argument between the deceased and the defendant. Where were you when you heard the argument?"

"I was at my post at the front counter."

"In the lobby of the Santa Rita Hotel?"

"Of course."

"What time of day did you hear the argument?"

"It was about nine-thirty at night. Maybe a little later. Maybe near ten."

"Did the argument take place on the night of October thirteenth of this year?"

"Yes, sir."

"How do you know?"

"That was the night Mr. Downing was murdered outside the hotel."

"And how do you know that was the night you heard the argument?"

"Because I thought of it immediately the next morning, as soon as I heard that Mr. Downing had been murdered."

"Thank you. Now, please tell us what you heard when you witnessed the argument."

"Objection," I said. "Calls for hearsay."

"Overruled," the judge said, and then hesitated. "Mr. Bartlett, is there something else?"

"No, your honor."

"Why are you standing up?"

I was simply too irritated to sit down, but I said, "I have a cramp in my leg, Judge."

The judge seemed to think that was reasonable, but Mr. Dale stared at me for a second, his mouth open. He said, "All right, then." He turned back to Billsley. "What did you hear, when you were hearing this argument between the defendant and the deceased?"

"Objection," I said. "Foundation. I believe the witness previously said he was listening to two live persons."

The judge said, "Sit down, Mr. Bartlett." He waited, his hand on the gavel, until I sat down. "The witness may answer the question."

Billsley turned toward the jury. "Well, they were standing close together, over by the window. I could see the Mexican pointing his finger at Mr. Downing, almost like he was poking him in the chest while he was talking. The Mexican looked real upset. I heard him say something about a report. Mr. Downing stood there looking at him. Kind of a little smile on his face."

I was shocked. Over the years, many other witnesses would say things on the witness stand that were completely at odds with what they had said to me previously. But that first time, in the middle of my first trial, I had no idea what to do, besides trying to hide my shock.

"Did he say what report?"

"No sir. He said something about a report."

"So you didn't hear what he said about the report?"

"Well, sort of. It was about a report."

Mr. Dale leaned on the prosecution table, looking down at his papers, his jaw muscles working and his lips pursed. When he looked up, he said, "Did you hear anything else that was being said?"

"Yes sir. Like I said, the Mexican was talking about a report. He was talking about a report, is what I remember."

"But what," Mr. Dale said, his jaw working again, "what did he say about the report?"

"Well, it was something about a report. And then he threatened him."

"Mr. Cordero threatened Mr. Downing?"

"Yes sir."

"What was the threat? Or did you only hear part of that, too?"

"No sir, I heard it."

"Well, what was the threat?"

"He was pointing at Mr. Downing, like this." Billsley held up a forefinger, with his thumb pulled back.

"He pointed at him like that? As if he were pointing a pistol?"

I jumped up. "Objection. Counsel is misstating the evidence."

The judge shook his head. "Proceed, Mr. Dale."

"Thank you, Judge," Dale said, moving around to the front of the jury box, rubbing his hands together like a fly preparing for a meal. He stopped once he was centered before the jurors. "So, when you observed Mr. Cordero threatening Mr. Downing, he did this?" He thrust out his hand to expose a thin, white forearm beneath the fabric of his sleeves. He pointed his hand at the jury, forefinger extended, sighting down the length of his arm as if sighting down the barrel of a gun.

"That's it, sir," Billsley said. "That's it, exactly."

"Objection," I said.

"Overruled."

Mr. Dale allowed his arm to relax at his side. "Mr. Billsley, was there anything else you remember about that evening, having to do with Mr. Cordero?"

Billsley said, "There is one more thing."

"And what is that thing?"

"Earlier, I was operating the elevator, because the regular elevator man was taking a break. There was an elevator call from the fourth floor, which is where the Mexican's room is. When I opened the gate, a Mexican woman got into the elevator. She held up one finger. I said, 'First floor?' and she nodded. I closed the gate and took her down to the first floor. She went out through the lobby."

Mr. Dale said, "Did you associate this woman with Mr. Cordero?"

"Yes sir. I did."

"Why was that?"

"Well, for one thing, she looked Mexican and he was the only Mexican man who was staying on the fourth floor that night. But I looked out into the hall before I closed the gate, after she got into the elevator, I saw him a few feet down the hall, standing and watching."

Mr. Dale said, "I believe Miguel Cordero's wife is with the family today in the courtroom." He gestured toward the family. "Do you recognize the young woman there as the woman you saw get into the elevator, with Mr. Cordero standing a few feet down the hall that night?"

"No sir. I'm pretty sure she's not the one who got into the elevator that night."

A stir went through the courtroom, as Mr. Dale said, "Was it a different woman, then?"

"I don't know. She had one of those shawls over her head, and I couldn't see her face."

I rose to my feet. "Your honor, I object. There is no reason to pursue this line of questioning. It doesn't sound relevant."

The judge said, "I'm inclined to agree, Mr. Dale. Where are you going with this?"

Mr. Dale said, "Judge, if I may ask another question or two, I think I can clarify the issue."

"All right," the judge said, "one more question. Maybe two."

Mr. Dale said, "Mr. Billsley, have you ever seen Mr. Cordero with a Mexican woman in the hotel before?"

"Yes, I have," Billsley said. He nodded toward the Cordero

family. "I have seen him with the woman over there. The one you said is his wife."

"How was it different, when you saw the woman in the hotel the night Stephen Downing was killed?"

"When I saw Miguel Cordero with his wife, she wore a black scarf on her head. When I saw the woman in the hotel that night, she had a long scarf, like a shawl, and it was wrapped around her head so I couldn't see her face at all. Like she was trying to hide."

"I see. From having seen Mrs. Cordero previously, was it your impression that the woman you saw leaving Miguel Cordero's floor of the hotel was Mrs. Cordero?"

"No sir. I couldn't tell. The woman in the elevator was shorter, I think."

"I see. Thank you. No further questions." Mr. Dale abruptly turned and walked back to his table. "Your witness, Mr. Bartlett."

I jumped up, not even waiting for Mr. Dale to be seated. "Your honor, may we approach the bench?"

The judge nodded, and once we were at the bench, he leaned forward. "I do see the problem, Mr. Bartlett," he whispered. "Mr. Dale, what did that fishing expedition have to do with this case? Is the jury supposed to infer something about the death of Stephen Downing from the fact that the defendant may have had some sort of congress with an unidentified Mexican woman?"

Mr. Dale whispered, "Your honor, my purpose in this line of questioning was to show that the defendant was up to something the night Mr. Downing was killed. That's all. Nobody seems to know what it was, but he was up to something."

"Judge …" I said, but the judge held up a hand.

"Mr. Dale," he said, "you're blowing smoke and you know it. I'm going to allow Mr. Bartlett some latitude in his cross-examination on that issue. Do you understand?"

Mr. Dale's face reddened. "Judge, I don't think …"

The judge's hand went up again. "I didn't ask for your permission. I asked if you understand."

Mr. Dale nodded.

"Good. Let's proceed, gentlemen."

Back at his table, Mr. Dale said, "I have no further questions of this witness."

"Mr. Bartlett?"

I glanced down at Hyram, whose legs were stretched out under the table, arms crossed on his chest. He appeared about to doze off.

"Mr. Billsley," I said, "you said earlier that you had heard the whole argument."

"Yes sir," Billsley said. "That I did."

"Every word?"

"Yes sir."

"But you also said the only words you heard were about a report. Correct?"

"Correct."

"You didn't hear which report they were talking about, did you?"

"No sir, but they were talking about it like they both knew what they meant. That much was sure."

"But you couldn't tell, from what you heard, which report they were talking about, could you?"

Billsley's chin went up. "Well I figured since, you know, everybody knows they were ..."

I held up my hand. "Wait, Billsley. What everybody knows isn't the question. The question is whether you could tell, from what you overheard, which report they were talking about. You couldn't hear that part, could you?"

"Well, no."

"You also couldn't hear anything else they said about the report, could you?"

"No. But I could tell it wasn't good, whatever they said. They both looked like they were about to fight."

Ah. I had my angle. "Let me get this straight, then, Mr. Billsley. You heard the whole thing, correct?"

"That's right."

"But you didn't hear any details about the report. Correct?"

"Yes sir."

"You didn't hear what they said about the report. Correct?"

"Yes sir."

"Even though you heard …" I held up two fingers of one hand and poked them in the air as if to make quotation marks. "… 'everything'?"

Amusement began to register on the faces of the jurors. They were catching on. I said, "You didn't hear anything else they said, except that Mr. Cordero said something about the report. Correct?"

"Yes sir."

I made a point of smiling at the jurors, some of whom grinned back. Juror Jackson frowned.

I paused. Billsley had told me that Stephen was red-faced and wild-eyed, during the argument, and seemed to be spoiling for a fight, while Miguel stood there calmly. On the other hand, he had just testified that Miguel was the one who had seemed more pugnacious, poking Stephen in the chest. I wanted to rub the contradiction in his face, but I couldn't think of a way to do it that didn't offer more proof of bad blood between Miguel and Stephen.

"No more questions, your honor," I said as I walked back to the defense table.

Mr. Dale stood. "Your honor, the Territory calls Doctor Hinkley."

The bailiff hurried out the back door. He returned with a gray-haired man in a rumpled shirt. He directed the man to the front of the courtroom. After the man was sworn in and settled into the witness seat, Mr. Dale said, "Sir, please state your name."

"Dr. Wilbur Hinkley."

"Are you a medical doctor?"

"You know I am." Dr. Hinkley's eyes panned calmly across the courtroom. I wondered how many in the room he had treated.

"Sir, have you been a medical doctor for long?"

"Thirty-seven years. I was educated in Chicago."

"Doctor, were you directed by this court to perform an autopsy on the remains of a deceased individual by the name of Stephen Downing?"

"I was. I prepared a report and submitted it to the court."

"You prepared the report after performing the autopsy?"

"That's correct."

"Would you tell the jury the results of your report, as to the cause of death to the deceased?"

I rose to my feet. "Objection, your honor. How can he talk about the results unless he explains how he arrived at the results?"

The judge said, "Counsel, please approach." Once we were at the bench, the judge whispered, "Mr. Bartlett, are you going to insist that the good doctor explain every gory detail of what he encountered with the body?"

"No, your honor." I glanced toward the back of the courtroom. Mrs. Downing was absent. "I simply want to make sure the jury understands the basis for whatever conclusion the doctor draws."

"Good. I did you a favor by ordering the autopsy. I don't want to turn this into a circus. I will allow testimony as to the cause of death, and nothing that is not directly relevant to the cause of death. Understand, counsel?"

"Yes sir."

Mr. Dale nodded. Back at his table, he went on. "Doctor, did you examine the entire body?"

"I did."

"Did you find any wounds or cuts or other disfigurements which were serious enough to have caused the death of Mr. Downing?"

"I did. I found a knife wound in the neck. To put it in layman's terms, the knife entered the neck about two inches, on the right front side of the neck, above the clavicle, traveling upwards at about a forty or forty-five degree angle. The wound was in such a place as to nick the jugular vein. It's a substantial vein, but not like an artery that would have spurted a lot of blood out real quick. Blood doesn't flow through a vein with the pressure that it does through an artery. But the nick was enough to let a lot of blood out over time."

"Did you measure the size of the wound?"

"I did. The entry wound was about three-fourths of an inch in width."

"Would that give you an estimate of the size of the blade that made the cut?"

"Yes. You see, all knife blades are tapered, at least for a short distance from the point. Some are tapered the whole length of the blade. As the blade penetrated the victim's neck, the entry wound would have widened because of the increased width of the taper. I estimated that the blade penetrated about two inches into the neck. Two inches from its tip, the knife blade would have to be about three-fourths of an inch across."

"How do you know it penetrated two inches?"

"Because I found the place where it struck the vertebrae, the spine."

Mr. Dale walked over to the clerk's table and held up the cloth containing Miguel's knife. "Sir, if I told you this knife, found in the defendant's room, was three-quarters of an inch wide, two inches from its point, would you agree that it could have been the knife used to murder the deceased?"

DAN GOSS ANDERSON

I jumped up. "Objection, your honor. Whether this was a murder is a question for the jury to decide."

The judge waved his hand impatiently. "Go on, doctor."

"It could. It sounds like it is the right size."

"Doctor, did you arrive at a firm opinion of the cause of death?"

"Yes. In my opinion, Mr. Downing bled to death as a result of being stabbed in the neck."

Mr. Dale nodded to the jury. "No further questions, your honor."

"Very well," the judge said, "Mr. Bartlett, you may cross-examine the witness."

I rose to my feet. "Doctor, you testified that you believe the cause of death to have been the wound in Mr. Downing's neck. Correct?"

"I did."

"Now, you didn't cut the torso open, did you? Just the neck?"

"That's correct."

"Did you examine the rest of the body? By that I mean, did you examine the torso and legs and so forth for wounds?"

"I did. There were no other wounds. One or two of his front teeth were loose, but nobody ever died from a loose tooth."

"But you didn't open the body to look for other evidence inside, did you?"

"No sir. When I saw the extent and location of the wound in the neck, I knew I had found the cause of death. I did open up the neck to get an idea of how deep the wound was."

"Did you take a sample of the blood to see if Mr. Downing had been poisoned?"

"No."

I glanced at the jury. Juror Jackson was looking closely at his fingernails, a slight smile on his face. Each of the other faces registered some degree of disapproval. The old man's mouth was

228

skewed into a pout. This line of questioning was getting me no-where. It sounded like I was fishing for nothing. I searched for a better line. "You mentioned that you knew the knife had struck the spine."

"The vertebra, yes. Specifically, the number two vertebra."

"What does that mean?"

"The bones of the spine are called vertebrae. For classification, we number the vertebrae from the top of the spine to the bottom. The number two vertebra is in the neck. That's where the point of the knife struck."

"How do you know it struck that particular vertebra?"

"Because I could see the chip there."

"You could see the bone was chipped?"

"That too. But I found a little chip of the knife lodged in the vertebra."

A rustle went through the courtroom. "You found a chip of the knife?"

"Yes. A bitty little thing. Smaller than a grain of sand. It was probably just the very tip."

"Did you preserve it? Did you take the knife chip out and save it?"

"No. I was asked to determine the cause of death. I did that, and then I had the body returned to the cemetery to be reburied."

"I see." I paced for a moment, thinking of my next move. "Let me get this straight. You were asked to find the cause of death, you found what you believe was the cause of death, and then you buried it where no one will ever see it?"

The doctor shrugged. "I suppose you could put it that way."

"You threw away the only remaining physical evidence of the cause of death?"

"If you mean the chip, it was really a tiny fragment. No bigger than the head of a pin, I would suppose."

"Then Doctor, how can you expect the jury to really know what the cause of death was?"

It was a stupid question, and everyone knew it. Someone laughed in the back of the courtroom, and almost immediately cut it off. But it had its effect. A quiet snicker spread through the room. Jurors put a hand to their mouths and looked at the floor, each trying not to laugh and upset the judge. I felt my face grow hot.

I waved off whatever the doc was going to say, and walked back to the defense table. "No further questions."

The judge said, "Mr. Dale, do you have any redirect for this witness?"

Mr. Dale rose and stood quietly, a little smile the only evidence that he was savoring the moment. "I have two questions, your honor. Doctor, this piece of whatever it was that you found imbedded in the spine of the deceased, I believe you said it was quite tiny?"

"Yes. As a matter of fact, it was almost unnoticeable. If the light hadn't been right, I wouldn't have seen it at all."

"Thank you. And if I might ask again the question put to you by defense counsel. If you did not preserve the tiny piece of whatever it was, how *can* the jury really know what the cause of death was?"

The doctor nodded. "Simple. It wasn't the little piece of metal itself that told me what caused the death. It was the hole in the decedent's neck, and the cut to his jugular vein. He bled to death. But the death was not inevitable. All somebody would have had to do is keep a hand with sufficient pressure on the cut, and I could have fixed it if somebody would have gotten him to my office in time. He could even have put the pressure on it himself."

I gasped, and Mr. Dale looked in my direction. When I said nothing, he turned to the jury and smiled. "No further questions," he said.

It was my good luck that no one was watching me, except Miguel. The implications of the doctor's testimony hit me hard, and I gripped the table as the shock of the words ran through me. Could have been saved. Could have been saved! Miguel's eyes were on me, and suddenly I really understood his fear, and felt it, because it was now my own. But just as suddenly, my head in a whirl, I was startled to hear the prosecutor call his next witness.

"Your honor," Mr. Dale said, "the Territory calls Mrs. Eva Downing."

I stood up, feeling like a fighter trying to buy a few seconds by distracting his opponent, after taking a hard punch. I needed to clear my head. "Your honor," I said, weakly.

"Yes?" The judge watched me, waiting. "Mr. Bartlett, do you have something to say?"

I couldn't think of what to say, or what to do. I stared at my table.

"Mr. Bartlett?"

I knew it was a critical moment. I knew the right thing to do, but my fear told me to be careful. I needed time to think, but there was no time. I had a job to do. Mrs. Downing was approaching the clerk. I needed to stay focused.

"Mr. Bartlett? If you have nothing to say, we'll proceed."

I shook my head and sat down. There would be time later in the day. I pushed my confusion aside as best I could, and watched Mrs. Downing. She wore the same black dress she had worn to the funeral, this time without the black veil. She raised her right hand, was sworn to speak the truth, and took her seat at the witness stand.

Mr. Dale said, "Would you please tell the jury your name?"

"My name is Mrs. Stephen Downing."

Mr. Dale rubbed his hands together, and watched the jury as he spoke. "I'm sure everyone here in the courtroom extends their deepest sympathies for the loss of your husband. I'd like to ask you some questions about some of the events that occurred not long before your husband's passing. Is that all right?"

She nodded. "Of course."

"Your husband had some business dealings with a man named Miguel Cordero, didn't he?"

"He did."

"Could you describe the nature of those dealings?"

"Yes. My husband and Mr. Cordero were working together on a mining project on the Cordero family property, in the Santa Rita Mountains. Stephen was a mining engineer."

"Tell the jury what you mean by a mining project."

"As I understood it, they had started a pipe line to bring water down from the higher part of the mountain to the placer mining area not far from Greaterville."

"Do you know what placer mining is?"

"I do. Placer mining is the type of gold mining where water is used to wash gravel and sand, so that the gold settles to the bottom. The washing process is called sluicing. I think the miners mostly call it panning for gold."

Mr. Dale's eyebrows went up slightly and he grinned at the jury. "You have an impressive knowledge of your late husband's business, Mrs. Downing. For a lady, I mean."

She folded her hands in her lap and looked Mr. Dale straight in the eye. "Please don't patronize me, sir. I'm not an idiot. My husband …"

The eruption of laughter brought an immediate loud rap from the judge's gavel. He scowled the courtroom into silence, and turned to Mrs. Downing. "Madam, I'm sure the prosecutor meant only to compliment you. Please take it as such, and let's move on."

Mr. Dale nodded, a smirk at the corners of his mouth. "I meant only to observe your obvious intelligence, Mrs. Downing.

Now, does placer mining, as far as you know, require quite a lot of water?"

"It requires a fair amount, yes. A number of prospectors and miners were placer mining in the Greaterville district, on the east side at the base of the Santa Ritas. It is pretty dry there, which is why they were trying to find a way to bring water down from the mountain. There was another company that was also trying to bring water down from the mountains for the sluicing, but Stephen had a plan to build a dam higher up than their dams, on land that belonged to the Cordero family. He thought he could bring more water down, year round. He also wanted to put in a lode mine even higher up in the mountains."

"And a lode mine is …?"

"Where they have a mine shaft. He believed that the gold being found around the base of the mountains must have washed down over many, many years from a certain spot higher up. He believed he knew where that spot was, and that was where he wanted to put a lode mine. The lode mine was his real goal. He believed there was a lot of gold up there."

"Do you know if he discussed these plans with the Cordero family?"

"He worked mostly with Miguel Cordero. He and Miguel discussed everything."

"Is Mr. Cordero the man sitting in the prisoner's dock?"

"Of course he is, sir."

"Now, those projects you mentioned. Did you yourself ever see any of these projects?"

"Myself? No. Stephen and Miguel would go out with pack horses for two or three days, while I stayed with the family at the ranch."

Mr. Dale began rubbing his hands together again. "Now, Mrs. Downing, in some marriages the husband tells the wife everything about his business. In other marriages, the husband tells the wife very little, if anything, about his business. How would you characterize your own marriage?"

Mrs. Downing looked first at the judge, and then at me with her eyebrows raised.

I rose to my feet. "Your honor, I don't see the relevance of that question."

The judge said, "Neither do I. Mr. Dale, what are you up to, here?"

"Judge, I'm only trying to ascertain whether the witness was made aware of all the details of her husband's business."

"I understand that, Mr. Dale. But why? What is the relevance?"

After a moment's hesitation, Mr. Dale said, "Never mind, for the moment. I'll withdraw the question. Mrs. Downing, how would you describe the relationship between your husband and the defendant?"

"They were friendly to one another. They spent a lot of time together, and they got along pretty well."

"When you say pretty well, do you mean to say they didn't always get along?"

Mrs. Downing glanced again at me. "They didn't agree on everything. They would argue sometimes. They never got violent with each other, and they always came to some kind of agreement. Miguel is a very calm man. I've never seen him get angry, even when Stephen was shouting."

"So your husband would get angry enough at the defendant to shout?"

"Well, yes. But it was never anything more than a spat, you see. It wasn't like something that could lead to, you know, this." She waved her hand to indicate the courtroom. "There wasn't ever any serious problem between them."

"Mrs. Downing," Mr. Dale said, holding up one finger and

speaking slowly, "my question was whether your husband would get angry enough at the defendant to shout?"

Mrs. Downing looked again to me, but I couldn't think of anything to help her. "Well, yes, as I said. Stephen had something of a temper. He would raise his voice."

"And he would raise his voice at the defendant?"

"Yes."

"Very well. That's all I was asking. Now, turning to the recent past, and by that I mean in the day or the week before your husband's unfortunate demise, were you aware of any reason for your husband and the defendant to have any disagreements?"

She drew a deep breath. "There were small disagreements. I don't remember anything that came up in Stephen's last … in his last day or two."

"Were there any new disagreements, even if they were little disagreements? Did anything come up in the last few days?"

She looked down at her lap. "No. Not … no. There was nothing."

"Were there any arguments about old disagreements? Or that resembled old disagreements?"

"No." Her eyes remained downcast.

"Let me ask again, then, Mrs. Downing, do you believe your husband kept you fully informed of the details of his business?"

"Objection," I said. "Relevance."

"Overruled," the judge said. "Mrs. Downing, please answer the question."

She said, "I assure you, sir, that I was fully informed about my husband's business affairs."

Mr. Dale smiled slightly. "Then, Mrs. Downing, would you please tell the jury what your husband was arguing with the defendant about, in the lobby of the Santa Rita Hotel, only hours before he was murdered?"

She blinked, looking down again at her lap. "I don't know."

Mr. Dale said, "No further questions." He gave the jury another slight smile as he returned to his table.

"Mr. Bartlett?" the judge said, "any questions for this witness?"

I rose. I fumbled for a question to ask her, unable to look her in the eye. "Mrs. Downing, you mentioned that you know Miguel Cordero. Have you known him long?"

She nodded. "Almost since my husband and I first came to Tucson. My husband met Miguel's father while Stephen was out riding, exploring around the mountains near the Cordero ranch. He told Don Antonio that the mountains might have a lot of minerals. Don Antonio liked my husband's ideas, and invited us to his ranch. We stayed there a few days. I became friends with Miguel's mother, and with Gabby ... Gabriela, Miguel's wife. That was when my husband and Miguel first started planning their mining projects."

I paused, thinking of Stephen's temper, and recalling something I'd learned in law school about character evidence. "Mrs. Downing," I said, "are you aware of Miguel's reputation for being a peaceful man?"

"Yes, I am," she said. "I believe everyone knows that he wouldn't hurt a fly. He is reasonable and ..."

Mr. Dale leaped to his feet. "Objection. The defendant's reputation is not at issue here."

My temper fired up at that. I said, "Your honor, everyone in this courtroom knows that the defendant's reputation really is at issue. We've all seen the articles in the paper about making the town safer from violence by Mexicans. The defendant is a Mexican. That fact alone means his personal reputation as a peaceful man is entirely at issue."

"Objection!"

The judge glared at me. "Sir," he said, "you are out of order. The Mexican race is not on trial here. Sustained."

Jackson and several other jurors scowled. I said, "No further questions."

"Mr. Dale?" the judge said, "Any rebuttal?"

Mr. Dale glared at me. I glared back. He said, "No questions, your honor."

The judge said, "Mrs. Downing, thank you for coming here today. You may step down from the witness stand, and you are excused if you wish to leave."

She nodded to the judge as she rose to her feet. Her eyes went to Miguel Cordero in the prisoner's dock. "I hope ..."

Before she could complete the thought, Mr. Dale jumped up as if to interrupt her. She left the sentence uncompleted, and followed the bailiff through the courtroom to the back door.

*   *   *

The funeral director, Margaret, comes to my pew. She whispers, "Mr. Bartlett, we need to close your wife's casket now, and you mentioned you would like one more moment with her. Would you come with me?"

I follow her out to the vestibule, passing the faces row by row, surprised at the number who've come. A man catches my eye and nods, and I don't place him until after I pass—one of the young airmen who used to come for dinner during the war, a dozen years ago. Another, a cowboy from the stable where Eva kept her horses for twenty-five or thirty years. Near the back, a woman in a pillbox hat smiles sympathetically. Beside her are two girls about the ages of my grandchildren. She might be one of the girls Roy dated in high school, grown up now and more appreciative of the kind of mother Eva was.

In the vestibule, Roy still stands beside the casket, dignified and looking tired. I tell him we're about to close up the casket, if he wants to say goodbye. He kisses his mother on the cheek, touches her stiff hand one final moment, and then steps back for me. I hesitate long enough for Margaret to realize I'm waiting for them to leave. She touches Roy's shoulder and says to me, "We'll give you a moment."

After they go through the door, I take out the letter opener wrapped in the handkerchief. I bend close to kiss Eva's cheek, and realize that, up close, her cheeks really are the wrong color, though only slightly off. Gabby was right. Gabby who knew her so well. And suddenly, I'm unable to do what I had planned—to stow the letter opener in the casket so it would be buried with Eva. For reasons of her own, she had hidden it in the music box instead of disposing of it. She kept it near. For most of our years she kept the music box on a shelf in the bedroom closet, but for a long while it sat on a bedroom bookshelf. She even kept it on her dressing table. How many nights and mornings, I wondered, had she sat brushing her hair, contemplating the dark secret hidden inside the pretty jewelry box on the table before her.

This morning, as I dressed for the funeral, it occurred to me that, if she so wanted it nearby, perhaps I should send it away with her in the casket. But now, reminded by the makeup of how much she and Gabby meant to each other, and how much they have both meant to me, I realize that burying this thing with her would, in my mind, separate us forever by leaving all the blame with her. I know she was not, alone, to blame.

I return the handkerchief with its contents to my coat pocket and hold her cool, rigid hand until Margaret returns for me. I stand back while she closes the lid, watching Eva's face until the last moment. I have never seen her look so peaceful.

I got the idea for my closing argument listening to Mr. Dale's closing. His hands grasped his lapels as he paced slowly back and forth before the jury, his eyes on their faces as he spoke, and when he needed to emphasize a point, he stopped in mid-step, hesitated, and made his point before resuming his slow pacing. He told them the story of the night Stephen Downing died.

The evidence clearly showed, he said, that Stephen had gone to the Santa Rita Hotel that night to speak with his business partner, Miguel Cordero. Miguel Cordero—that man sitting right there in the prisoner's dock. And at the hotel, an argument ensued between the two men. No one could be sure what the argument was about, but the evidence was clear that they had argued. Not long after that argument, Stephen Downing was dead, having been stabbed to death by a knife similar to the very knife found in Miguel Cordero's hotel room. He held up the wrapped knife for emphasis. "In fact," he said, "the evidence showed that this very knife must have been the instrument of death."

It was all too much coincidence, Mr. Dale said, to be a coincidence at all. Miguel Cordero had a motive for the killing, as seen in the fact of the argument itself. He therefore must have had plenty of time to think the act through before he committed it. Therefore, the killing was premeditated. Miguel Cordero had murdered his business partner, Stephen Downing.

Mr. Dale finally centered himself before the jury and let his hands fall to his sides. "Members of the jury, justice for Stephen Downing and for the Territory of Arizona demands that you return a verdict of guilty of murder in the first degree." He paused for effect, and then turned back to his table.

The judge said, "Very well. Mr. Bartlett. Your closing?"

I had scribbled a final note to myself while Mr. Dale was speaking. I fixed my eyes on the note as I stood up, focusing not on the butterflies in my stomach but on what I would say. I walked over to the clerk's table and picked up the cloth-wrapped knife. I pulled back a corner of the cloth for a quick peek to make sure I had my facts straight. I did. I walked back to the center of the courtroom, exactly where Mr. Dale had concluded his argument. I looked straight into Jackson's eyes, because he was the man I had to convince. If I could get through to him, he would convince the rest. His shoulders stiffened visibly under my gaze. I had his attention.

I held up the little package as if I were showing it only to him, pulling the knife from its wrapping and holding it there, point upward.

"This," I said, "is what is wrong with the prosecutor's case. This knife. This knife that probably has the right dimensions to match whatever knife it was that stabbed Stephen Downing. This knife may very well be the right size. It certainly was in the hands of Miguel Cordero, because it was his own knife."

I turned to look at Miguel. "This knife proves that Miguel did not kill his partner, Mr. Downing. How can we know?"

I held the knife a little higher and pointed to the tip of the blade. "Do you see how sharp this knife is, at its point?"

I paused, remembering how Mr. Dale had used his pauses to emphasize what he was saying. "You heard the doctor's testimony. He testified that he found a tiny chip of metal stuck in the bones of Stephen Downing's neck, in the vertebrae. In other words, members of the jury ..." I turned to find Jackson's eyes again. "In other words, the knife that killed Stephen Downing was broken at the tip of the blade. A small, perhaps almost imperceptible break. That knife, if it is ever found, will be missing a tiny little chip, the chip that Doc Hinkley found in Stephen Downing's neck. We can't know exactly how much of a chip, because the good doctor disposed of the evidence. But he was very clear. It was a chip from the knife that killed him."

I paused. "This knife," I said, as slowly as I'd heard Mr. Dale speak, "is whole. There is no chip in the blade." I held Jackson's gaze until he looked away.

I lowered the knife slowly to my side. I nodded to Jackson, ever so slightly when he looked back at me, but he did not respond. I said, "The prosecutor's entire case rests on the unbroken tip of this knife. His case is missing an explanation for how this knife could have suddenly healed itself of being broken."

I took the knife back to the clerk's table and I turned back to the jury.

"The hotel," I said. "The Santa Rita Hotel. Tucson's largest. Two hundred rooms, with a telephone in every room. Possibly a hundred hotel guests, perhaps even more, that night. We don't know. We didn't hear anything about what all those other people were doing. It was a Friday night, a night when there would probably be a number of men out and about on the streets. We didn't hear any evidence about what any of them were doing. We heard testimony from Billsley, Mr. Billsley, from the hotel, that he heard every word of the argument between the two men, but he couldn't remember much if anything of what they actually said."

I turned again to Jackson. "Which proves he heard nothing. He heard some voice tones that sounded angry, or upset, and he interpreted what he heard to be an argument. The conversation could have been about anything at all. What time they were supposed to meet the next day. Whether Stephen would be available. Whether one of them had done something he wasn't supposed to do. Whether one of them had *not* done something he was supposed to do, leaving something undone that the other one ..."

I stopped. "I could go on, of course. We could all speculate, all day. The point is that we don't know what the conversation was about, we don't even know whether it was an argument at all, and we can't possibly determine from Billsley's testimony whether anything happened between the two men that would have led to one of them being killed. Remember, these were men who had been in a fairly long business relationship. They had spent time together riding and hiking through the mountains, far from anyone else. If one of them wanted to kill the other, wouldn't it have made sense to do it out in the middle of nowhere, where the evidence could be disposed of? Wouldn't that make more sense than doing it right in the middle of town, on a busy Friday night, when anyone could have witnessed it?

"Another thing. You heard the testimony about all the blood around Stephen Downing's head, and how it had soaked into the street. If there was so much blood, why was no bloody clothing found in the defendant's hotel room? Surely, whoever did the stabbing had blood splashed on him. Yet nothing like bloody clothing was found in Miguel Cordero's room. Just some boots that did not match the footprints in the sand in the street."

I paused again. I turned back to the clerk's table and retrieved the wrapped knife once again. I took it out from its covering and held it up. "No broken tip," I said. "Therefore, no proof, either from this knife or from anything else Mr. Dale presented to you. You must find Miguel Cordero not guilty of the crime with which he is charged. He is not guilty."

I held the knife up for another two seconds, trying to catch Jackson's eye, but he was looking at the floor. Hyram gazed at the jury as I resumed my seat, giving me no sign at all of how he thought I'd done.

The judge said, "Any rebuttal, Mr. Dale?"

Mr. Dale was still scribbling at his table. "Yes, Judge." He continued to write for another moment, and then stood up quickly, holding his notes as he took his place in the center of the courtroom. Gone were his dramatic pauses and measured pacing. He spoke quickly, referring often to his notes.

"The defense attorney," he said, "is wrong when he says that the Territory's case rests on the tip of the knife found in Miguel Cordero's room. He is wrong when he says there was no evidence of an argument. He is wrong when he says we needed to produce evidence of what everybody else in the Santa Rita Hotel was doing the night Stephen Downing died. He is wrong."

He glanced at his notes. "In fact, our case rests on the whole picture of the situation. Stephen Downing's widow testified that her husband had a temper, and that he had been known to raise his voice when he was angry. Mr. Billsley testified that he heard the deceased and the defendant have just such a loud argument in the hotel. Mr. Billsley may not have heard every word that was said, but he did hear mention of a report. It is clear from what he heard that the two men were arguing about something connected with their business dealings, something serious. Mr. Montano testified that he found Stephen Downing's body early in the morning, while it was still dark outside and while he was on his way to work. The fact that no other witnesses have come forth about seeing a fight in the night is a good indicator that the killing took place in the wee hours of the morning when everyone else had gone to bed. Sheriff Pacheco testified that Miguel Cordero, the man accused, was present in his hotel room on the morning after the killing, so it is clear that he was nearby at the time. He wasn't out of town. He wasn't twenty miles away, at home at his father's ranch. He was within a few yards of where the murder took place. And he had a motive to kill Stephen Downing, which was evidenced by the argument between himself and the deceased."

Mr. Dale took another quick look at his notes. He fetched the knife in its wrapping and held it up to the jury in the same way I had. "This may have been the murder weapon. It certainly has the right dimensions. If you recall the testimony from Doc Hinkley, he said he believed the murder weapon had struck the spine because he found a small piece of metal lodged there. But if you think about it, we don't really know how that tiny speck of metal became lodged in the bones of Mr. Downing's neck. Perhaps he had a childhood accident. We don't know."

I jumped to my feet. "Your honor, I have to object to that. It isn't what the doctor said. He said ..."

"Overruled," the judge said over my raised voice. "This is argument, Mr. Bartlett, not new evidence. The jury will make its own determination of what the doctor said, from their own individual memories. Sit down."

I looked over at Jackson, whose eyes were on the prosecutor. I sat down.

Mr. Dale went on, holding up the knife again. "In fact, perhaps this wasn't the murder weapon, after all. The defense attorney himself has actually given you a good argument for why that fact, all by itself, would prove premeditation by the defendant. The defense attorney indicated his belief that a different knife might have been used, and he also pointed out that no bloody clothing was found in the defendant's hotel room. He also raised the question of whether the defendant would have been smarter to commit the murder out in the mountains somewhere, where the body could be disposed of.

"These arguments, taken all together, indicate how clever the defendant was, and how he must have planned, executed, and tried to get away with killing Stephen Downing. There was no bloody clothing, because he must have disposed of it in a way that no one has discovered. He had all night, after all. And in the same way, if he did not do the killing with this very knife, then he disposed of the true murder weapon along with his bloody clothing.

"No matter how you look at it, gentlemen of the jury, Miguel Cordero has been proven to be a murderer, and perhaps a very clever one at that. He deserves your verdict of guilty. You must do your duty."

He paused to look at his notes. Then he raised his eyes and said, "Thank you."

As he sat down, the judge began to speak. He explained what murder in the first degree meant, and the difference between that and murder in the second degree. "It has to do with *mens rea*," he said. "The guilty mind. A first degree murder involves malice aforethought, which is the intention, formed before an act, to seriously harm or kill another person. A second degree murder could be a crime of passion, something done in a moment of anger, for example. You must decide if Mr. Dale has proven beyond a reasonable doubt that this defendant, Mr. Miguel Cordero, caused the death of Stephen Downing, and if he did cause the death, whether he did it with malice aforethought or not."

The judge went on to explain that, in deciding the case, the jury could not consider the penalty to be imposed. Their job, he said, was simply to decide what evidence had been proven, and from that to find whether the defendant was guilty or not guilty. Then he instructed the bailiff to take the jury into the deliberation room to begin considering the evidence.

The jurors stood up stiffly. They had been sitting for hours. None of them looked toward me or the prosecutor, but several glanced at Miguel as they filed out. He sat stoically in his seat, chained to the metal loop in the floor, his chin high, eyes on his family seated in the front row of the gallery. He did not look at me, and I was glad. I could not have held his look.

After the jury had shuffled out, the judge said, "That will be it until we have a verdict. I will send the bailiff to inform counsel when that happens."

We all rose as the judge made his exit. Mr. Dale gathered up his papers and headed for the door without a word to me. The

Cordero family stood expectantly, seeming to be waiting for me, so I stopped to talk with them. Miguel's mother's eyes were red. His father's face was drawn and stern, but he otherwise betrayed no outward emotion. The brothers were as stoic as their father. Gabby's lips trembled, and her cheeks were wet. All of their eyes were on Miguel as he was led from the courtroom.

Don Antonio spoke first. "What do you think, *Licensiado*? Do you think he will be guilty, or not guilty?"

"I don't know," I said, looking from face to face. "I like to think I found some major weaknesses in the prosecutor's case. I hope the jury takes those weaknesses very seriously. If they do ..." I shrugged. "Perhaps they will acquit him."

Gabby said, "And if they don't?"

It was the question I was afraid of. "Then we'll have to see. It's possible they will decide that the case was proven about the killing, but not proven about the malice aforethought. If that happened he would be convicted of second degree murder. He would get a long prison term, I think it's ten years, but then he can come home. But right now, I'm hoping for an acquittal."

Eva's sealed casket is centered before the altar as gray-haired Father Anselmo makes the sign of the cross and begins, "*Introibo ad altare Dei.*" *I will go to the altar of God.* Beside him, an overly solemn, teenage altar boy intones, "*Ad Deum qui laetificat juventutem meam.*" *To God who gives joy to my youth.* In the old days I would have chuckled at a sad-faced, pimply boy ritually attesting to the joy given him by God. Not today. Today is Eva's day. She was never amused by my acerbic insights about Catholic ritual, or my occasional dinnertime imitations of the facial expressions—bored, or pompous, or sanctimonious—of the various priests who passed through our parish. When Roy was growing up, she forbade any sharing at all of my observations at the dinner table.

Which was fine, I suppose. She knew my conversion to Catholicism never really took. I tried, but could never generate in myself an earnest faith like hers. I studied the liturgy, I studied church history, I studied Latin and over the decades I even memorized the entire mass. I still did not get it. Only now, finally understanding what really happened to Stephen, how it all fit together, do I understand her intensity during mass as she lip-synced the priest's words, "*Mea culpa, mea culpa, mea maxima culpa.*" *Through my fault, through my fault, through my most grievous fault.* At each *mea culpa*, the old priest's fist taps his chest ceremonially. My own hand rises almost involuntarily to my chest. My own *mea culpa*, which I always refused to face. My fingers press through the fabric of my coat against the hard dagger in my breast pocket.

The jury deliberated not much more than a half-hour, which I spent fidgeting at the defense table, agonizing over whether I had handled the trial the right way, afraid to turn around and face Miguel's family. Finally, the bailiff came and announced there was a verdict. The clerks and the stenographer entered. Miguel was brought in and his chain was locked to the loop in the prisoner's dock. The prosecutor arrived from somewhere and took his seat. He folded his hands on the table and we nodded to each other. Hyram had left and had not yet returned. I hid my trembling hands under the table. My whole body suddenly felt as if I might shake to pieces.

The bailiff finally intoned, "All rise!" The judge entered briskly, took his seat and called the case as the stenographer scribbled away.

247

The jury filed in. Two or three, as I recall, glanced at Miguel, but I couldn't tell anything from their manner about what they had decided. I have long ago quit trying to read anything into the mannerisms of jurors entering the courtroom with a verdict. The friendliest glance my way can precede a guilty verdict. A scowl could mean anything. Or nothing. Jackson kept his eyes on the judge.

Once they were seated, the judge said, "Members of the jury, I understand you have reached a verdict."

Jackson stood up, and my heart went cold to realize he had been chosen foreman. "We have, Judge," he said. He held up a piece of paper.

The bailiff walked ceremoniously to Jackson, took the paper from his hand, carried it to the judge. The judge glanced at it and then handed it back. The bailiff carried it back and handed to Jackson.

The judge said, "The defendant will stand."

As Miguel rose to his feet, I rose as well and, without being asked or directed, walked over to stand beside him at the prisoner's dock. His eyes were a mix of defiance and fear. Across the courtroom, the Cordero family sat rigidly upright. Eva held her kerchief to her mouth, her eyes on the floor. Mr. Dale had his elbows on his table, his fingers playing with a pen.

The judge said, "The jury foreman will read the verdict."

Jackson held up his paper. "We the jury, upon our oaths, do find the defendant, Miguel Cordero, guilty of the crime of murder in the second degree."

A cry from Eva pierced the courtroom. She jumped up and ran for the exit, followed after a moment by Josue. Gabby, eyes wide with horror, stared at Miguel. My heart pounded. Miguel sank back into his seat, mumbling, "No, no. No."

Mr. Dale turned to watch as Eva ran out, then looked back at the judge with something like a smirk on his face. I rested a hand on Miguel's shoulder as the judge thanked the jury for following its duty, and excused them. They stood and at Fred's direction shuffled in a line out the back door. Miguel's mother bent forward in her seat, sobbing quietly. Don Antonio stared at the judge.

The bailiff closed the door behind the jurors and returned to his seat, as the judge said, "Does either counsel wish to put anything on the record? Good. I'll set sentencing for one week from today. Ten o'clock. The defendant will be held without bond until that time. We are adjourned."

The bailiff intoned one last time, "All rise," as the judge rose to exit. Only the prosecutor rose. Everyone else seemed frozen in their places as the enormity of Miguel's conviction settled into the room. Mr. Dale left. The jailer came over to collect Miguel, whose eyes had glazed over. I tried to take his hand, but he shook me off. "No," he said. "No, no, no."

I think I said, "I'll come to see you tomorrow, Miguel."

He was led from the courtroom, chains rattling, seeming unaware of his family until the last moment before the door. He stopped suddenly and looked at Gabby. "*Te quiero, mi amor*," he said quietly.

She nodded and tried to smile, her eyes wet. "I love you, too."

He waved, and then he was gone.

That night was one of the longest of my life, the voices in my head replaying the trial over and over, even during the brief snatches of sleep I did manage. I stared out my window at the street below, trapped with my thoughts for hours. Dawn came, then daylight. I dressed and went down to the lobby. While I stood there, mired and indecisive, Eva arrived with her friend Chela. Eva's face was a rash of red blotches, her breathing coming shallow, her black dress wrinkled and creased as if she had writhed in her bed all night. Her voice was hardly audible. "I must speak with you. In private." Without waiting, she went to a corner of the lobby where there were two chairs separated by a small round table. Chela took a seat nearby, watching Eva, her eyes dark with concern.

I sat down and took Eva's hand across the table. I'd realized during the night I needed to confess my secret to her. But I hesitated, unsure how to begin, and she pulled her hand away. She said, "There is something you must know. What happened isn't what people think. I mean, what happened to Stephen. You see …"

Just at that moment, the worst happened, and fifty years would pass before she finished what she tried to tell me that morning. My own secret would remain unconfessed.

Many of the details seem like a blur now, probably because they happened in a blur. In the wild scene I recall, Josue rushes into the lobby, his eyes wide. I can feel the tight grip of his fingers on my shoulder as he blurts out in Spanish what has happened. I see my own hands reaching for Eva as she collapses in slow motion from her chair onto the tile floor. I hear Josue's voice telling me again and again, "He is died. *Está muerto.* He is died."

Later that morning, I learned that, after the verdict, Miguel had been put into the small isolation cell in the jail overnight, to make sure he calmed down. Early the next morning, as a new guard came on duty, he was moved into one of the main cells with the other inmates. Shortly afterward, insults flew, about Miguel killing a white man. A fight ensued. It was said that Miguel attacked the inmate named Jericho, but I have always had my doubts. Several other inmates jumped in, all of them white. Miguel's head was smashed into the bars, again and again. No one helped him. He died face down in a pool of his own blood.

It looked, declared Mr. Dale, like self-defense. After all, Miguel had just been convicted of murder. No one was prosecuted.

"*Agnus Dei, qui tollis peccata mundi, dona nobis pacem.*" I am crying now, as the priest entreats the Lamb of God to grant us peace. In the corner of my eye I see Carol turning toward me, holding out a white handkerchief, and I feel Gabby's hand on my shoulder. I dry my cheeks with the handkerchief. "*Sed tantum dic verbo, et sanabitur anima mea.*" *But say the word and my soul will be healed.*

Eva was bedridden at Chela's home for weeks after Miguel was killed. I could not bring myself to attend the funeral mass, but they said it was well attended. Afterwards, in a long caravan of wagons and buggies, Miguel was transported home to his family ranch for burial. The Mexican community was outraged. White citizens were edgy for a while and cautious if they went to the south side at night. Eventually, life returned to normal, as it always does even after such a tragedy.

I stopped by at Chela's every day to see how Eva was doing. I would sit in a chair by her bed with Chela hovering nearby as chaperone. I held Eva's hand and talked to her about inane things like the weather, which was getting cooler, and about how I was looking for a place to set up a law office, which wasn't really true. I didn't want to tell her I was thinking of leaving town and going somewhere else to start my life over. Hyram had been right. I was foolish. Miguel was dead. There was no way to take it all back.

At one point, during those weeks, I dug out Mr. Norman's letter of introduction to Epes Randolph and left it open on the table in my hotel room. Each afternoon, I read it over and considered the options it offered. Mr. Randolph could open doors. At that time he was somehow involved with a flood control project on the Colorado River, between California and the Arizona Territory. He had lung problems, like so many other people who came west to the desert in those years, and everyone knew he would return to Tucson because of the dry air. Perhaps he would need an assistant.

He seemed to be well known in both Arizona and California. Perhaps he could introduce me to influential people in California who could help me get my start.

In the end, I put the letter away. My old life was behind me. I came to realize, visiting Eva day after day, that I did not want to leave her behind. As she improved, our afternoon times together grew longer. She was the first thing on my mind when I awoke each morning. The image of her wan smile or the memory of her soft voice led me off into sleep at night.

The mild desert winter came on. She and I began to take walks together to the stables to visit Molly, who was growing shaggy with her new winter coat. Her ears pricked forward as soon as she heard Eva's voice. Eva, in a wool sweater, would spend a half-hour grooming her, and then give her a little hay. One day, on our walk, Eva took my arm and held it tightly all the way back to Chela's house, her eyes on the ground. By the time we arrived, I knew I could not leave Eva.

A few days later, I rented a buggy and driving horse and arrived with the announcement that we were going off on a picnic. The day before, with bilingual hand signals, Chela and I had made a secret arrangement for her to prepare a basket of tortillas, salted carne asada, and vegetables. When I showed up, Eva brightened at the prospect of a picnic, and was undaunted when she saw that the gig had only enough seating for two riders—we would have no chaperone. I patted Chela's hand gratefully, grabbed the basket and a couple of blankets against the winter chill and off we went, just Eva and me.

The trail we followed meandered along the bank of the Santa Cruz Wash, and we found a nice spot in a grove of cottonwood trees. I helped her down and spread a blanket. She untied the chin ribbon of her wide-brimmed hat, and unpinned her hair to let it fall around her shoulders.

Chela had wrapped the food in a heavy cloth to keep it warm. We ate without much conversation, and the silence felt comfortable. I remember the way the breeze brushed her hair across her forehead. She caught me watching. The dark circles under her eyes gave her smile a haunted look.

Finally, leaning back on her hands and looking off toward the mountains, she said, "You have been sweet to me, Owen. Maybe one of these days I can find a way to thank you. This has been such a terrible time."

I said, "Terrible doesn't begin to describe it. I can't imagine how you've managed."

We were quiet again, as the sun moved down toward the horizon. She said, "I cried every night, after Stephen died. And every morning I pulled myself together to face the day. I told myself if I could only hold myself together until after Miguel's trial, everything would be better. They would let him go. I was sure of it. Because I know he was innocent. I never imagined what would happen. I don't think I'll ever get over it."

I took her hand. "Perhaps you should move away from here, someplace where you won't have reminders everywhere you look."

"No. I am tied to this place forever now. Forever. And you? You've only just arrived, practically. You could go anywhere. You have a bright future."

"To be honest, I don't know what to do next. I've thought about giving up law and doing something else."

Unexpectedly, she put her hand on my wrist. I could feel the warmth moving through her fingers into my skin. She said, "Don't throw away all your studying and preparation. What happened to Miguel was not your fault. Believe me. Besides, you have a talent. When you were speaking in that courtroom, people listened. I was watching them. Maybe you could go into politics. There is talk about making Arizona a state. Think of it. And you could play a part."

Politics and statehood were the furthest things from my mind. I leaned forward and kissed her. It was a long kiss, and her lips were softer than I expected. She let the kiss happen. She did not pull away.

I leaned back a little, looking into her eyes. "I want to be with you."

She looked away and smiled the barest of smiles. "You don't know what you are saying."

"I do. I've thought about you since the moment I first saw you. I can help you get through this. I would take care of you."

"I know you would, Owen. That's not it. Too much has happened, too fast."

"Marry me. I will make you a happy woman."

Her smile widened. "That's a tall order."

"Even if it takes years, I can do it. Don't say no. Think about it. Wouldn't it be nice to have a safe place? Someone to take care of you while you heal?"

It was a quiet ride back to town, with only the crunching of horse hooves and the buggy wheels on hard ground. She sat close, her shoulder pressed against mine. In front of Chela's house on Meyer Street, I helped her down. Standing with me beside the buggy, she gripped my hand tightly and said, "Don't do anything foolish."

"Such as what?"

"Don't do anything foolish here on the street, with what I'm about to say."

I looked up and down the street. "All right. What?"

"Tomorrow we can pay a visit to Father Arnold. I need to know how serious you are."

"Serious about what?"

"About getting married."

I jumped a foot in the air, but she held my hand tightly. Her eyes were smiling. "Don't. Now, good night. Come for me at ten, tomorrow."

We walked to the door, hands clasped tightly together. I said, "May I kiss you on the cheek, at least, here in front of the neighbors?"

Smiling, she shook her head. "We aren't engaged yet, sir."

We were married by Father Arnold on the first day of spring, 1906, five months after the terrible events of October. It was a Wednesday. Two weeks before, at Eva's insistence, I had begun instruction with Father Arnold, who knew immediately, by my questions and objections, that my conversion to Catholicism was going to take more than the usual year or so of instruction. Having been raised essentially in a religious vacuum, I found certain of the Church's eternal truths were larger than I could swallow whole, starting with something as basic as the concept of original sin. Why, I kept asking, would a loving God punish children for the sins of their parents? It made no sense to me. He would sigh and begin anew. God showed his love for us by sending his only begotten son as a sacrifice, in remission of our sins. But what sins, I wanted to know. And so it went on. He was very patient with me.

So was Eva, fortunately. After one particularly difficult session with Father Arnold, she and I went for a walk to the stables, and I assured her that I was determined to work through it all, and I passed on Father Arnold's estimate that my conversion would take much longer than the average. To my surprise, she told me the next day that she wanted to go ahead with the wedding, rather than wait. Looking back and knowing now what she told me on her deathbed, I think she may have been secretly desperate for midnight company to protect her from terrible dream visits by the spirits of Stephen and Miguel. I recall, in our earliest years, how she would awaken me in the wee hours, her face drenched in tears, and I would hold her until she finally found sleep. She never explained the nightmares.

Father Arnold knew of no canonical reason for a delay, as long as I continued my instruction and agreed to raise our children as Catholics. At our wedding, Eva wore a pale yellow dress that fell narrowly to her ankles. I wore a business suit. Chela served as maid of honor, and young Josue was my best man. I had no other men friends at the time, and he was so eager. We invited no one else, because Eva wanted the wedding to be private. Chela and a few of her friends held a small reception in Chela's garden, where Eva and I had first met. Afterwards, Josue delivered us in a borrowed buggy to the train station, where our baggage was already being loaded onto an overnighter to Los Angeles. We rode to Santa Monica, at the end of the Southern Pacific line. We spent our wedding night in a sleeper compartment, our window curtain open to the moonlight and the vivid desert stars. We made our first love in the gentle rocking motion of the train. And as we drifted off into sleep, she whispered, "I hope I can be a good wife to you. I'll try very hard." Exhausted in my wedding bliss, I could only kiss her in response.

We spent a week walking hand in hand along the Pacific surf, wandering through the Santa Monica shops, and wrapped tightly around each other in our little hotel room. Upon our return, Josue met us at the train in the same borrowed buggy. I found out later that, unsure when we would return, he had met every eastbound train from California for two days to make sure he didn't miss us. He delivered us to the adobe house I had purchased shortly before the wedding, on 17th Street a couple of blocks from the old armory. He helped me port the luggage to the door. He bowed a stiff bow, shook my hand and then Eva's hand. In Spanish he wished us all the happiness in the world. He bounded back into the buggy and was gone.

I opened the door, swept Eva into my arms, and as a proper young husband should, I carried her into her new home. Before the wedding I had installed a new bed and a sofa, but little else. While we were gone, Chela and Josue had brought in dishes and pots, several new chairs, a couple of towels and a wash basin—enough to give us a comfortable start. There wasn't much that Eva wanted from the old house. Bad memories, she said. Most of her old things, she sold off. When they were gone, she sold the house. But hidden away in her music box, she kept the letter opener wrapped in a white handkerchief monogramed with Stephen's initials. All those years.

* * *

Just after the *Agnus Dei*, the priest recites, "*Pacem relinquo vobis, pacem meam do vobis.*" Peace I leave you, peace I give you.

Despite all the prayers, all the masses, all the other sacraments, she never found her peace. She made a good life, but even though she was devoted to a religion based on redemption and forgiveness, she never felt forgiven, because she never forgave herself.

"Owen," she said to me in those last moments in the hospital, "I'm so sorry. I never meant ... like that." Scarcely getting through a sentence without gasping for air, she told me how Stephen had taken the forged assay report to Miguel, returning angry that Miguel still wouldn't listen, wouldn't even look at the report.

Stephen stormed around the house, shouting "This is OUR time! This is MY opportunity!" and she shouted back, "No! Not this way! Miguel is honest. You be honest, too."

She is quiet for a few seconds, eyes closed, chest barely rising and falling, and I hold her hand firmly. Her eyes open and she goes on. Stephen turned on her, raised his fist, furious that she was defending Miguel. He hesitated with his fist raised, and then turned for the door. Time to get even, he swore, stomping out. Time to get even!

She sat alone, waiting and waiting. As the night grew later and Stephen did not return, she went out to search for him. She wrapped her shawl around her head to keep others from recognizing her, and she took her sharp letter opener for protection in the dark streets. She spoke to Miguel at his hotel room door. He told her that yes, Stephen had come back. The two of them argued in the lobby, but nothing else happened. Stephen left. Miguel did not know where Stephen had gone.

Outside once more, she must have looked up and down the street. No Stephen. For some reason she went around to the back of the hotel. And there he was, coming toward her.

"He called me Miguel's whore. He ... called ... me ..." She shuddered against the words and shook her head no, her breath coming in rattling gasps. "I was not ... I would not ..."

There, in the ghostly silver moonlight, Stephen's fist must have gone up again, this time to be used. She stumbled backward—she said—as he came at her and the force of his swing threw him toward her as she fell. Her back hit the ground as he fell onto her, his face contorted, her arms up to deflect his falling weight—her hand still gripping the sharp letter opener tight, now pointing it purposefully, as it punctured his neck. She must have felt the warm splash of his blood. Somehow, she escaped from beneath him. Looking back, she saw him writhing on the ground, holding his neck. And she ran.

"Owen," she said, "I killed my Stephen. And ... I killed Miguel, too, because ... I was a coward. I was afraid. Oh God, I meant it ... only for that second ... but I meant him ... to die, like he meant to hurt me. Poor Miguel. I was too afraid to tell. So ... afraid. And then ... and then it was too late to tell. Poor Gabby."

She closed her eyes. "God forgive me."

Then, as I held her hand and watched, she smiled. Just barely, but she opened her eyes and smiled, her eyes off somewhere beyond where I could see. "Amen," she whispered.

Now, before her casket, the priest recites, *"Sed tantum dic verbo, et sanabitur anima mea." But say the word and my soul will be healed.* Around me, Helen and Roy, Carmen and Josue, and the grandchildren are all rising to go to communion. They shuffle in a line passing the coffin. They each touch it as they pass, or lay a hand on it. They take their places kneeling side by side at the communion rail, waiting in faith for the priest to make his way along the row to them. Eva shared their faith. Week after week and year after year, as her turn came at the communion rail the priest would hold the round white wafer above her and murmur, *"Corpus Domini nostri Jesu Christi custodiat animam tuam in vitam aeternam." May the Body of our Lord Jesus Christ preserve your soul unto everlasting life.* She would dutifully respond, "Amen," and receive the body of her Lord on her tongue. She would bow her head in a moment of prayer before rising to return to her place in the pew beside me.

Amen. So be it. Not until those final moments in her life could amen at last mean for her what it implies for us all—acceptance, which must come before forgiveness. She smiled as I held her hand. She whispered "Amen." So be it. And then she died.

"I tell you," Gabby says, "I should have bought the convertible. This would be a perfect day for it. The salesman said he could tell I was a convertible kind of girl. But I wouldn't listen. I should have listened."

We are on the Catalina highway in her Chevy Bel Air, headed up to Mt. Lemmon for a picnic. The V-8 engine purrs without difficulty as the car begins the climb into the foothills. She telephoned me yesterday and told me to find a sweater, because I needed to get out of the house and she wasn't taking no for an answer. This is my first time up this highway. It has been open for five years, after being built by prison labor over some fifteen years. A few of those hardworking prisoners were my former clients. I ran into one of them last year, on the sidewalk downtown near the new courthouse. Bud Jackson. Bud did a five-year stretch for stealing cars. His grandfather, I happen to know, was William Harshaw Jackson, whose wife was killed in an Apache raid and who later served as foreman on the jury that convicted Miguel Cordero. Bud told me how much he appreciated the chance to work on the highway, instead of being cooped up on a prison yard all those years. "It was hard labor, Mr. Bartlett," he said. "Awful hard. I tell you what, though, it made me what I am today. It made me a man. I'm not like that kid I was at nineteen. I got a family, and I got my shoe repair shop. I'm doing good, Mr. Bartlett." I shook his hand and said I was proud of him, as I have told other former clients who, bumping into me somewhere, often simply wanted me to know they're doing better and they're not like that anymore. Neither am I, though I have never felt the urge to justify myself to anyone. Perhaps I'm like this from having grown up carrying a secret, my mother's heavy secret, everywhere I went. And unlike my clients, I've never been caught in the crushing jaws of the justice system.

Gabby holds her hand out her window in the wind stream. "It feels so good. Put your hand out. See what I mean?"

I give it a try but the November air is too chilly. I crank my window back up. "I'm a warm weather desert rat, Gabby. The mountain air smells good, though."

"Yes." Gabby closes up her own window and the car is abruptly quiet. We cruise past cliffs and outcroppings, moving up into the country of manzanita and juniper. Greener, less deserty. I regret that Eva and I never made it up here. I've heard there are pines and firs at the top, and even aspens. Two or three years ago I tried to talk her into the drive, but she pointed out how old I was, and said a drive like this would be dangerous with such an old man negotiating these curves and switchbacks. What if I had a heart attack? The car would go right over the edge and crash down the mountain, with us in it. I didn't press the idea, but I'm sorry I never saw all this beautiful ruggedness until now—so different from the desert we lived in only a few miles below for so many years.

Gabby says, "How are you, Owen? How are you doing?"

"Oh, I'm getting along. I'll be all right. The kids take good care of me. Helen comes every day. Carmen had me over for dinner, and I played nine holes of golf with Josue on Monday. I'm doing all right. It's already been two weeks since the funeral. Time flies."

I don't mention the process of going through Eva's things, sorting them, deciding what to do with them. I've been doing it by myself, despite Helen's offers of help. The quiet time is good and I can feel my sadness passing on through me, deep and full of memories, like a slow, sorrowful river toward some distant ocean. Almost every object I touch in the house is a memento of something, mostly of the mundane and the daily routine. The blue and white gingham apron Eva kept handy on a hook beside the fridge. The long, thin screwdriver on a shelf outside the kitchen door, which I sometimes used to adjust the carburetor on her car—that carburetor never seemed to hold an adjustment. The six-inch statue of the Virgin of Guadalupe that I won in a church raffle in the early years of our marriage. For a while it rested atop a bookshelf, then it was on a window sill, then here and there on various shelves in the bedroom, then other places. Over the decades it must have rested on every flat surface in the house that was waist high or higher. It was always in view, somewhere. Or perhaps, as I think about it, we were always within its view, and within its care. That's what Eva would have said.

I handle all these mementos, move them to the coffee table in the living room for packing, then reconsider and put them back where Eva last saw them. I'm not ready for our house to become something else, something besides our house together. I'm not yet ready to start going through her clothes. I'll probably have to enlist Helen's help, but not yet. The blue and tan jewelry box remains on the coffee table in the living room.

Ever since the funeral I have carried the letter opener in my pocket. It was some sort of fetish for Eva, and, because I now carry the secret—her secret—of what it means, it is a fetish for me as well. Her story that last night in the hospital has been like a tint washing back over time, changing the color and the meaning of so many things.

Like the times, sometimes weeks, when she withdrew inside herself and I thought she was still merely grieving Stephen's death. Like the perplexing way she spoke of what she owed Gabby, and the baffling sense Gabby and I both had that Eva wanted somehow to share me—her husband—with Gabby. It is all clearer now, but still somehow baffling. The notion of sharing me with Miguel's widow must have offered Eva some bit of release from the guilt she bore over Miguel's death. Murder is a heavy burden for a guilty heart to bear, but even worse must be the crushing weight of knowing that one's own cowardice contributed to the death of an innocent man.

And me—why have I never felt guilty? Perhaps because I didn't know until nearly the end of Miguel's trial that I may have killed Stephen myself. Perhaps because I've never known whether he would have died anyway. I can't recall Doc Hinkley's exact words, but he testified that although Stephen bled to death, he might have been saved by keeping pressure on the wound until he got medical help. I stopped Stephen, there in the street, and he died because I stopped him.

I thought he was just a drunk. I took a wrong turn on the way from the train and came upon the Santa Rita Hotel from behind instead of the front. Rounding the corner of a building, I saw him, on one knee, one hand at his neck and the other holding to the ground, steadying himself as he straightened and rose to his feet. Eva must have run away only moments before. Seeing me, he rushed at me, one hand still at his neck and his free hand grabbing for my coat. I dodged away, irritated, and impatient. I was so tired and it was the middle of the night. He turned, staggering. In the moonlight I could not see the blood that must have coated the hand he held to his neck. All I saw, or all I thought I saw, was an aggressive drunk rushing me as if to fight. As he came on, I brought up my fist, and stepped forward into the blow, all those boyhood bare-knuckle fights powering my fist to a spot just beside his mouth, knocking his head backward and sweeping his feet from under him. He landed on his back and lay still, arms outstretched. I glanced around to see if he had any drunken friends I should worry about. We were alone. I straightened my coat and left him there. To die, as it turned out.

After I checked into my hotel room and removed my coat, I looked out the window. He lay there, unmoving in the moonlight. I was sure he would sleep himself into a bad hangover and eventually be fine, except perhaps for a mysterious bruise beside his mouth. Short minutes later I was deep asleep on the bed, still fully dressed, exhausted from my long train ride. As the days went by and as I got more information, I wondered about the connection between that drunk and the stabbing of Stephen Downing. I decided the drunk must have awakened and staggered away. The stabbing, I decided, must have occurred later, after my encounter with the drunk, while I slept. Not until the trial, not until Doc

Hinkley's testimony about holding a hand over the wound and trying to get medical help, did I realize what must have happened. The drunk must have been Stephen, rushing at me and grabbing for me because he wanted help. He was trying to save his own life. I stopped him, and he died.

Gabby glances over at me in the car. "I know something about what you are feeling. I lost my Miguel. Of course, I was twenty-two and it was different, but I think not so very different from what you are going through. I used to wish Miguel and I had children, but God did not see fit to give them to us, even though we tried very hard to change His mind, if you know what I mean."

She gives me one of her salacious winks, and I have to smile.

"Yes," she says, "we tried very hard. God was good to give me Miguel for those three years, anyway. After I lost him, that part of my life was over. There could be no other man for me, except, you know, to scratch my itches now and then." She glances over with a little grin. "You were a good itch-scratcher. And we scratched your itches, too, no? A little. But you had your Eva. At least, *mi amor*, we both knew what love is."

I nod but don't answer. In the past Gabby would talk about what life could have been like if Miguel were still alive, and how she still missed his strength and his dignity. I never said it to her, but I did wonder sometimes, through the years, whether Miguel had stabbed Stephen, after all, leaving him there in the street. And I could never tell her about my encounter with Stephen behind the hotel. What good would it do?

For years after the trial, I would sometimes awaken in a sweat from dreams about being back in the trial, or from dreams about Miguel. Sometimes I would see Stephen's desperate face, mouth open in a soundless cry for help, coming at me. I would sit awake in the darkness, remembering the courtroom faces, the sounds, even the smells from that moment when I realized what I had done. I would parse my legal culpability—self-defense, lack of intent, the incident unreported because I did not know the damage I'd caused. I couldn't be guilty of anything. Next to me lay Eva, startled awake sometimes in the middle of her own hell, of which I knew nothing. How could I not have known? It seems so obvious now, looking back, after her last words. Why did I never suspect her? Perhaps because it all happened so fast. Not even two weeks had passed between my arrival in Tucson and Miguel's brutal death after his conviction. Eva collapsed in my arms, and after that, my concern was for her well-being. Culpability, anyone's, was no longer my concern. But what a pair we were as we made our long life together, neither suspecting that the other held the secret second half of the puzzle we did not know we shared.

Those terrible events faded eventually into the haze of time, as newer, closer details passed through our days. For me things must have been much easier than for Eva. I never felt a real sense of guilt, not consciously anyway, though my dreams might have told me otherwise. I could remind myself that I simply hadn't known of Stephen's mortal danger. I thought him to be no more than a drunk who wanted to fight, and I knew how to deal with guys who wanted to fight. Eva, on the other hand, meant to kill Stephen. She meant it only for a moment, only in an instant flash of anger, but in that deadly moment she happened to be deliberately pointing a sharp instrument at his neck so that he would fall on it. Everything changed in that moment, for her, for me, for Gabby.

The old dreams have returned since Eva died. Only a couple of nights, but they still carry that old power. I awakened last night with my heart pounding. All I recall from whatever I was dreaming is that Stephen was watching me, just watching me, and behind him there was another, shadowy figure I knew to be Miguel. I got up and sat in the living room, in darkness. I could barely make out

Eva's jewelry box on the coffee table before me. My mind replays yet again that moment in the courtroom. Doc Hinkley. Pressure on the wound. Could have been saved. My mind tumbled in confusion, and in real fear. In the pit of my stomach, I suddenly understood Miguel's fear in the prisoner's dock. What had I done? What should I say? Should I say anything to the judge? To the jury? Had I actually done anything wrong? Should I be the man in the prisoner's dock, instead of Miguel? I recall how the courtroom air almost turned to fog for an instant, and how much I wanted to run. Many times since, talking to my clients caught in the nets of the criminal justice system and caught in their fear of what would happen to them, my own fear has come back to me, secretly. The big desk between us always sheltered me, reminding both of us that I was the lawyer—the defender, not the defendant. I understood their fear in a way other attorneys did not seem to. I would have grasped Eva's fear, as well, had she shared her secret with me. But she never did.

Had I been a better man, or more experienced attorney, I'd have risen to my feet in Miguel's trial the moment I understood my role in the crime that had taken place. But I wasn't, and I hesitated, and the prosecutor called Mrs. Downing as his next witness, and I decided to think things over later, and the moment passed. I thought I would have more time.

Except that, by morning, time had run out and there would never be another moment. Just when Eva came to me in the lobby and began to confess, and just as I was about to confess to her, Josue rushed in with the news. Miguel was dead. He is died! He is died! The time to do the right thing was gone.

I remember that my immediate feeling was relief. Relief that there was nothing else I could do. Relief that, with Miguel dead, there was no longer a reason to reveal my secret. Relief that my culpability no longer mattered and I would not be swallowed up by a legal system I barely understood. I was catching Eva as she collapsed. I was carrying her to the wagon that brought her home. I was riding with her, mystified at her immense grief about the death of Miguel. I was holding her hand.

As the Chevy Bel Air passes smoothly up the steepening mountain road, I recall the first moment I saw Eva through my hotel window. I think about her relaxed easiness when she played with the grandchildren. I remember her erect attentiveness as she rode her horses, and how deathly fragile she was, her last days in the hospital. What strength she must have had to carry that burden of guilt all those years. I touch the hard letter opener hidden in my jacket pocket. The secret is mine now. I feel a small inkling of why she did not want to share it. It is hard, and sharp, and painful.

Gabby keeps glancing over at me as the car rounds the curves and we climb higher. For all our history, she is not the person I can have this conversation with. I say, "It's too bad this highway wasn't built back in the old days. I'm sure Miguel would have enjoyed it."

"Let me tell you, my Miguel knew mountains. He was always riding his mule up over the rough country by the ranch, exploring, looking around. He loved the mountains. If he was here, he would want to get out of the car right now and start walking. Even if he'd be a very old man now. He would want to walk."

A minute later, she adds thoughtfully, "Miguel never rode in a car. There weren't any in those days. Or only a couple. Now they are everywhere, and even most of the roads are paved."

"Back in those days, we didn't even call them cars. They were automobile machines."

She laughs. "We sure have gotten old, *verdad?*"

Before long we come around a curve and happen upon a wide view of the Tucson valley. Gabby pulls off to the side and we climb out of the car for a look. Holding hands because we are old and she is in heels, we pick our way carefully across the wide, flat rocks to the edge of a cliff. Before us, lower hills undulate down toward the valley. I can make out the town in the hazy distance. Gabby's eyes are not good enough to quite see it, so I try to describe what it looks like. I tell her the view is breathtaking. "It all looks so small. We spent our lives down there, your house and my house and the stores and the streets. The town looks so small and fuzzy. As if it's almost not really there. Like a mirage."

She says, "Did you ever fly in an airplane?"

"I can't say I have. Have you?"

"Just once. Four or five years ago, I took the train to Los Angeles for a fashion meeting. Somebody dared me to fly back home instead of taking the train, so I did it. I rode in a Trans World Airlines airplane. Big propellers outside the windows. Very fancy inside, but it made me nervous with all the rumbling and vibrations. When you looked out the window, this is what it looked like. Everything tiny and far away below. Far away."

On an impulse, I pull out the silver letter opener and hold it between my hands.

"What's that?" she says. Without a word I hand it to her. She turns it over in her hands. "Why are you carrying an old letter opener?"

"I don't know. The memories, I suppose. It belonged to Eva."

She turns it over, then back. She has no clue what this thing represents in her life. For a second I'm almost sorry I brought it along, but I leave it in her hands, because she has as much connection to what it represents as I do.

She holds it out to me. "I don't know why you are carrying it all around, but you must have a reason. Probably just because it was Eva's."

I take it and feel its slight weight. "Yes. It was Eva's, but it was mine too. Sometimes things are hard to get rid of, and you have to carry them with you."

At that, she reaches over and takes the letter opener back. "No," she says. "You don't. You don't have to carry it. You can carry whatever you want in your heart, but you have to let the things go. Listen to me. I know a lot about this. Things ..." She shakes her head and I sense that she is talking about Miguel. "You have to let things go." She runs her forefinger along the letter opener. "I'll tell you what. Let's have a ceremony."

Something grabs me uncomfortably in the stomach. I don't feel ready to let things go. "What kind of a ceremony?"

She smiles. "We'll call it a moving on ceremony. Like, life is moving on. We love what we have. You have to grieve, but we love our life. We love the ones we lost, and we love the life we still have. Our ceremony is about all that. It's about life is moving on, and whether we like it or not, we have to move on with it. Are you ready, *mi amor?*"

The answer, though I can't say it aloud, is no. I can't be ready. There is too much to sort. Too much has happened. Maybe later. Not now.

She takes my hand. "You aren't ready. That's ok. It's just a little start. That's all. Let me help you. Come." She tugs at my hand and I follow as we move up nearer the edge of the cliff. In almost a literal way, my whole life is out there before me. Farther into the hazy distance, other mountains rise, and beyond them is the edge of the sky. I feel something hard in my hand and realize Gabby has put the letter opener back into my hand.

"Go ahead," she says. "Throw it. I know it has memories for you, but it's just a cheap silver letter opener. I'll buy you ten more. I have a feeling this one is not good for you."

"Why do you say that?"

"I just know."

I laugh, suddenly. She can't know that those were Eva's words when she wanted me to defend Miguel. When I asked Eva how she knew I would do a good job, she said exactly those words. "I just know." And I did a good job.

The connection comes to me. Gabby's idea, her quixotic notion of a ceremony, is exactly the right thing to do. She is watching me as if I look like I'm about to jump over the cliff.

"Don't worry," I say, still smiling. "I'm not crazy. You just reminded me of something. Here." I hand her back the letter opener. "It should be you who does it. Don't ask me to explain. You're the perfect person."

Her eyes narrow as she looks at me. "You are a strange man sometimes."

"Perhaps. But let's do it. Come on. I'll hold your hand."

She takes my hand and steps closer to the edge, her grip tightening as she steps. "Like this?"

"Maybe a little closer, so when you throw it, it goes far enough over the edge."

We inch a few baby steps nearer and she leans forward. Then, with an awkward underhand toss, she sends the letter opener up into the air and it falls beyond the edge of the cliff. After a moment we hear a clink, and then another clink.

She steps back. "I don't think it went very far."

"I think it did. Much farther than you can imagine."

We hold hands, gazing off at the valley, the town in the distance. So many memories. In my mind's eye, way off, I can once again see Eva riding her horse among the creosote, across the desert. Her black hair blows back in the breeze of the rhythmic canter, and she rides erect, one hand holding the reins and the other down at her side. They move in harmony, she and her graceful white horse, as if they are one. In my mind's eye, she glances for a moment in my direction. She is smiling. She is free.

I try to smile back. One of these days. Yes, one of these days, by and by, I will be free too.

Photo by JOHN SHASKY

Dan Goss Anderson grew up mostly in the desert southwest. After a stint in the military, he worked as a janitor, factory worker, and landscaper, until finally returning to school to study creative writing. He completed a Master of Fine Arts in fiction writing at the University of Arizona, and went on to teaching college writing courses and freelancing for various magazines. In his forties, he once again returned to school, this time to study law, and became a public defender. He now lives in southern Arizona, where he divides his time between fiction writing and the practice of law.

THANKS

It doesn't take a village to write a book, but having a village behind me made this a much better and truer story. My thanks to Jacquelyn Kasper, who found every century-old law text I needed from the deepest archives of the University of Arizona law library. Also to Mary Ann O'Neil, 9th Circuit Court of Appeals librarian in Tucson, who exhumed details of the life of Judge George Davis. Ray Vermuelen, at the Pima County Clerk of the Court's office, got me a look at several early-20th century Arizona murder case files. John Bolm and Stephen Richard helped me unearth background on early mining practices in Arizona. Maria de Lourdes Avila ensured that the Spanish language and Mexican cultural details are realistic. Damon Atchison told me far more than I would have even thought to ask about early telephone technology. Dr. William Neubauer confirmed my sketchy knowledge of puncture wounds to the human neck. Meg Files's advanced fiction group read a few passages early on and cured me, gently, of certain miscreant tendencies. Mary Martha Miles offered great editorial suggestions.

Other generous people have read all or parts of various drafts and helped guide my path, including John Levy, Joy Athena, Alicia Cata, Gina Fischer, Peter Hormel, Patrick Doyle, Fred Runk, Eli Hyland, Neil Hyland, Marilyn Goulden, Keith Provan, Neil Anderson, Dan Wemple, Dian Johnstone, Frances Causey, Rebecca Gelenberg, Birdie Stabel, Nick Bleser, and Sherry Sass. In particular, I recommend to any writer the very professional services of The Editorial Department and its staff.

Finally, a special thanks to my sweetheart, Sherry Mullens, who, besides making significant contributions to my thoughts about how this story ought to unfold, patiently encouraged me through years of my alternating silences and whining as the story came together.

CPSIA information can be obtained
at www.ICGtesting.com
Printed in the USA
FSOW02n0302050216
16534FS